Life, Death and Cellos

This edition published in 2019 by Farrago,
an imprint of Prelude Books Ltd
13 Carrington Road, Richmond, TW10 5AA, United Kingdom

www.farragobooks.com

ISBN: 978-1-78842-111-9

ISABEL ROGERS

LIFE, DEATH AND CELLOS

THE *Stockwell Park Orchestra* SERIES

Stockwell Park Orchestra

Conductor

First violins

Second violins

Violas

Cellos

Double basses

French horns

Flutes

Clarinets

Oboes

Bassoons

Trumpets

Trombones

Tuba

Percussion

To Pearl's tea urn and custard cream stash...

Chapter 1

By Saturday morning, Erin and Joshua were regretting both the prawns and the brandy, but not the sex. They didn't feel like accomplices to a murder.

On Friday evening they had met for a curry on the Clapham Road, where Erin watched Joshua's fingers break a poppadom and gesticulate with a shard. She kept her hands carefully at plate level, chasing a lump of mango chutney round the edge as she listened to him.

'Hear that? The sitar's using quarter tones.'

From then on, hearing a quarter tone scale would be tangled up in her head with the taste of mango chutney and mint cucumber raita in some weird musical synaesthesia.

'Stop conducting,' she said. 'We're not in orchestra now.'

Joshua brought his poppadom down from pointing somewhere high up the flock wallpaper and crunched it in two bites, pushing errant triangles back into his mouth with his finger.

'Sorry,' he said, around the geometry. 'I'm always listening if there's music around. Bit rude, when someone's right in front of me trying to have a conversation. Sometimes I need... to be corrected.'

Erin saw his raised eyebrow and wondered if she wanted to take it seriously, but the waiter was suddenly at their sides.

'Two more Kingfishers, please,' said Joshua, as he drained a bottle.

She slid her hand around her glass, wiping clear trails through the condensation with her thumb. It was still nearly full. Joshua was already on his third. At some point she knew she would have to decide. She wondered if it would involve having to read *Fifty Shades*. It had been so long she wasn't sure if sex dungeons were a given these days, but at twenty-six she felt she really ought to be more up-to-date and less nunnish.

'So,' she said, deciding not to decide for the moment and flailing away from sex dungeon questions, 'where do you see yourself in five years' time?'

'Bloody hell, this sounds like a job interview.' Joshua leaned forward. 'Are you interviewing me, Erin?'

She folded her napkin into a fan on her lap, feeling the heavy thread of the linen. 'Don't be daft. I just… well, all I know of you is from rehearsals and a couple of pints in the pub. Would be nice to know a bit more. You know – your dreams. Desires. Peccadillos.'

'Five years? That's a bit long-term. Five minutes? I can be quite specific. Five hours – even more so.' His eyebrow lifted again. 'Yes, if pushed for specifics I can do the next five hours in exhaustive detail.'

She folded a few more pleats into her napkin. 'That would mean a very late night and not much sleep before tomorrow's concert.'

He laughed. 'I could conduct tomorrow night in my sleep, honey. Despite what Rafael and David think, Stockwell Park isn't exactly the Berlin Phil.'

'So you want the Berlin Phil in five years, then?'

'Ha! I wish. Even Rattle took longer than that. But yes, something good, sometime… you lot are just a stepping stone. A rather beautiful stepping stone,' he added, a bit too hastily, 'but I can't pretend I'm going to be swilling round the amateur orchestras of London for ever.'

'Swilling?' Erin felt her petulance rise. 'Thanks.'

'Sorry. Wrong word. You know what I mean. It's no crime to be ambitious.'

'No. Of course it isn't.' She stopped, then smiled. 'But are you up to deflecting the trombones' ambition tomorrow? Concert adrenaline makes them almost invincible.'

She congratulated herself for navigating a sticky conversational corner, and caught the restaurant staff smirking by the bar. It was a Friday night. Must happen every week. She guessed they witnessed the start of a lot of affairs.

Joshua stared at her as the waiter brought their dishes and tessellated them on the metal warmers. Prawn vindaloo with an unfeasible number of accompaniments, which had seemed perfectly normal when they had ordered ravenously half an hour earlier.

She surveyed the table when it was all parked. 'Ambitious. You did warn me.'

'I am.'

She shivered. She knew why she was here. Experiencing all his charisma focused on her shorted out her logic circuits. She felt herself blush. It was different when he had a whole orchestra to control: he broadcast mostly over the cellos' heads to the other sixty people relying on him to nuance the music and bring them in on time.

She didn't know whether conductors developed an ability to project their personality onto their surroundings, or whether they had it innately and were drawn to careers where it was a definite advantage. Maybe they were born confident show offs? She couldn't imagine Joshua as a data entry clerk or a car mechanic. He needed people, not machines. He was a basker. She was part of the mirror.

They ate king prawns with their fingers. By the time Joshua had licked his fingers a few times, then leaned across, caught her hand and licked hers, the decision had been taken. She drained her glass and poured the next bottle, and didn't notice under the spices that the prawns were crawling with vibrio parahaemolyticus: bacteria that were ambitious in their own small way.

As it was, they all ended up in a cab together to Erin's flat, and she only fleetingly worried that her bedroom might not have enough hooks and chains to be fashionable.

Joshua left Erin at two o'clock and made his way home across London, and in the morning he told his wife he'd been working late, had slept in the spare room so he didn't disturb her and was going to go back to bed because he felt something like flu coming on. One lie. Keeping it simple.

Erin woke early, alone and unwell. After hours shuttling between bed and the bathroom, she phoned the orchestra manager to apologise for a sudden and virulent attack of food poisoning. The concert would be missing a cellist.

An hour later the orchestra manager, David, received a second call – this time from Joshua. Working on his proven theory that a successful lie is a simple lie, he merely repeated what he had told his wife about flu, and omitted to mention multiple evacuations in his en suite. Flu sounded less intimate. More socially acceptable. Definitely not seedy affair in a dodgy curry house. So far so duplicitously slippery.

By Saturday lunchtime David was in possession of two excuses and an alarming deadline. He spent a few minutes looking through his address book weighing up whom he could ask to conduct an orchestra at four hours' notice. Haste always undermined a negotiating position. After skipping a few people he knew would either be booked elsewhere or take offence at being a clear second choice, he saw Oscar's name. Oscar, like Joshua, was young and ambitious. Unlike Joshua, Oscar was petulant, spiteful and entirely humour-free. He threw blame around a rehearsal like a sulky teenage Thor might fling Mjölnir, not caring who got pulverised. David knew the orchestra would hate every minute under Oscar's baton, but figured a few hours of resentment were worth not cancelling the concert. Besides, his seat in the horn section was too far back to catch the worst of Oscar's legendary body odour. He would make it up to the front desk string players later.

He interrupted Oscar's lunch to see if he could be tempted by John Adams' *Short Ride In A Fast Machine* and a Tchaikovsky symphony. If Oscar had only known, he might have indulged in the two-sausage-two-eggs-bubble-and-squeak cholesterol-fest he was craving. As it was, he measured a portion of wholegrain rice onto his kitchen scales and steamed some broccoli. It was a Saturday: day six of his new diet. The one that was going to work. Why this one rather than previous attempts he wasn't quite sure, but his GP's alarm when revealing his cholesterol and blood-pressure test results persuaded Oscar to take it seriously. A pity he hadn't ten years earlier.

Oscar finished his coffee (black, no sugar) and went to his music room to look out scores for a spot of revision before the rehearsal.

Chapter 2

The last minute of Oscar's life was one of his happiest, driving Adams' Fast Machine for an even shorter ride than usual. The orchestra gathered momentum like a wave about to break, and he imagined he was surfing with the easy skill of a Californian wearing Speedos and an all-year tan. All conducting lessons were forgotten. He flung his head back as the *fortissimo* crashed over him, circling both arms furiously in a classic novice error ('The Cervantes Windmill'). Drops of sweat sprinkled the front desks as he tossed hair out of his eyes. The strings persevered with their four-ledger-line squeaks: ever-dutiful despite being inaudible underneath all the razzing brass. A few players cursed him, including Marco – first violin, inside second desk, a bit sweat-spattered – but even Marco wasn't being literal when he thought, 'Oh just sod off and die, you tosser.' When the horns, trumpets and timpani joined the home straight, the sheer climax of it all was too much for Oscar's diseased heart and button-straining girth. He stopped mid-beat and, with a puzzled expression, fell slowly backwards off the podium.

His landing was cushioned by a lady in the front row, her surprised yelp drowned out by dogged chords from the trombones who hadn't looked up. By the time a hushed awfulness settled, Oscar was already dead.

As the musicians peered over the edge of the stage, a second shock rippled round the onlookers. Oscar's right arm spasmed. His lax fingers had let the baton fall and they seemed – to some of the more imaginative audience – to be searching for it, feeling around the parquet in increasingly desperate jerks. Clearly the conductor was not ready to face the afterlife without his baton. Nobody moved.

After a moment, the supernatural mystery transpired to be merely Mrs Ford-Hughes trapped underneath a quarter-ton of spent musician and his voluminous jacket, suffering from claustrophobia, imminent suffocation and a broken collarbone.

Amateur orchestral concerts do not usually end in death, no matter how badly some solos are played, and an air of bewilderment swirled round the hall as two ambulances arrived. The players reverted to their native buoyancy more quickly than the audience. When they realised there would be no more music that evening, most of them left by a side door and buggered off to the pub.

Cancelling the rest of the concert annoyed some of the audience who reasoned it had only been the first half and they'd paid for the whole thing. To their mind, the orchestra clearly knew the notes: surely all someone had to do was start them off and the symphony would unroll of its own accord? The dead conductor had, in any case, been a stand-in for the regular one. Why should anyone care?

Marco – curser of dead conductors – seldom went to the pub. That evening, however, he followed his fellow musicians through back streets to the nearest one, as if slotting into a determined column of ants zigzagging through a maze to their favourite food. The crush in the bar was unprecedented. Brass players (soldier outrider ants, twice as big as the rest of them) had stacked up triple pints quickly, fearing this very emergency, and stood in their accustomed corner glaring as the other sections of the orchestra invaded their territory.

'It's a first. We haven't actually killed anybody before.' Marco was still feeling trembly at the dramatic unveiling of his new power.

'It is an extreme reaction.' His desk partner, Maureen, spoke with venom. Maureen's mouth pressed downwards: evidence of a cynicism that had thickened, year by year, to cover her like tree rings. 'Murdering music, now *that* we do on a weekly basis.' She did not leaven this with any hint of a smile, but snorted softly into her drink.

Most people spending any time with Maureen soon found their ideas wandering towards stabbing themselves in the back of the hand with a fork, or anything within reach, to distract from her black hole effect that sucked out any humour within six feet.

While the orchestra drank, back at the concert hall the doors were propped wide open as paramedics manoeuvred a covered stretcher to a second ambulance. Mrs Ford-Hughes, given the preference afforded to the living over the dead, had already gone.

The orchestra's committee watched. They remained as the blue light turned a corner, was reflected in the windows of the building opposite and disappeared into London's nighttime shimmer. The police had been and gone, taking names, statements and telephone numbers. They had implied with all the subtlety of their kind that they were ready to swoop for more information, were swooping to be required in future. DCI Noel Osmar was the last of his team to leave, nodding his thanks and noting to himself that he could be more familiar with the classical music scene on his Stockwell patch. But then again, they didn't tend to harbour violent criminals. The days of machine guns in violin cases were over. And Morse, with his opera-loving ways, wasn't even real.

'Committee' is perhaps too grand a word to describe the three people who were left in the hall: David, Pearl and Rafael. David managed practicalities, booking soloists and venues, fielding calls from sick people and finding last-minute replacement conductors. He regarded the open foyer doors over his bifocals, swaying up on to the balls of his feet and down to his heels in the repetitive manner of an asylum inmate. He was extremely tall and thin, so this height looming towards the others and receding could have been as soothing as waves on a shore, but nerves had been frayed to such an extent that evening that it was not appreciated.

Pearl broke first. 'Oh, do stop, David. It's bad enough having to cancel the second half without you swaying about like that.'

In her mid-sixties, Pearl ballooned her black concert dress into ample curves. She fulfilled the essential administrator role any amateur orchestra needs, which included hiring music and – far more importantly – ensuring the smooth running of the rehearsal coffee break. Pearl never ever ran out of biscuits. She played at the back of the violas, very quietly, with her bow microscopically above the string if the tempo went faster than *allegretto*.

'At least you don't have to decide on refunds,' said Rafael, an accountant who relished the prestige enjoyed by Financial Director of the Stockwell Park Orchestra. 'Some people came up to me asking for one as they were loading poor old Oscar onto the stretcher. One even demanded we reschedule the whole concert.'

David and Pearl swung round, giving Rafael their whole attention. With orchestral finances being on such a constant knife-edge, any danger of funds being clawed back closed their ranks like nothing else. Rafael did not immediately amplify, however, and all three eventually resumed gazing at the spot where Oscar's ambulance had been.

'Mr Ford-Hughes may sue, you know,' said Rafael, after some reflection. For the second time, the other two stared at him in horror. Rafael shrugged. 'At the very least, they might withdraw their annual bursary. His wife was not entirely unscathed.'

Pearl sighed, unable to banish the vision of Mrs Ford-Hughes struggling underneath Oscar. 'Let's not count chickens. The horse may not have bolted just yet.' Pearl never used one metaphor when there was the slightest opportunity of using two. 'Mrs Ford-Hughes could be fine.'

'They did call that second ambulance,' mused David. 'Since Oscar's had turned into a hearse. But yes, perhaps she may prove to have only minor injuries.'

Rafael was thoughtful. 'I wonder how much our insurance premium will be now, to cover being crushed by a falling conductor. I've never enquired.'

This was considered carefully by the other two, more urgently by Pearl, who was rapidly trying to work out how she could conflate her previous bolted (or not) horse and the question of lightning ever striking in the same place twice, but after trying out all permutations of 'bolt' in her head she gave up with a small sigh of defeat. The men were doing maths and didn't notice her struggle.

All three resumed their vigil by the open doors, until David realised everyone else had gone. He stirred.

'Fancy a drink?'

'I think, just this once, yes,' said Pearl.

'Coming, Rafael?'

'Oh, why not? Just the one.'

They locked the doors and headed to the pub.

'A quiet drink is just what I need, actually,' said Rafael, as they approached. 'It's been quite an evening.'

He opened the door. The entire orchestra was crammed round the bar, and the noise level rivalled that of Oscar's final minute: a result of an hour's hard drinking coupled with the shock of seeing someone die. Rafael looked back at Pearl and David.

'Found them, then,' said David, going past him. 'Come on. I'll get the first round.'

The door swung shut, leaving the street quiet again.

Oscar, the dead conductor, was by then sliding into a fridge in the local hospital morgue. As his body finally stopped moving, the settling momentum dislodged some internal gas, and thus the aroma of Oscar's last earthly fart was shut in with him to start eternity.

Death, the highest accolade for vibrio parahaemolyticus, was so far removed from the guilty prawns nobody would suspect, but perhaps that is the beauty of chaos theory.

In another part of London, in another vault, stood a cello in an old-fashioned brown case. It was three hundred years old and for the last twenty of those it had been imprisoned underneath a bank. There was silence and appreciation. It had been accruing noughts on the end of its value ever since Antonio Stradivari had sent it out into the world from his workshop in Cremona. It had been played by dukes and composers, soloists and novices. Inside its belly were dust particles from great halls of the rich and appointed, from Italian palaces to chateaux in revolutionary France.

In the dark, below twenty-first century London, there was no glint or vibration to betray that once more it had outlasted an owner and was about to start a new adventure.

Oscar, who had never seen it, had just given it to someone else.

Chapter 3

The story made it on to the local news. Editors had found the only publicity shot of Oscar available on the web, taken to capture his flamboyant conducting style: his lank hair enjoying a brief gravity-defying moment away from his scalp as he was caught in a downbeat. Either the focus wasn't quite deep enough to reveal his trademark sweating or the photographer had taken careful heed of who was paying for the photo. The headline CONDUCTOR DIES IN CONCERT was repeated on local bulletins and news sites.

Erin made her way to work on Monday morning feeling weak but OK to move, having spent the weekend with her head in a toilet. She stopped for a coffee on the way and idly eavesdropped on two women behind her in the queue.

'Hear about that conductor bloke at the weekend?' The first voice oozed with salacious anticipation of a good gossip.

'No – what?' The second was immediately alert. They had rehearsed this many times. The subject didn't matter: the importance lay in the telling. If they had both heard of The Thing, emphasis would shift to rivalry over who could insert the most shocking detail. If nothing factual sprang to mind, it was a matter of a moment to select something plausible and use that instead. As long as this was accompanied with an eyebrow lift of sufficient height and really committed nodding, it was usually accepted. And repeated.

Erin froze, hyperaware of anything related to Joshua. She waited for a skinny two-shot latte, but focused all her attention behind her. If she had possessed directional ears, like a horse or dog, they would have swivelled straight back.

'He was doing a concert with that local lot – whaddya call 'em?'

There was a pause, during which it became clear that her companion shared equal ignorance of the orchestra's name. It continued for so long Erin almost told them herself, to jump-start them before her coffee was ready.

'Dunno. That lot that play in the Civic Hall. Anyway, there he was conducting away like nobody's business, then fell over into the audience!'

'No!' The second woman didn't doubt the veracity; she merely delivered her required line.

'Yes! Just like that! Squashed some poor lady in the front row 'n' all!'

Erin snorted as she rummaged in her wallet, enjoying the image of Joshua toppling onto an unsuspecting member of the audience.

'No!' The second role in this melodrama employed limited vocabulary. 'Was he alright? Poor bugger.'

'No, that's the thing!' The first woman was practically salivating at the prospect of the next bit. There's nothing like imparting news of a surprise death to get the juices flowing. Erin handed over money and picked up her coffee. 'He died, see! Dead even before the ambulance got there, they say!'

Erin replaced her cup on the counter and clutched the edge, dizzy. The blithe conversation went on.

'Dead?'

'Yes! And then they had to get a second ambulance for the audience lady, and she's ended up in hospital too—' A death and a maiming in one fix. The woman was apoplectic with excitement.

'Who's next?' called the barista. Erin half-expected to see him brandishing a scythe.

'Oh, it's us!' said Number Two. 'Two cappuccinos, with sprinkles. 'Scuse me.' This last was to Erin. 'You alright, dear?'

Erin straightened and breathed a couple of times. 'Yes. I'm fine. Thank you.'

She went blindly to the office, and couldn't have said afterwards how she had got there. Sitting down at her computer, she kept her coat on and stared at the blank screen.

The news presented Erin with a number of difficulties: a new affair with a married man is not something to boast about or mourn publicly. She felt a prickling resentment that she had no chance to celebrate it before it had been cut short. Then she reasoned how much worse it would have been if they'd been together for months.

She sat at her desk sipping coffee, and with each mouthful she tamped down the tears threatening to swell upwards. By the time she had finished her cup, her equilibrium had recovered enough to allow her to pretend to be working quite calmly. Colleagues noted her pallor, but her muttered reference to food poisoning was accepted. Her hand went repeatedly to her phone to check her emails and Twitter feed, searching for news of Joshua. Nothing official from David about that night's scheduled rehearsal, apart from confirming it would go ahead. No mention of who would conduct. A few wide-eyed tweets from some players: Erin even replied to some of them asking if it was true, but after the first few came back with shock and exclamation marks she switched her phone off.

It never occurred to her to ask the name of the man who died.

The oppression of that Monday swirled around her in monochrome until she could reasonably make her excuses for an early exit. She went home, opened a bottle of Talisker, poured an inch into a tumbler and drank it straight down.

She decided to go to the rehearsal, reasoning that if she really couldn't go through with it, the tummy bug story would cover her. She felt impelled to find out what had happened, otherwise she would just roll it endlessly around her head without any answers.

Carrying a cello through London's rush hour isn't easy, and that evening she really wasn't in the mood for the half dozen jokers who imagined they were the first people in the world to say 'That's a big violin!' or 'Machine gun?' She turned away from the High Road towards the school they used for rehearsals, walking as usual in a broken line of players who had turned up on the same tube. Pushing open the doors, she saw some people standing about chatting while they got out their instruments as David got stands out of the cupboard.

Erin couldn't see anything different. There were no whispers, no shock. Pearl was rustling about down the corridor with packets of biscuits and filling the urn. Erin began to wonder if she had imagined everything.

She lugged her cello over to where a couple of other cases were already open and two cellists, Ann and Charlie, were tightening and rosining their bows. She was about to ask in a suitably roundabout way if she had dreamed Joshua's accident, when Ann looked up.

'Erin – how are you? David said you'd not been well.'

'Oh – thanks. Much better now.'

Erin didn't know how to ask the next bit. She pressed her lips together to stop a betraying wobble and busied herself with her case.

'You look a bit shaky – sure you're OK to play?'

She nodded. Why was nobody mentioning Joshua?

Charlie assessed her. 'Well, you missed all the excitement.'

Ann, bending over her cello, didn't notice Erin blinking. 'God, yes! Bloody nightmare!'

Charlie warmed to his theme. 'You at least expect a conductor to see it through to the end of a gig.'

Erin felt her hands shake. I should never have come, she thought. I can't do this. 'So – it's true, is it?' she said.

'Keeled straight over nearly at the end of the Adams,' said Charlie.

Erin couldn't do it any longer. She felt her knees go and ended up sitting on the floor between the cello cases, staring up at Ann and Charlie with tears on her cheeks, making weak flapping motions with her hands.

'So it is true. I heard these two women talking behind me this morning, and then nobody said anything else – and—'

Charlie and Ann exchanged glances. They'd been as shocked as anyone when it happened, of course, but since Oscar had not met any of them before Saturday afternoon, and had certainly not endeared himself to them in the short duration of their acquaintance, nobody else in the orchestra was shedding tears. Ann leaned down and stroked Erin's shoulder.

'Did you know him well?'

This merely put Erin into such a fit of sobbing that she couldn't speak. As the other players arrived and started to get instruments out and distribute parts, Charlie and Ann exchanged bewildered shrugs over Erin's head. Pearl, returning from urn duties, stopped on the way past and asked if Erin was alright.

'She's a bit upset,' mouthed Ann, with exaggerated consonants and not much volume, as if a stage whisper would gloss over the display of raw emotion at knee level.

'Well, I can see that,' said Pearl. She cast around for anything she might possess which would help the situation. Not being gifted with either emotional insight or much vocabulary of a soothing nature, she opted for her strengths. 'Can I get you a cup of tea and a biscuit, Erin?'

Erin tried hard to regain control, and blew her nose. 'I'm sorry,' she said. 'No, I'll be fine. Thank you, though, Pearl.' She stood up and blew her nose again, and took a deep breath. 'It's just the shock of hearing about Joshua, and—'

'Joshua?' Charlie was in quickly with his query.

'What about him?' asked Ann.

'Is something the matter with Joshua?' Pearl was confused. 'I thought he'd got over his flu?'

Erin was flicking from one face to another, trying to catch the truth, but was a jump behind each time.

'He looks OK to me,' said Charlie, nodding to where Joshua was walking into the hall, his shoulder bag slung on one side and his cylinder of batons on the other. His eyes, as usual, searched for Erin first, and gave a cheery wave in their direction.

'He looks positively fighting fit,' continued Charlie, looking at Erin and neglecting to keep a laugh out of his voice.

Erin squeaked, and fainted.

Chapter 4

Why play in an amateur orchestra? The answer is usually either to have sex, gossip about who else is having sex, have a crush on the conductor, pretend to read Proust in the trombone or timpani rests or wait for the pint after the rehearsal. There are those who join for a love of music or a desire to expand their cultural knowledge, but frankly they are usually at the back of the violas and nobody talks to them much.

There are orchestras in most of the cities and towns across Britain, of varying degrees of competence. If you're lucky, you get a professional conductor. Sometimes you get a young soon-to-be professional conductor, about whom you can then say smugly 'Oh yes, of course, I worked with him before the LSO snapped him up'. Sometimes you get a conductor who should be doing something else: almost anything else (you can identify this type as their nose gets increasingly close to the score in the tricky bits, only to emerge with a beaming smile at the next big tune they recognise, hoping the terrified first violins didn't notice he let them get on with it themselves round all those semiquaver corners). That type of conductor doesn't even know any viola jokes. There is no point to them. The hive-mind of an orchestra can instantly perceive this, and usually chews them up and spits them out within a few months.

Joshua was on the cusp of making it as a professional. At twenty-three, he was at the very lean and hungry end of his career, with the energy to make himself believe he could be the next Rattle. He regarded his stint with the Stockwell Park Orchestra as a rather dull but necessary step before he got 'proper' professional gigs, and was blinkered enough to believe the collateral damage he caused admitting this to people like Erin was inevitable.

Because of the knot of people around Erin, he didn't realise she had fainted. Pearl, in any case, seemed flustered no matter what the occasion, so to see her flapping an ever-present tea towel at something by the cello cases didn't draw undue attention. It could have been an errant wasp. It was only when he heard people calling Erin's name that he realised something was wrong. By the time he got there, Erin was opening her eyes. He crouched down.

'What's the matter?'

Erin went from pallor to flushed in an instant. She looked at the faces looming over her head from all directions, heard Joshua's voice, and experienced the crash of waking from a really embarrassing dream and realising it was all a dream. Except that this hadn't been a dream, and instead of waking on her own in her own bed and being embarrassed in solitude, there was most of the cello section and others staring at her while she experienced that moment. It was clear to read, and Charlie read it perfectly. She was silent and struggled to sit up. Joshua held her arm.

'I'm fine. Really,' she said, eventually. As if to emphasise this, she got to her feet and leaned on her cello case. Smiled. Tried to erase the last five minutes of her life.

'I think Erin thought you'd been the one to snuff it on Saturday,' Charlie said. He started to laugh, to signal he meant it in a helpful, light-hearted way, and a few others joined in.

Erin tried to salvage the situation. 'A silly misunderstanding!' she laughed. 'And on top of not feeling well all weekend – I've been keeling over regularly!' She could feel her voice coming out unnaturally high, and knew she'd added exclamation marks.

'Well, if you're sure…' Joshua said, his hand still on her shoulder. He saw Charlie looking, and snatched his hand away. 'Why don't you get a drink of water and we can start the rehearsal?'

Pearl bustled off to fetch rehydration. Charlie looked at Erin. Joshua's hand hadn't moved fast enough.

'Well, well,' he said softly, turning to get his cello out of the case. 'Erin, my girl, you are a dark horse.'

Erin just looked at him and almost smiled. She unclipped her bow, tightened and rosined it. It is a ritual string players go through at the start of rehearsals. It keeps their hands busy enough for their conversation to take off absent-mindedly, as if the distraction of motion lets a voice say more of the truth.

'Just because you think he's a dick doesn't mean the rest of us do,' she said quietly. Ann was not far away.

'I don't think he's a dick,' Charlie said, but saw Erin's cynicism. He tried again. 'Well, I don't *just* think he's a dick.'

'Now we're getting to it.'

'When you get as old as me you'll share some of this cynicism.'

'What are you – thirty something?'

'Yeah, well, the experienced end. And I started out cynical.'

They didn't have time to continue as most of the orchestra were already in their seats and shuffling through the music on their stands. The first rehearsal after a concert always had an element of pot luck: sight-reading a new piece exposed some players beyond their abilities. How far they would get by coffee time was anybody's guess before the first downbeat.

Erin looked at the pages in front of her. *Fingal's Cave*. Mendelssohn had written it when he sailed along the Scottish west coast to that amazing rock formation, accessible only by boat. It starts with a cello tune that has enough semiquavers and accidentals to make an amateur cello section sound ropey, even at a sedate *allegro moderato*. The fact that they were supposed to be waves on the sea made the whole thing a bit too nauseating for her comfort.

Joshua looked up and checked everyone was ready.

'Evening!' he said. 'Sorry to have missed the concert on Saturday.' There was a collective murmur from the players: a mixture of remembered shock, correct respect for the dead and inevitable musicians' gallows humour rising to the surface. 'I didn't know Oscar well – none of us did – but I'm sure you'll join me in sending our sincere condolences to his family for their loss.'

'Their huge loss,' muttered someone in the trombone section, to local chuckles. Even Joshua's lips twitched.

'Anyway, I think Pearl will be collecting for some flowers at the break, so if any of you want to contribute, do go and see her.' He looked down at his score, and flicked it open. 'Have we all played this before?' he asked generally. Another murmur: mostly of 'yes's, some 'no's. Anyone who had started playing in a youth orchestra would have crashed their way through it at some point. Mendelssohn has that dubious honour of being popular without ever quite being admired, and very seldom played well. 'Right then. We're doing a beefed-up version of this, to give our horns and trombones something to do. So: horns, you're doubling the first and second parts, and Carl, grab yourself a double bass part, OK? Nobody can accuse us of being authentic. Don't worry, we won't muck about with the Beethoven later. Cellos – ready for this?' He smiled at Erin, who blinked back at him. Joshua swept everyone together in his upbeat and off they went.

Almost immediately, the cellos were sent alarmingly high up their A string. The section bravely went for it, but were relieved when the violins took over. First flute had a go at the interminable tune, then the whole wind section joined in (almost at pitch), while the strings got more and more worked up. Joshua was encouraging them to give a bit more. Erin started to feel seasick. Wind increasing, bigger waves, strings all joining on a rising scale into… nothing. Bloody Mendelssohn never delivered. A little oboe chirrup and they were thrown back into the interminable waves.

Erin's left hand ached. Clarinets had a perky bit of tune, answered by the horns. A couple of bars of cello *soli*, then the tune was handed over to the violins, who were soon back into the semiquavers. They weren't much better than the cellos at coping with them, but got them in scores more often so their miming technique was better if it was all totally beyond them. The back viola desks grimaced into their music stands. Pete, at the very back, had got so flustered that he started sawing the neck of his viola from side to side and keeping his bow arm more or less still: a sign he was truly struggling. Joshua shouted out the timpani cue as it went past, but the two percussionists were arguing silently about how many bars each had counted and who was wrong.

The piece finally wound itself up via *arpeggios* of increasing desperation into regimented scales that sounded as if the orchestra was doing the splits (violins up, cellos down) and into interminable cadences, like Beethoven. The whole thing disappeared into a lone flute note and some string *pizzicatos*. Brian slid flat off the flute note, as he always did, so the more musically attuned members of the orchestra felt their eyebrows stretch higher and higher into their hairline in an effort to compensate. It never worked.

Joshua put his baton down and sighed. Then smiled, quickly. He knew that an orchestra encouraged was an orchestra more likely to keep watching him, and less likely to fantasise about the post-rehearsal pint.

'Great.' There had to be more he could say. He looked around the room at the faces turned to him, mostly earnest, some bored; Pete, sweating slightly and trembling, was blinking fast. 'Well, that's outlined some of the work we'll be tackling over the next few weeks…' he trailed off, but then gave himself a mental shake and concentrated. He rolled up his shirtsleeves and flipped the pages of the score back to the beginning. 'Right, upper strings at Letter A…'

There was a slow turning back of pages as the players listened to what Joshua had to say, and the rehearsal loped its way through its first half to coffee. Pearl slipped out five minutes early to get the urn up to temperature, spoon instant coffee into plastic cups and arrange biscuits on plates. She felt content doing this: more so than sitting next to Pete and trying to dodge the scroll at the end of his viola as it invaded her personal playing space during heated moments. There was more rhythm in her solitary spooning then there ever was in her playing: coffee granules fell into white plastic cups with the precision of a genetic scientist letting DNA drip from a pipette, and the grains' dry rattle came to fall on every offbeat quaver, without her knowing. Nobody saw, and Pearl herself didn't notice.

'Feeling better now after your little turn?' Joshua asked Erin as they both shuffled forward in the coffee queue. There was a hardness in his tone that she hadn't heard before. Or was it just that she hadn't noticed?

'Yep, thanks.' She reached forward to pick up a cup from the table where Pearl was lining up full ones. 'No problem.'

Charlie was just in front of her, and half turned, blowing steam off his coffee to try and get it down to less than scalding temperature in the fifteen minutes they had before playing again. 'She's a tough nut,' he said to Joshua. They all moved away from the table to let the press behind them surge towards caffeine. Erin glanced at Charlie. Clearly he had guessed about her and Joshua. What she didn't know was what he was going to do with that information. He was currently wrong-footing her with displays of support and concern.

'Oh, I know that,' said Joshua, smiling at Erin. He felt like ruffling her hair, but thought he'd better not. 'But it's not every week that we have to resuscitate a cellist before attempting Mendelssohn.'

Erin thought she'd better join in the conversation, or it would be batted over her head without her. Charlie got there first.

'We might have to resuscitate the whole bloody section after much more of that. We don't take kindly to feeling seasick. Who chose it anyway?'

David, who had been approaching to speak to Joshua, cleared his throat just behind Charlie's back.

Erin flicked a glance at him, caught Charlie's eye, and muttered 'Awkward…' into her coffee cup.

Joshua embraced the situation. 'David, we seem to have a small rebellion in the lower strings – was it you who chose *Fingal's Cave*?'

'Well, yes, I did speak up for it at the last committee meeting.' He looked over his glasses at Charlie. 'To which everyone is invited, as you know.'

Charlie smiled broadly. He knew that a few hours practising a mildly irritating piece was nothing to the torture of sitting through even one hour of the orchestral committee meetings. David knew that Charlie knew. They both twirled metaphorical revolvers round an index finger and replaced them in their holsters, agreeing to go back into the saloon for a companionable drink without having to go through the messy shoot-out.

Joshua wasn't quite ready to let it go that easily. For a conductor, he was a bit too fond of the 'divide and conquer' rule of orchestras to get unswerving support from the players, most of whom saw what he was doing for the power play that it was.

'It does have nice horn parts,' he mentioned, as if in passing. David played fourth horn: the lowest notes in the chords without requiring the steel balls to do the high solos (first), the worryingly exposed duets (second) or the almost equally high harmonies (third). He arranged his face into an insouciant expression to convey that someone choosing pieces because of a lush part for themselves had never crossed his mind. Anyway, he had more pressing matters on his mind.

'We need a quick word – can you come over and have a chat with Rafael after the rehearsal?' said David.

'Yeah,' said Joshua, a bit perplexed at the urgency of the request. 'What's up?'

'We'll talk about it later.' David made a *pas devant les enfants* face, indicating Erin and Charlie. 'Just wanted to catch you in the break.' He walked back to where Rafael was standing, looking worried. They nodded at each other, and started talking too quietly for anyone else to hear.

Charlie laughed. 'All a bit cloak and dagger, don't you think?'

'I think he enjoys it,' said Joshua. 'It'll be about waiving my fee from last Saturday or something.'

'Don't you get sick pay?' asked Erin. She'd never thought about it before.

'Ah, the innocence of her!' said Joshua. 'Bless you. No. It'll go to Oscar. Or Oscar's widow – or somebody.'

'Was he married?' said Charlie. 'If he was, there must be something about the animal magnetism of a conductor driving a pheromone bull through girls' defences, cos he certainly wasn't going to get points for personality.'

Erin snorted into her coffee.

'Dunno, actually,' said Joshua. 'I think David only had his contact details and stuff through Fenella.'

'Fenella?' asked Erin. 'What's she got to do with it?'

Fenella, the leader of the cello section, was a willowy young woman who was mistress of the middle class long hair flick. She was one of the better players, but nowhere near as good as she thought she was, and it was rumoured that her recent place to study at music college was more the result of her family's social networking skills than her musical abilities. Apart from fainting near Fenella's cello case earlier, Erin had little to do with her normally. She was not quite as far down the unpopular road as Maureen in the violins, but was supercilious enough to alienate most other players in the orchestra. Quite why she should have anything to do with a dead conductor was unclear.

'Wasn't she related?' Joshua said. 'Niece, or something? Or niece-in-law? Fuck knows. David does, anyway.'

'Now that's a family resemblance nobody spotted,' said Charlie.

'I dunno – maybe it's by marriage. Can't remember, but David mentioned ages ago that she had some relation who was a conductor, if ever we needed extra help with a sectional or something.'

'Or your successor,' suggested Charlie.

Joshua glared at him. 'Yeah, well, he's dead now, so that little idea hasn't panned out.'

Erin wasn't sure where all this rivalry had come from, and she wasn't enjoying it. She looked over to where Fenella was standing with the rest of the cellos, in the traditional way of orchestras' socialising by section.

'She doesn't seem very upset,' she said. 'I don't think Oscar can have been a close relation.'

Charlie laughed. 'Fenella wouldn't care if her pet chinchilla had just died. All she'd think about is how to get the fur made into fingerless gloves so she could show them off at the next rehearsal.'

It was almost true. Fenella's life was focused on Being A Cello Player. Not actually as far as working on being much good, but Being A Cello Player involved a lot more than that. There was hair flicking, swaying unnecessarily in your chair when playing, sending printed notelets to your friends with pictures of cellos on the front, and having a cellocentric handle on Twitter. The cellist aura shone around Fenella with such a dazzling shimmer, people often forgot to listen very carefully to her playing. She was working very hard on having the reputation of a player to watch, and was busy cultivating her contacts in the musical world to make that happen.

The others were saved any further temptations to bitch about her because David started to chivvy people back to the hall to start the second half. Charlie, Joshua and Erin dropped their cups into the bin and left Pearl doing the same with the paper plates, popping any spare biscuits into her mouth to keep everything tidy.

As they were tightening bows and getting spikes to the right length, Charlie asked Fenella about Oscar, phrasing it as tactfully as he could while still not really caring whether he upset her or not. She was not fazed at all, picking up all the long hair lying on one shoulder and tossing it across her back before answering.

'Oh yes, he was my mother's step-brother. She was so much older than him she never really saw him much.' Fenella had the habit of keeping her eyes closed through most of what she said, only opening them at the last few words as if to check whether the person to whom she was speaking had wandered off. Similarly, a lot of the time she was lost in the inner world of her musicality, which was why, quite often, she was behind whatever beat the conductor had chosen to set. Charlie saw her pupils return to the centres of her lids and just in time arranged his face into something approaching concern, ready for Fenella to see.

'And was he married? Any children?'

'No. I don't think he even had a girlfriend at all.' Fenella looked momentarily sorry for Oscar. 'Mummy certainly never mentioned one.'

Charlie and Erin exchanged glances at 'Mummy' being used without hesitation by someone in their twenties, but Fenella's face was hidden behind her curtain of hair as she leaned down to secure her spike, and she spoke upside-down through it.

'His father – my grandmama's second husband – was terrifically supportive of Oscar's music, and I think all he ever did was that. But, as I said, we never really kept in touch.'

Joshua had started riffling through his score by then, and there was a general settling and attempts at concentration amongst the players, so the potted history of Oscar as told to the cello section had to stop. Fenella dropped one more fact into the quietening atmosphere before leaving the subject altogether.

'His funeral is next week. I've got to go with Mummy.'

'Right, OK everybody?' called Joshua over the chatter. 'Can we go from letter G?'

The orchestra lumbered up to speed again, and Joshua felt them suck some of his life force from him with every dragged note. At times like this he thought there had to be a better way to earn a living. He had to step out of this sea of amateurism and get some professional gigs soon, or he would go mad. There was only so much exposure to David's fourth horn and Pearl's viola playing a man should have to take.

Chapter 5

At the end of the rehearsal, Joshua saw Rafael and David were loitering together as he put away his baton and gathered his scores. He sighed, only partly for the concert fee he'd missed out on. The financial side of orchestral administration shimmered outside his usual area of focus, but he constantly felt it pressing in, narrowing down what was possible in terms of repertoire or soloists. He wandered over.

'You rang…?' he said, hoping a mock-butler tone might lighten the atmosphere, but there was little chance of that when those two got together. Rafael pursed his lips and frowned.

'If you could restrain yourself for five minutes from inappropriate attempts at humour, we'd be grateful.'

Christ, thought Joshua. This was going to be worse than he'd thought.

'Yes,' added David. 'I'm afraid we have some rather bad news.'

'Pearl's retiring?' tried Joshua. Two stoney faces told him to forget it and just get this little interview over with as quickly as possible and bugger off to the pub, which was where Erin and most of the others had gone already. 'Sorry. Is this about my fee? I'm not expecting you to pay me for the gig, you know. Absolutely understood.'

'Would that it were so simple,' said Rafael.

Joshua received this opinion with the glassy-eyed stare most people employ when accosted by a subjunctive. Rafael continued.

'It's not just your fee from last Saturday we're worried about. There have been other complications. You'll be aware that when Oscar fell, he injured a member of the audience?'

Joshua nodded.

'The lady in question was Mrs Ford-Hughes.'

Clearly Joshua's reaction was not quite aghast enough. David clarified.

'Mr and Mrs Ford-Hughes have been stalwart supporters of this orchestra for many years, giving a substantial annual donation.'

'Oh,' said Joshua. 'Shall we send flowers to her as well?'

'Please, Joshua,' said Rafael. 'Try not to be flippant about everything. The result of this unfortunate—'

'Flattening…?' Joshua couldn't help himself.

'…accident,' Rafael glared, 'is that Mr and Mrs Ford-Hughes have declined to continue their support, with immediate effect.'

'Oh.'

'And that's not all,' added David. 'Mr Ford-Hughes is currently taking legal advice about whether to sue us for damage and injuries suffered by his wife.'

There was a small silence as the implications of this sunk in. The smell of warm lino wafted around them as the last stragglers put their instruments into cases and left, some sketching a wave at the trio as they went. Most of the chairs had been stacked against the walls, leaving just Joshua's stand on the empty floor and half a dozen small puddles where the brass had been emptying out their various bits of curly plumbing.

'Ah,' said Joshua. 'So – um – where does this leave us? Are you saying we have to close down or something?'

David smiled, albeit grimly. 'No. At least, not yet.'

'But we're on a bit of a sticky wicket,' said Rafael. He caught David's eye. Each might have been thinking of what Pearl could have said at that point and breathing a silent prayer she wasn't there to say it. 'We can't survive on ticket sales alone. Never have been able to. So we all need to come up with some creative solutions for this season's concert to try and stay afloat.'

Joshua tried to work out if they needed him to work-shop some blue sky thinking then and there, or whether he was allowed to go to the pub and get back to them. David smoothly closed the impromptu meeting.

'If you could give it some thought, Joshua, we'd be grate-ful for your input. Whether or not they decide to sue, we're looking at a considerable hole in our budget for the coming few months. If we do nothing, we won't have an orchestra next year.'

'Yes, of course,' said Joshua, turning to drag his stand into the cupboard along with all the others. 'Shall I ask around the players? See if any of them can come up with something brilliant?'

'No, not just yet, please,' said Rafael. 'We want to see what ideas the committee can suggest first, and then perhaps give them a few alternatives.' He straightened his shoulders and inhaled sharply, as the generation just before his had done during their national service. 'Wouldn't want them to think they were without leadership in a crisis such as this.'

'Right,' said Joshua. 'Yes. I mean, no. Indeed.'

He was momentarily caught off-balance by the implication that he was a member of the committee. He hoped he wasn't going to have to start going to meetings. Before David or Rafael could mention that, he darted out and walked to the pub, hoping Erin hadn't been too far ahead of him and got herself wedged behind a protective flange of cellists. There was some serious teasing to be done about her misunderstanding earlier.

David and Rafael exchanged another look, assessing how the meeting had gone.

'It'll be all round the orchestra by closing time, you know,' said David.

Rafael nodded and shrugged. 'Can't be helped. We had to tell him tonight.'

They straightened the last few stacks of chairs and turned off the lights in the hall, going out into the gloom. The September nights were darkening fast. Bidding each other good night, they parted: David towards the tube and Rafael to his Audi parked a little way up the street. He stopped as he reached the driver's door, noticing the scratch running all the way along his paintwork. With a moan that sounded as if he were in real pain, he put his fingers over it, leaning down and stroking it as it crossed the door line and dug in deeper towards the back, as the tosser with the key had given their attack a bit of extra muscle on the final section. He knew parking the Audi in Stockwell was risky, but he lived so far from a tube station that his journey home was a nightmare otherwise. Just another shitty Londoner doing something shitty to another Londoner without a moment's thought. Nothing new there. He saw that his own car was only one in the unbroken line down the street, each of which had a deep horizontal mark cut into their side. He sighed, unlocked the door and got in.

As he started the engine, his music started playing from where it had left off when he'd parked three hours earlier. He felt his blood pressure subside as a Chopin piano sonata trickled out of the dashboard like dry ice. There were more important things than a scratched car. He let the clutch in gently and drove home, where he knew there was the second half of a rather nice bottle of Médoc waiting for him in the kitchen.

Chapter 6

The players were already halfway through the first round when Joshua arrived: Erin pressed in close to Charlie, Fenella and some of the other cellists, with the violinist, Marco, and a few others. Marco – and indeed everybody else – was grateful that Maureen didn't often drink. They could at least have conversations that lasted a few minutes at a stretch before being sucked out of existence down her plughole of doom.

Erin thought she felt Joshua come through the door, while she was laughing at an anecdote Charlie was telling about his famously unreliable car. They had already carried out the initial dissection of the rehearsal, which was usually dealt with first and got out of the way before the conversation ranged more widely. There was always an undercurrent of bitchiness, of course, especially if Fenella was around, but sometimes post-rehearsal drinking was genuine shared time between 'almost' friends: that temporary feeling of closeness you get in a pub with people you see regularly, where an acquaintance may blur into a friend for the evening. Musicians are not a group to shun alcohol.

Erin had been intoxicated by Joshua for weeks before their date. When he was in the room, a locator beam seemed, to her, to scan until it locked on to its target, and then deliberately, inevitably, all the cells in her body were tuned to him like an array of tiny radio telescopes. She could be in a far corner talking to someone else, and feel her skin lift and sense the subtle realigning of her blood. The longer she was exposed, the greater the effect, but since there is no Geiger counter for pheromones – except for impartial observers – few can quantify. If she turned and they looked at each other, she felt utterly helpless: flotsam on a swell of the tide.

Charlie saw this change in Erin, even though her back was to the door. He looked over and saw Joshua and, in that moment before the rest of the group waved him over, Charlie marvelled at the mysterious sense some people had of their surroundings. He was not a scientist: he could not say how fast a pheromone trail spreads through molecules of air. He could not know if Erin was reacting to something chemical, or to something subtle in his own body language as he saw the door open, or whether there was any truth in what people laughingly call 'being on the same wavelength'. Surely he wasn't starting to fall for the woo-woo claptrap of psychic connectivity? Yet he had witnessed Erin's alignment shift right in front of his face. He felt a first – startling – needle of envy. A mere three hours after he had learned of Erin and Joshua's affair, and he was already running his fingertips along its surface to locate any cracks of weakness. He would almost have said that he *liked* Erin. Which was odd, because he'd never thought of her in that way before.

Joshua breezed past, offering another round as he went. Charlie thought the moment had gone for his car story, but Erin nudged him.

'So, what happened? The exhaust fell off and…?'

The others finished giving their orders to Joshua, and he was surrounded again by their faces, each expecting a decent punchline.

'Half the exhaust,' he corrected, 'was falling to its rusty death down a famously deep Camden Town pothole, and the other bit was clanging about under the car like the bloody Tin Man doing an Indiana Jones under-the-Nazi-truck routine. Without stuntman.'

The group laughed. This was what they expected: silliness over a pint. But Charlie decided to cut it short because of the difficulty he was having concentrating.

'That was Sunday. This morning saw us in Kwik Fit and now she's as shiny as anything down below, and the decibels have got a bit more manageable too. Sorted.'

Charlie smiled generally at the circle of faces around him, and took a gulp of beer, signalling the end of the story. It was someone else's turn now. He had to recalibrate some unfamiliar emotions, and couldn't do that *and* talk.

Joshua elbowed his way towards them balancing pint glasses, before handing them out (Stella for Marco and bitter for Charlie and Erin) and plunging back to the bar to get the last couple. Fenella emptied her wine glass and re-crossed her legs, settling herself more comfortably on her bar stool with a flick of her hair from one side to another. She was the only one seated: the one fixed point around which the others found themselves forced to shuffle. Nobody quite had the guts to wander off altogether and trigger a communal herd migration. When Joshua returned with her refill, she smiled her thanks in such a focused way that it caught Charlie's attention. Now he had discovered the complicated meta-conversations that seemed to be happening that evening, there were more happening all the bloody time. Erin had also noticed Fenella's flirting and flexed in an involuntary defence of something which was not hers to own.

Charlie downed the rest of his first pint quickly, wondering how interesting the evening was going to get.

'So,' said Joshua, after his long first swallow, 'were you all discussing world-shattering events or do you want to know the latest Forecast of Doom from Rafael and David?'

The others laughed. Joshua's temperamental differences with the committee were widely known.

'God, what are they up to now?' said Marco.

'Do we have to learn everything off by heart in the first week so they can return the parts to the library and not pay?' said Erin.

'Getting closer,' said Joshua, sharing a look with Erin that nearly blew Charlie over. Fenella warmed up with another hair flick, and was in there straight away.

'So it's money, then?' she asked. 'Rafael never talks about anything else.'

'Yep. Well, you know Oscar caused some collateral damage on his way out?'

There was an equal measure of giggles and pointed head tipping towards Fenella. Even the most unpopular person in a crowd doesn't deserve to hear her recently dead relative mocked in public. To his credit, Joshua took the hint.

'Oh God, sorry Fenella, I'd forgotten he was family.' Joshua put his hand on her shoulder, which seemed to have a remarkable healing effect.

'No, no, don't worry at all!' she said. 'Really. He wasn't a close relative. I hardly knew him. This sounds much more interesting.' She laughed in such a high-pitched, self-consciously musical way that the surrounding people were left in no doubt they were witnessing someone trilling. It really did exist.

'Right, well then. Old Ford-Hughes is a tad upset that his wife was injured. He's only gone and cut off our funding.'

'Oh no,' said Marco. 'That'll be what Rafael was muttering to David about all through the break. I thought he looked even more uptight than usual.'

'Plus he's thinking about suing the orchestra for injuries and compensation and whatnot,' continued Joshua.

'But Oscar couldn't help falling!' said Fenella, her voice still rather high. 'It was an accident.'

'If you call "daily McBreakfasts and no exercise for decades" an accident,' said Charlie, unable to keep his silent observer status going any longer. This was too much fun.

'You can't start making fat people responsible for their own deaths,' said Erin.

'It would save the NHS a packet,' Joshua pointed out. 'But anyway, that is a whole other debate and I suggest a Stockwell pub is not the place to have it. By the way, I'm not supposed to have told you any of this, so zippo my friends, if you please. The esteemed committee has to come up with some suggestions as to how we can stay afloat, and then we are going to give you considered options from which you can help choose the way to paddle out of this shit.'

There was a small silence as they all drank. Joshua looked at Erin, but she was the far side of Fenella's crossed legs and completely out of reach.

'Surely we're insured?' said Marco.

'Can you get insurance for being squashed by a dying conductor?' asked Charlie.

'I mean, public liability insurance – stuff like that.'

'Well, David's looking into that now,' said Joshua. 'Even supposing we are covered, if Ford-Hughes sues it could get very expensive. Isn't he a barrister, or something?' Nobody seemed to know. 'He'll wheel out the big guns and all we'll be able to get is Smeg & Co. from round the corner and it'll be like nuclear deterrent versus a pop gun.'

'So, we need to do two things,' said Erin. They all looked at her. 'First: we need to make some money somehow to keep afloat. And second: someone needs to be very nice to Mr and Mrs Ford-Hughes and persuade them not to sue.'

There was genuine appreciation of her clarity of thought, even a grudging one from Fenella, who was now fully in female rival mode and not used to dispensing favours to the enemy. She was not of the Sisterhood.

They all spent the rest of the evening talking round those two tasks, not really getting any further forward but realising how much they valued their weekly musical escape in each other's company, and how much they would fight to defend it. There were a few drunken hugs later with declarations of barricade-building prowess come the revolution, but it was agreed there should be no singing or radical haircuts.

Chapter 7

Some time in the 1640s (the exact date is not known) a baby was born to a couple named Alessandro and Anna in Cremona, Italy: the city famous for the talent and skill of its luthiers. Much of the city revolved around this industry, which attracted and created wealth and formed a reputation which would travel the world.

Nicolò Amati was his family's third generation to make stringed instruments, and his grandson would still be making them when he was dead. Nicolò was already in his seventies by the time Alessandro's son was apprenticed to him as a teenager. When Nicolò died, nearing his eighty-eighth birthday, the young Antonio had already been working on his own for four years, adding his full name to the labels on his instruments: Antonius Stradiuarius Cremonanfis Faciebat Anno...

By the time he died, possibly aged ninety-three, still in Cremona, Stradivari had made over eleven hundred stringed instruments including violins, cellos, guitars and harps. Around six-hundred-and-fifty of them survive.

Only sixty-three cellos remain, from the eighty or so he made. Some are more famous than others, and are known by name. Those who play them say his best instruments date from between 1700 and 1720, when he was at the peak of his knowledge before physical signs of ageing showed in his work. Perhaps the best cello he ever made is the 1701 'Servais', which is owned by the National Museum of American History and was played by Anner Bylsma to record the Bach Suites. Pablo Casals played the 1709 'Boccherini'. Heinrich Schiff played the 1711 'Mara'.

The 1711 'Duport' was owned by Mstislav Rostropovich until he died in 2007, when it was thought to be worth $20 million (despite having been dented by Napoleon who briefly borrowed it in Paris from its titular owner Monsieur Duport. The dent can still be seen). There is the 1712 'Davidov', played by Yo-Yo Ma. Steven Isserlis plays the 1726 'Marquis de Corberon'. Jacqueline du Pré played a number of them, and passed Yo-Yo Ma the 'Davidov' upon her death. Even Julian Lloyd Webber played the 1690 'Barjansky', which just goes to prove that connections are all important in the music business.

Some do not have names, but all are probably better than any other cello which exists or has existed, and possibly ever will exist. They all cost many millions of whatever currency you measure it in. Baroque composers like Corelli and Scarlatti were writing music for the well-respected Amati instrument, which had beautiful tone and agility. By the time Vivaldi was writing, Stradivari was already making his best violins and cellos, and they allowed Vivaldi to write more complex and technically demanding music than had ever been heard before. There was a symbiotic development process in those northern Italian provinces (not yet Italy) that allowed music to soar as it never had before. When Vivaldi wrote his *Four Seasons* in 1723, he was writing music nobody had heard before: he described real things in the world people could see, like running brooks and frozen trees with his music. Stradivari's instruments turbocharged Western baroque music. It was a revolution.

Chapter 8

Oscar's funeral was on Tuesday the following week. It had been organised by members of his mother's family, who had informed Fenella's mother with a curt, black-edged postcard. That was the first communication between the estranged family for twenty years.

When Oscar's father married Fenella's grandmother, Oscar had stayed with his mother, who then poured such vitriol into his nine-year-old ears that Oscar had not been inclined to search out his stepfamily at any point during his adolescence. What his mother failed to mention is that perhaps her husband's bank account might have held more attraction for her than the man himself. Admission of this, of course, was impossible. She chose her divorce lawyer well, and she and Oscar were well-provided for. When his father eventually died after a few years of marriage to Fenella's grandmother, he left the bulk of his estate to his only child, neatly bypassing his ex-wife. Oscar, then only eighteen, was released from the drudgery of having to earn a living, and was free to indulge the two things which were most important to him: his mother and his dream of becoming a conductor.

His father's estate was complex. It comprised a great deal of money in various kinds of accounts around the world and an investment portfolio with so many noughts it was managed with quiet care by men dedicated to this task alone in a wood-panelled office in London. He owned a number of original and appreciating works of art, and also a cello made by Antonio Stradivari.

Fenella and her mother drove to the funeral together, west, out of London, away from the September sunrise. The tiny Norman church was in the village where Oscar had grown up and, as Fenella and Mrs Stroud walked under the lychgate into the churchyard, they saw a woman dressed in black, standing by the church door, extending her hand to the mourners as they went in.

Mrs Stroud leaned towards her daughter's ear as they picked a puddle-free path past the graves.

'There's Oscar's mother. I think that's her. I wonder if she'll speak to me. She didn't send the card herself.'

Fenella hadn't known her mother to be unsure of herself in any social situation.

'Oh, I'm sure she will. Oscar's father was nothing to do with you, was he?'

'Quite. We are here to pay our respects to that poor young man.'

'Absolutely.'

Mrs Stroud's footsteps sounded more firm on the path. 'But let's not stay too long afterwards.'

They both stopped talking as they approached the church door. Oscar's mother was a very short woman: draped in a fringed black shawl, she wore a wide-brimmed black hat, festooned with several inky ostrich feathers and a black chiffon veil. The whole ensemble had the air of a hurriedly drawn crow. She turned from her last greeting to see Fenella and Mrs Stroud approach. Her eyes narrowed.

'You must be the Strouds.' Her voice accused them of something unspecified, but perhaps after a life as full of bitterness as hers had been that is how a voice becomes naturally.

'Yes, hello. I'm so sorry.' Mrs Stroud extended her hand but, when it was clear that it was not going to clasp anything other than empty air, she let it fall to her side again, where her fingers and thumb pinched their way along the hem of her jacket repeatedly, as if reassuring themselves that this was the true function of a hand and it wasn't to worry about what had just happened in mid-air.

Oscar's mother looked up at Fenella, drilling her eyes into her with such venom that Fenella felt physically repelled. 'You,' she spat, 'are to see Mr Montgomery after the service.'

Fenella looked confused. 'Pardon?'

The hat trembled, setting the feathers ticking like independent metronomes. 'Mr Montgomery.'

Fenella showed no sign of understanding any more than the last time his name had been mentioned.

'Did you receive his letter?'

'No... um, what letter?' Fenella was by now so flustered she could barely speak.

An arm emerged from the serriform black shawl wings under the hat, to gesture inside the church in the manner of someone flapping away an irritating fly. 'He will find you,' she hissed. 'After the service.'

Fenella and Mrs Stroud entered the church, looking at each other with absolute confusion, and fed themselves sideways into a pew. Turning room was not generous. There were a number of Oscar's family mourners who were, in homage to P.G. Wodehouse, settling themselves into their pews as if the pew had been built around them by someone who knew they were wearing pews tight about the hips that season.

The church was half-full. Or half-empty, depending on your psychological outlook. The breadth of Oscar's coffin was further exaggerated by the slimness of a long-stemmed rose on the lid, trailing black ribbon. Entwined in the ribbon was a conducting baton.

Fenella looked around the church and, after passing over a number of people she assumed were part of a family she had never met, she became intrigued by the elderly organist attempting Bach. He was as bony as many of the guests were rotund. His wrists emerged from cuffs in an uncomfortably cadaverous way – given the occasion – as he reached for the upper system in *Jesu, Joy of Man's Desiring*. A church organ can usually be relied upon to dispense balm, but that day there were so many wrong accidentals and an alarming choice of stops that it just made people nervous. The organist was also trying to use the pedals. His buttocks caterpillared along the stool, accompanied by syncopated clicks of two replacement hips.

The vicar's signal to start the service drew a welcoming murmur. His organist's momentum, however, was not easy to divert. It took four attempts, ranging from a glance in the organ's rear-view mirror to the vicar walking up behind him and shouting. Startled, the organist crouched onto a defensive Schoenberg-like chord. A moment later he snatched his hands and feet back, and the organ wheezed into merciful silence.

There were a couple of hymns and eulogies. The vicar was appropriately saddened by the funeral of someone who had yet to reach thirty, but his sadness was tempered by not having seen Oscar in church since his occasional Christmas visits as a child. He had been persuaded to take this funeral by Oscar's devout mother, who had leant heavily on the church, and this vicar in particular, since her husband's desertion and remarriage, exhibiting classic abandonment behaviours without any inclination to move on. She would not be calmed. Whale music irritated her tinnitus. Joss sticks brought on her asthma.

The vicar suffered panic attacks thinking about how she would cope with a real bereavement, and had already mentioned delicately to his Bishop about a possible transfer. There was only so much responsibility a man of the cloth should be asked to shoulder.

When it was Oscar's mother's turn to speak, she made her way to the front and turned to face her audience, but found she was too small see over the lectern. A number of stout hassocks were stacked at her command: she climbed up and began to speak, swaying as if perching on a windblown branch.

'My dear friends and family, thank you so much for coming today to say goodbye to my beloved Oscar.' She clutched a handkerchief and between every sentence lifted the veil away from her face so she could dab at her eyes. It was not only Fenella and her mother who were reminded of an emotional actress accepting an award. Even the mention of Oscar fitted. Instead of clapping though, this audience merely waited in silence, broken only by the click of the organist's hip if he shifted in his seat. 'He was young – too young – just starting out on the career he'd set his heart on. I remember as a boy he would stand next to our radio, conducting the orchestra with a wooden spoon…'

Oscar's mother reminisced at great length about his childhood and her part in his upbringing, missing no opportunity to mention the father who had abandoned both of them and skilfully presenting herself as a resourceful woman, singlehandedly shaping this genius boy's future. Fifteen minutes later, listeners were not only numb with boredom and from cushionless pews, but also unsure whether they were listening to a eulogy about Oscar or a pitch from his mother for her own sainthood. The ostrich feathers on her hat drooped so far she nearly inhaled them and, after a few attempts to blow them back up, she decided to draw to a close.

'So, we shall follow Oscar outside and see him laid to rest with God. His body may be returning to the dust but he has left me memories more precious than gold.' At the mention of what Oscar left behind, she stirred and looked towards a man at the back of the church. 'I would like to thank Mr Montgomery, who has been a staunch supporter of our family for more years than either of us cares to remember,' she paused for the ripple of obligatory smiles of almost-laughter to settle, 'and who has guided me through the legal tangle of these past few days. If only death could be as simple as life.'

At that perplexing aphorism she finally stopped talking, and half-turned to step down from her hassocks. As she did so, she again flung a pointed look of absolute hatred at Fenella, which was not unnoticed by others. Mr Montgomery had the decency to lower his eyes and feign ignorance.

Outside, the vicar, aware that the service had gone on much longer than everyone had been expecting, opened his prayer book beside the grave to read the minimum acceptable. The coffin began its last downward journey. Oscar's mother, who had carried the rose and baton out of the church, stepped forward and dropped them both in, with a quiet moan and more handkerchief flourishing.

Mr Montgomery, who had been waiting at a respectful distance under a yew, straightened and made his way over to Fenella and Mrs Stroud, looking very much as if he wished he were somewhere else entirely.

'Miss Fenella Stroud?' he asked, looking with carefully neutral eyes at a point equidistant between Fenella and her mother. He adhered at all times to precise methods of not causing offence.

Fenella started, even though she had seen him coming. 'Yes?'

Mr Montgomery pressed his lips together in something that wasn't quite a smile.

'I did write, but it appears my letter could have gone astray.'

'Did you have our postcode?' asked Mrs Stroud, eager to play her part in whatever family drama was about to unfold. 'Because we find it's on the Post Office computer wrongly, and if people look it up online our letters tend to go to the old people's home in the next lane...' She trailed off as it became clear that Mr Montgomery's knowledge or otherwise of their postcode was of no consequence to him. He was looking intently at Fenella.

'It is of no matter,' he continued, reaching into his inner coat pocket. 'I have a copy here, together with all relevant paperwork.'

He gave Fenella a flat bundle of envelopes and folded papers. They were the heavy cream colour of the law.

'What's this?'

'The estate of the deceased has been disposed of according to his wishes, laid out in a will I myself arranged a number of years ago.' His face softened a little. 'Of course, I did not expect to be returning to it so soon.'

'His will?' Fenella was confused for the second time that day. 'What's that got to do with me?'

'There is a codicil specifying you as a beneficiary of an item from the estate.'

Fenella and her mother took a moment to prise the meaning out of his legalese.

'He's left *me* something? But I hardly knew him.'

'Nevertheless, that is indeed the case.'

'So that's why his mother was looking daggers at you all morning!' said her mother. 'Oscar must have left you something she wanted. Quick – open it and find out what it is!'

Fenella sorted through the thick pages in her hand in confusion, eventually handing them back to Mr Montgomery for help. He unerringly picked out a single sheet, laid it flat on top and gave it back to her to read.

'It's probably just his old batons or something, don't you think?' she said carelessly, wondering what on earth she was supposed to do with a dead man's batons. Give them back to his mother, who clearly didn't want her to have them? 'He knew I was musical.'

Mr Montgomery cleared his throat, but then thought better of saying anything. He waited.

Fenella scanned the print, fighting her way through the dense prose, and then stopped as she reached the salient paragraph. She read it twice. It remained on the page. She looked up at Mr Montgomery and then at her mother who, by this time, was getting impatient.

'Well? What does it say?'

'Um… he's left me a cello.'

Mr Montgomery swallowed.

'Well, that's nice,' her mother said. 'He must have known you were learning when he made his will. It's kind that he thought of you – though he probably didn't know you have a very good one already. I must say, I didn't know he had one. He certainly never played – he was a pianist, if anything.'

Mr Montgomery cleared his throat again.

'Mummy, you don't understand.'

'Understand what, dear?'

'It's a Strad.'

There was a pause as Mrs Stroud looked at Fenella, then at Mr Montgomery, then back at Fenella, with her mouth dropping wider as she turned her head. The only sounds were a breeze through the yew tree, a pair of greenfinches calling to each other in its branches and the steady thudding of earth as Oscar's grave was refilled behind them.

'What?'

'He's left me a Strad.'

Mrs Stroud took a pace closer to Fenella and looked at the page.

'Well I never. I suppose that must have come from his father, though goodness knows why he had one either. He didn't play.'

'An investment, I believe,' said Mr Montgomery.

'So the rest of his stuff went to his mother?' asked Fenella. 'Is that why she is so angry with me? For getting this?'

'It would appear to be so, yes,' said Mr Montgomery. He extended his hand, as he realised his work was complete. 'Good luck, then, Miss Stroud. The instrument is currently being held at our bank. The address is on the paperwork. If you telephone for an appointment and bring all the required identification, you may collect it at your convenience. Subject to arranging suitable insurance, of course.'

'Oh yes,' said Mrs Stroud, rather breezily. She was keen to convey her credentials as a musical mother, quite used to sorting out the administration behind the musical endeavours of her children. 'We have a policy covering all our instruments at home. I'm sure we can add this to it.'

Mr Montgomery looked at her sternly. 'I suggest you contact the present insurer prior to making any changes,' he said. 'Do read through all the papers I have given you.'

Fenella could see that her mother had not quite grasped the enormity of what had just happened. A musical mother she may have been, but the purchasing of increasingly expensive cellos for her daughter had not introduced her to the world inhabited by Stradivari owners.

'Just out of interest, before I read through everything,' Fenella asked. 'How much is it insured for at the moment?'

'Six-million US dollars. Goodbye.' He shook her hand, turned and walked out of the churchyard.

Fenella and her mother were the last remaining mourners.

Six feet down in the dark, a wooden box Oscar had never seen started its doomed fight against rot and worms. The other wooden box he had never seen remained in a dark vault of its own, unaware that it had just been transferred yet again between two transient human links in the fungible line it had known since leaving Antonio's workshop in Cremona more than three hundred years earlier.

Chapter 9

The following week, Rafael stood up just before the rehearsal started and waited for everyone to hush. After it became clear that the percussion were never going to stop chatting and the oboe was going to carry on warming up her reed with decoy duck calls, he raised his voice above it anyway and tried to get everyone's attention.

'Ah – just to let you know – everybody? Thank you. Just to let you know that the last few minutes of tonight's rehearsal will be a short presentation of our rather serious financial situation, together with a few suggestions from the committee.'

There was a mixture of speculation about how bad the money situation was with some groaning (mainly from the brass section) that the rehearsal would now overrun and they'd be late to the pub. Rafael caught some of that, and tried to reassure them that it wouldn't take very long. Anyone who knew anything of the committee (and this was most of the orchestra) knew he was lying out of his arse, which was why none of them ever went to any committee meetings. Life was too short. They all assumed that Rafael, Pearl and David were single people with a limited hobby spectrum, which did not often include frequenting the pub. That was why only those three had been on the committee for more years than they liked to relate, with no great press of new blood itching to join them. That was also why it was assumed they rather liked their overly long meetings. The facts were very different, but not bothering to find out the facts has never stopped a general view being accepted, based on nothing more substantial than a couple of rumours and half-hearted observation.

Rafael sighed as he went to sit down, picking up his instrument on the way. He played second bassoon and was happy doing so. A bassoon doesn't get many opportunities to shine as a solo instrument in an orchestra, but at least playing second meant that even if they ran into one it wouldn't be his to play. Indeed, bassoons are famously subtle, blending into orchestral texture like the musical equivalent of camouflage fabric. Practically the only well-known solo happens at the very beginning of Stravinsky's *Rite of Spring*. When Sir Simon Rattle conducted the Berlin Philharmonic on 31st August 2003 at the Proms, he had just brought in the bassoon solo – a very tricky passage – when someone's mobile phone rang, easily louder than the bassoon. Rattle stopped the music and allowed the Prom audience (famous for turning on their own for minor infringements such as a persistent cough or noisy sweet wrapper) to fall on the miscreant and punish him according to their own penal code, accompanied by mutterings of 'wanker' from those too far away to get in on the action. Once the sounds of the probable murder had dissipated, Rattle encouraged the bassoon player to start again, and the eerie, slightly strangled melody started again.

Rafael had never played that solo, and was glad of it. Quite apart from anything, because it starts the whole piece.

All the player ever gets by way of support from a conductor is a general wave of permission to begin, with none of the regimented pre-beats given to the whole orchestra to get them to kick off in some order and at vaguely the same speed. The conductor then stands there for a couple of bars, either looking on admiringly in the case of the Berlin Phil., or extremely nervously in the case of a youth orchestra conductor, who knows that in a very few bars the whole ensemble could crash to the floor. Some might argue that most audiences would not notice a mistake in Stravinsky, but that is hardly the point.

As well as the Mendelssohn on Rafael's stand, there were symphony parts too – for Beethoven 7, written in A major. Joshua had already steeled himself for the first run through: each section of the orchestra would take it in turn to forget about that tricky third sharp: the G# they weren't expecting. No matter that it was there in plain view at the beginning of every stave, there would be G naturals dropped liberally throughout like stones in a cement mixer, accompanied by exclamations of varying levels of profanity. Joshua knew by the third go all but the most challenged player would have got the hang of them, but that didn't seem to sweeten the forthcoming pill. The only benefit he could see of choosing it – apart from the fact that any Beethoven was a perennial favourite of audiences and therefore more likely to attract the bums on seats they so desperately needed – was that it was scored for only two horns and that meant David wouldn't be playing. He could only imagine what kind of Faustian committee meeting had taken place where the deal between the Mendelssohn and the Beethoven had been struck.

In the cellos, there was the usual spike adjusting and, in the case of Fenella, a lot of hair flicking going on while they arranged themselves ready to play.

'Ooh, lovely!' Fenella said as she spotted the Beethoven on the stand. 'I adore this!'

She had arrived later than the others, and was only just sitting down in her chair as Rafael went to fetch his bassoon. Being the section leader at least meant she didn't have to squeeze through other instruments to reach her seat. She was still trying to decide on how to break the news about her recent inheritance to her fellow cellists. (She had not brought the Strad with her that evening: it was still in its bank vault waiting for insurance to allow it out.)

Erin could see she was more excitable than usual but, along with the others in the section, she had no idea why. She occupied herself with the usual pre-rehearsal tasks of moving her music stand out from under Fenella's recently flicked hair and placing it slightly closer to her and Charlie's seats, which then had to shuffle back, looking behind her apologetically at the third desk, who, in turn, tried to shuffle back a few inches, and so on to the fourth desk, who shifted themselves into the double bass's laps. The impact of Fenella's hairstyle choice was felt throughout the lower strings. No matter how much room Erin tried to leave when setting up at the beginning of the rehearsal, it was never enough. Perhaps Fenella's hair grew faster than other people's?

There was a constant battle between all the strings and Joshua. He, like all conductors, preferred a tight string section arranged around him so they were near enough to pick up on each nuanced beat and change of expression he tried to convey. The first desks all wanted a bit more room, partly so they didn't have to move their heads to see Joshua's baton in their peripheral vision and partly because of collective sectional memory: they preferred not to get drenched in another man's sweat or smell his body odour as a concert progressed. A conductor cannot keep his arms demurely by his sides, and the combination of plain exercise and stress sweating often produced an intensely unpleasant aromatic area around the rostrum. This is not to say Joshua had personal hygiene issues (unlike Oscar), it's just that string herd-memory is very strong. They are not an individualistic breed.

Fenella was busily turning through her Beethoven part to identify any *soli* sections, so she could allow the rest of the cellos to benefit from her musical insight about how best to approach them. It was of no matter to her that she was one of the youngest players in the section, or that Ann, who sat quietly at the back, had spent half a career playing professionally before having children and had probably played more Beethoven symphonies than Fenella had dreamed of. Fenella had never bothered to find out about Ann, or any of the other cellists.

'We haven't done Beethoven for simply ages,' she was saying. 'It's so rewarding to play.'

'You mean it's a damn sight easier than Shostakovich,' said Charlie, remembering an ill-fated programming experiment the year before. Fenella's extravagant style of leading had become miraculously more introspective during the more rhythmically challenging passages. It was almost as if she had got lost and was letting the section make its own way to the next obvious cue. Charlie was not going to let her forget this, and grinned at Erin.

Fenella was spared having to think of a comeback by Joshua getting the rehearsal started, smiling at Erin as he found the page he wanted in his score. He had heard the cellos bitching a hundred times and felt as little sympathy for Fenella as the rest of them did. Quite apart from Erin's inside information about her behaviour, he was at a loss to know why Fenella had blagged herself the lead seat in the section. He had dropped some hints to the committee, but had been rebuffed, being informed that she was a great hope for the future of classical music in the country and that one day the orchestra would be proud of their association with her as a young, developing musician.

He turned to the first movement of the Beethoven as the strings tuned. Fifths approximated, they all set off together in search of G sharps.

A couple of brass players sulked on chairs at the side of the hall, wondering whether to interrupt the rehearsal now Joshua had got it started. A blindingly obvious rehearsal rule had been broken: do the stuff using all the players first, and then the rest that uses smaller forces towards the end so those who aren't needed for that get to leave early. It is no accident that some trombone and tuba players (a) have a vast library of paperbacks coupled with an uncanny ability to count bars rest while also reading (non-challenging texts are preferred, such as Wilbur Smith) and (b) can slip out of a rehearsal almost silently yet bounce immediately back to full volume as soon as they get to the pub.

The Beethoven was scored for only two horns and two trumpets, leaving nothing for the trombones or the third and fourth horns to do.

Their resentment ratcheted up with every G natural that escaped.

David was late to the rehearsal, unusually for him, but as soon as he pushed the door open he frowned. The fact that he had rushed across London to get there as soon as he could, only now to realise he was not even needed, was too much. With a nod of uncharacteristic solidarity to the side-lined brass, he marched up to Joshua and stood behind him. Not quite brazen enough to interrupt the music, he relied on the passive-aggressive approach. When enough string players' eyes had flicked in his direction, Joshua knew something was amiss and turned round. Beethoven dribbled to a halt as his baton rested on the rostrum. He forced a false smile at David.

'Hello? Yes?'

'Sorry, but why are you doing the Beethoven now?'

'Why?' Joshua bit down several possible replies. 'Apart from introducing most of the string section to the lesser spotted G sharp, I thought I'd go wild and rehearse some of the music we have to perform in a few weeks. Is there a problem?'

'Well, it's not the most efficient use of resources.' David gestured at the now glowering brass players on the side chairs. 'Why don't we do the full orchestra bits first and then the Beethoven in the second half and we can let these guys go instead of making them sit around twiddling their thumbs.'

Rafael and Pearl had the decency to look a bit awkward during this, because neither of them had given a second thought to the uneven use of the brass. They also simultaneously remembered the planned financial crisis meeting at the end of the rehearsal. They wanted everyone there to be on board for whatever plan they ended up following. If David had his way, half the brass wouldn't stick around to talk about their options, and would moan about whatever decisions were taken, in their absence, later on.

Rafael did his best meerkat impression to get Joshua's attention, elongating his neck and half-standing, but wasn't noticed.

Joshua sighed, not for the first time that evening.

'OK. We'll do the Mendelssohn now. Sorry guys…' This apology was spread with a wave of his arm to include the forgotten brass and also the rest of the orchestra, now muttering and sorting out all the paper on their stands. Quite a lot of them dropped one or the other part as they tried to sort it out with one hand, the other holding their instrument. Logistical changes took on gargantuan proportions when applied to an orchestra. The other brass returned to their seats in the orchestra.

Meanwhile, Rafael scurried round to talk to Joshua and David. Pearl saw him go, and was relieved he was clearly taking charge of a potentially very confusing evening. She decided to give herself an extra five minutes urn-warm-up time before the break to ensure a good supply of enough hot fluids, whatever the situation.

'What about our financial crisis meeting?' asked Rafael. 'We were going to hold it at the end of this rehearsal and, at this rate, we'll miss all the brass.'

'Oh fuck,' said Joshua, not enough under his breath and noted by several people. 'This was never going to be simple.'

'Ah, yes. I'd forgotten about that.' David had the decency to look sheepish about his part in the current confusion.

'Look,' said Joshua. 'Why don't we have the meeting bit over coffee, then the brass can bugger off to the pub and we can play some Beethoven, and then everyone will be happy. OK?'

'OK.' David nodded, relieved his actions hadn't ruined the whole rehearsal. He was beginning to feel guilty for disrupting it at all, now his latent rage, always induced by London tube travel, had begun to dissipate.

'Yes,' said Rafael. 'That's a good idea. Perhaps you could mention it before the break?'

'Gotcha,' said Joshua, returning his attention to the orchestra. 'Could we have an A for the brass, please?'

Soon the journey to Fingal's Cave was being enacted once more, as the sun tried to slant through encrusted windows too high for the caretaker to clean.

Pearl was true to her promise and the extended coffee break/meeting was liberally supplied with hot caffeine. She even broke into her emergency chocolate Bourbon biscuit packets. Desperate times called for desperate sugary measures. The cellos had got out first and were standing together with their triumphal Bourbons as the queue looked at them enviously and hoped Pearl had done her calculations better than usual: often any superior biscuit supply caused such a spike of demand there was instant inflation and backroom deals. The worth of the basic currency unit of a digestive was lost in the rising exchange rate.

Ann was asking Fenella about Oscar's funeral.

'Thank you,' said Fenella, nodding with her eyes closed in the vague direction of Ann. 'It was fine. His mother was a bit odd, but I only thought that before I found out why.'

She was hoping to finesse the correct enquiries out of her audience without having to announce it baldly. The ability to assess the mood of an audience is impaired, however, if you seldom look at them. You can hardly *smell* interest or empathy.

Charlie was more preoccupied with the physical mechanics of the funeral to notice.

'Did they have a winch at the grave?'

'Charlie! Shut up!' said Erin. 'What a thing to ask.'

'Don't tell me you haven't been thinking about it too. Or was it a cremation? Did he fit in the oven?'

'Actually,' said Fenella, 'it was a very dignified service. Apart from his mother, who was—'

'But how many people did it take to lift him?'

'Charlie,' said Ann. 'Stop being so size-ist. And Fenella might not want to talk about the funeral.'

Fenella, on the contrary, was itching to tell everyone about her conversation with Mr Montgomery, but felt the conversation slip away from her.

'I'm guessing at least six – maybe eight. Was it eight?' Charlie went on. 'You wouldn't normally get that many round a coffin, but Oscar's would have a bigger perimeter of course.'

Joshua caught the end of this as he joined them, sidling up behind Erin and making the hairs on the back of her neck rise as she caught his familiar scent. He too had no qualms about making blatant fat jokes when Oscar had been such a poisonous personality. His size was probably the one attribute they could at least pretend they were ribbing affectionately.

'Well, he was wide but not tall. You've got to factor in leg room along the sides. Nobody wants to be tripping up when you're carrying that kind of weight.'

'Joshua!' Erin tried to stop him. But he and Charlie were off, leaving the others and any semblance of sensitivity way behind.

'Maybe they had to stick someone on each end as well,' said Charlie. 'A sort of "all points of the compass covered" approach?'

'Ha! But then you couldn't have the front guy walking backwards, could you?'

'Some sort of sling?'

'A harness?'

'Like a carthorse!'

'Enough, boys!' said Erin in a strangled sort of shout. They both turned to her, looking rather sheepish, making her feel more maternal than she liked to around Joshua. That wouldn't do at all.

Ann stepped in, pouring her own kind of balm onto the situation.

'Sorry, Fenella. Though why I feel I have to apologise for these two unreconstructed morons is beyond me. You were saying? Oscar's mother was a bit on edge, was she?'

Fenella smiled her gratitude at Ann.

'Yes, she was. It was all a bit odd. Mummy and I tried to say hello to her when we went in, but all she did was get cross and splutter a bit.'

'Well, she must have been very upset,' said Erin. 'That's understandable.'

'Ah, but I found out why later on!' Fenella scented her chance to tell them. Which was a good thing, given her eyelids were doing their best to obliterate visual clues.

'Go on then,' nudged Charlie, but couldn't resist adding, 'I bet it was a dark family secret. Oscar's not hers or something?'

Erin nudged him sharply with her elbow.

'No – it was just that Oscar left me something in his will,' said Fenella. Now the time had come to tell fellow cellists, the enormity of what she was about to say was making her chest flutter. 'A cello.'

'But he didn't play, did he?' asked Joshua. 'I thought he was a pianist.'

'Yes, he was. But this was something his father had collected, and just left to him along with a load of other stuff, I think. I don't think he'd ever played it at all. Which is a shame.' She paused as long as she dared. 'Because it's a Strad.'

For once, Fenella kept her eyes open to see what kind of effect that statement would have on the cello section of Stockwell Park Orchestra. She was not disappointed.

Joshua recovered first, not having the inbred cellist's inculcated reverence for such an instrument. His reaction encapsulated his years of musical training and verbal dexterity at conveying complex ideas to musicians of all ages and abilities.

'Fuck me.'

'Well,' said Fenella. 'Quite.'

'A Strad?' repeated Charlie. 'You're kidding.'

'No. I had to get all sorts of papers from their lawyer and everything.'

'But you haven't brought it here?' said Ann. 'You're playing your usual one, aren't you?'

'Yes, for the moment.'

'For the moment?' said Joshua. 'You don't mean *you're* going to play it, do you?'

He realised the meaning of this would become absolutely clear as soon as the sound had evaporated off the sentence. He knew, and didn't care.

'Have you tried it yet?' asked Erin. 'Is it any of the famous ones?' She, along with the other cellists, were processing information threads very fast indeed. The lead role in a future Oscar Best Picture film had just landed in the lap of a talentless starlet who knew how to network with the big producers.

There is a subtle and nuanced grid that overlays every section of every orchestra: that of talent. Most of those who play in each section know, to the millimetre, exactly where they are positioned on it, except for those like Fenella who find their confidence leads them to home in on a place a few clicks higher than they should have come to rest. Conventional seating arrangements are supposed to reflect that, with the star players at the front and the ones with more ovine flocking qualities sitting obediently towards the back desks. However, it doesn't always work like that.

Charlie, Ann and Erin were now trying to factor in the news that Fenella now owned, and would perhaps shortly be playing, a Stradivari cello: a da Vinci in a world of disposable stick drawings would be wielded by a crayon-clutching child.

They were not left to do this for long, as Rafael had already started to waft people back to the hall. He wanted to get some decisions out of the orchestra quickly, but didn't know how much more in subs they would be willing to stump up. The gradient of a demand curve is what economists wish they could know in advance of any foray into the market.

You want inelastic demand for what you're selling, and then people will pay almost anything for it. Rafael just didn't know how much his fellow players loved playing in the orchestra. He was about to test it.

They drifted back to their seats. Joshua leaned on the edge of the stage at the side of the hall. Pearl had already told David and Rafael to start without her, as she wanted to clear away the rubbish. They propped the door open so she could hear anything important. It also meant everyone else could hear the cellophane scrunches of dead biscuit packets and Pearl's occasional forays into Cole Porter.

Rafael started the ball rolling. 'I don't know if you've heard any rumours, but the orchestra is facing some rather grave financial problems.'

Looks were exchanged amongst the players and enough of them intersected with Joshua's eyes to confirm to Rafael that the pub telegraph had indeed been put to use the previous week.

'Not only have we lost a substantial regular donation from Mr Ford-Hughes, there is the added possibility that we may face legal action and potential liabilities.'

Gwynneth, the ex-pat from Merthyr Tydfil who played oboe, raised her lilting voice to contribute. 'Is that 'cos that bloody lard-arse flattened his wife?'

The whole hall erupted into laughter. Even Fenella pressed her lips together in what could have been a smile.

'It is an unfortunate result of Oscar's – um… accident – yes,' agreed Rafael, when the laughter had subsided.

'But, lest we are carried away with what happened at the concert,' said David from his seat in the horns, 'let us remember that the result is a big hole in our finances. We, as

a committee, have come up with a couple of ideas. Rafael?'
He gestured to Rafael to carry on.

'Yes.' Rafael looked round at the faces giving him more or
less their full attention. 'Well, as I see it, we have a number
of options. Firstly—'

'This isn't a committee meeting, Rafael,' called a trombone. 'Give us the bad news and we can get on.'

'Right. One: we increase subscriptions.'

There was a rising chorus of disapproval. Players already
dedicated a lot of their spare time to the orchestra, and paid
for the privilege of doing so. In asking much more of them,
Rafael knew he would be flattening off that demand curve.

'Two: we increase ticket prices.'

Again, the murmur of disagreement.

'But we can't sell them at the price they are now!' said
Gwynneth. 'There's only so many concerts me mam can
travel up for, and there's her with the bad hip and being
under the doctor and everything.'

Joshua rolled his eyes at Erin while Gwynneth was speaking. He didn't care about ticket sales as much as he should
have, and the fact that they were now somehow linked to
an octogenarian's health problems in South Wales seemed
surreal. Joshua had not, so far, made the connection between
the broad sweep of culture and music, and the individual
people (apart from himself) who made it an actuality.

'Three,' continued Rafael, gamely.

'Five, sir!' called someone from the back of the violins.
Monty Python would have been proud to be invoked at such
a moment.

'Three,' repeated Rafael, frowning at the violins in general (they operated a cabinet-like collective responsibility

for everything from wrong notes to inappropriate jokes during their accountant's speeches), 'we get a new sponsorship deal.'

For once, there was silence. A sort of 'Is that it?' kind of silence from a group of people who had not quite realised how terminal this situation could be until this moment.

'So,' said David. 'What do people think?'

'You mean, what is the least-worst scenario?' said Marco, from the violins, trying to counterbalance his section's bad karma both from the recent heckle and latent guilt about the string of events on his part. He still half-believed he had cursed Oscar to his death during the concert and had said as little as possible to anyone in the intervening days. He had tried not to think articulated thoughts, concentrating on nebulous coloured shapes instead, while worrying it was too late for him to learn how to meditate.

His desk partner, the ever gloomy Maureen, wasn't so kind.

'You mean we're broke and might as well give up now.'

'Maureen's contribution is as constructive as usual,' said Charlie. All those within hearing distance laughed, all those outside it realised they'd missed something. Nothing new there in orchestral rehearsals.

'Perhaps we could throw it open to you?' asked Rafael, realising the meeting could be slipping away from him. 'Do you have any suggestions?'

There were quite a number, some more serious than others.

'Get someone to do a reality TV documentary on us.'

'Cake stall?'

'Jumble sale.'

'Promise a free death every concert.'

'Leaflet the whole town.'

Erin listened, remembering what they had talked about in the pub. She cleared her throat.

'Why don't we go and see the Ford-Hugheses? Apologise, you know? Take flowers. Wouldn't that go some way to patching things up?'

Joshua looked at her admiringly, as did David and Rafael. The hubbub subsided and the only thing to be heard was a faint trail of 'Do You Want to See Paris?' from Pearl in the corridor. She produced a surprisingly wide vibrato. A giggle rippled round the orchestra.

'It would take more than a pretty apology to change his mind,' said David. 'He is a businessman renowned for his acumen.'

'A tight-arsed bastard,' qualified Charlie.

For once, David smiled, and didn't disagree.

'Well,' continued Erin. 'What about a deal then. Is there anything they want that we can give?'

Ann raised her hand from the back of the cellos. 'How about? – well, I know Mrs Ford-Hughes is a keen amateur singer. How about offering her a small solo? We could do a Bach thing towards Christmas, surely?'

There were openly admiring looks beamed towards her, only slightly tinged with surprise that it had been she who had come up with the best idea so far. A Bach aria, or better still, a duet, would be a manageable event which could contain any damage done by employing other soloists to corral any mistakes. There were any number of Bach oratorios with multiple solo parts.

Joshua's mind was racing through the oratorios he knew, trying to come up with something suitable.

'Do you know, that's an excellent suggestion,' said Rafael, smiling warmly at Ann.

'Right, well, why don't we try that before any of the other more difficult options?' said David. 'Erin, would you care to accompany me to visit Mr and Mrs Ford-Hughes this Saturday to put it to them?'

Erin gulped with surprise. This had not been part of her plan.

'Oh go on,' said Joshua. 'I've got to go too. We could make it a threesome.'

Erin blushed as the whole orchestra exploded in a salacious imagining of what that threesome might look like. As soon as some of them started to visualise David in that scenario, the sniggering came to an abrupt halt.

Erin looked at Joshua, wishing he could sometimes rein his flirting in, but partly thrilled he couldn't. Charlie could see she was right in the middle of the dangerously conflicted zone of clandestine romance, and that he could do nothing to help. To give him credit, he did nothing to expose her further either.

'Oh. OK then,' she said.

'Good,' said David. 'That's settled.'

'Thank you for your time,' said Rafael. 'On with the rehearsal.'

Joshua sauntered back to the rostrum, grinning at Erin.

'Right,' he called to the orchestra in general. 'Let's do ten more minutes on *Fingal*, then the brass can bugger off to the pub and we can get stuck into Beethoven for the rest of it.'

There was a cheer from assorted trombones, horns and trumpets.

'As long as you get me a beer in,' added Joshua, only half joking. 'If I'm going to have to go and talk to the Ford-Hugheses, you all owe me one!'

There was a general murmur of agreement, and the music started again.

Chapter 10

The Ford-Hughes's house was a substantial detached building on Prince of Wales Drive, overlooking Battersea Park. Erin and Joshua met on Albert Bridge, by the sign warning troops to break step as they cross. Everyone who reads those signs crosses the bridge hypersensitive to any tremor. These days not so many foot soldiers march out from Chelsea Barracks and the old bridge still stands.

They strolled south through the park, past tennis courts and kids' football games and municipally planted flowerbeds sprawling into hairy middle age. Gone were the feverish council clipping sessions of spring and summer. The park was already feeling autumnal. The smell of rotting weed at the pond edge was less pungent, and mallards poked their bills into it to chase burrowing invertebrate snacks.

Joshua took Erin's hand and in an instant she was seventeen again, giddy with it. He really did not leave her with any defences. She knew she should grow some. Her last heartbreak had been embedded into almost forgotten teenage years, leaving her with an unlined face and most of her lifetime allocation of trust left. You can't plan ahead through the hormone rush of an affair.

'So – Fenella's got a Strad, eh?' he said as they stopped to look at a pair of coots in the pond.

'Yeah. I still can't believe it.'

'What I can't believe is that she's planning on keeping it.'

'What do you mean?'

'It should be on loan to a professional: being played.'

'Well, she seems to think she can play it.' Erin was trying to steer her course around the bitchiness trying to ooze out of her skin: a mixture of envy and resentment over the whole set of Fenella's life circumstances. Knowing you can play better than someone else does not necessarily equip you with what is necessary to fulfil your promise. It requires a single-minded purpose that few people develop, with some not wishing to barter away what must be lost in order to possess it.

They walked south, towards their appointment with David at the Ford-Hughes's mansion.

'You know what I mean,' said Joshua. 'Someone who can take it round the world and play concertos to thousands of people. Who can make recordings with famous conductors with unpronounceable names.'

'Yes, yes, Hector Projector,' said Erin in a mock soothing voice. 'We all know you are destined for the big time. All you need now is an exotic name.'

Joshua glanced at her as they walked, smarting at her implied criticism. Their relationship only existed in the moments of their meetings, and he engineered it that way deliberately. One must compartmentalise in order to survive. Erin had not yet felt to the edge of the box he had put her in, and he was quick to use all the tricks he knew to obfuscate the boundary as she neared one side or another.

'Talent, my dear, is what will get me to the big time,' he said. If she could play at tweaking a view of the future, so could he.

'Oh, look! There's David. Crikey, is that where we're going?' she said.

He followed her gaze and saw David standing on the other side of the road bordering the park, outside a four storey, stuccoed mansion. Joshua dropped Erin's hand as they went through the gate out of the park, opening up a more suitable distance between them as platonic friends out for a walk, and David smiled and sketched a wave as he caught sight of them approaching.

'Good morning Joshua… Erin.' He nodded at each in turn. 'Glad you could make it. These things are never easy on one's own.'

'Some pile!' said Joshua, nodding up at the immaculate building.

Erin wished she had spent a little more time that morning deciding which shoes to wear. Even the gravel on the way to the front door looked as if it had been raked, perhaps several times that day already. The end-of-season feel of Battersea Park a few feet away didn't seem to have encroached. There was not a leaf on the ground.

'Shall we?' David asked, gesturing for Erin to go first. Three pairs of feet announced their arrival on the pristine gravel. Erin half-expected a gardener to materialise from behind a geometrically clipped bay to brush over any flecks of gravel their footsteps had dislodged from their positions of perfect zen enlightenment. However, they reached the highly polished door unmolested. David lifted the ring and let it fall with an oiled thud, and the heavy sound wave pushed inside the house with all the assurance of conspicuous wealth.

'Do you think there's a butler?' whispered Joshua.

David frowned quickly, and mouthed 'behave' just before the door swung inwards.

Mr Ford-Hughes opened the door himself, looking as if he rather regretted agreeing to see them. He was wearing elephant cord trousers almost the same shade of gold as the gravel, and clearly made no sartorial concessions to the weekend: a silk tie, expertly knotted, and what looked like a cashmere jersey seemed to be as informal as he was prepared to get.

He stepped back and pulled the door wider to let them in. 'Well, come on then. Come on in.'

'Thank you,' said David, grateful for his last-minute decision that morning to polish his shoes. 'And thank you for seeing us.'

Mr Ford-Hughes muttered something between a cough and a 'hmm', shut the door firmly and walked with purpose along the hall and through double doors into a drawing room. David, Joshua and Erin followed him over the Persian rug. Erin trailed her finger over the edge of the hall table as she passed, feeling the solid, waxy surface and inhaling the scent of beeswax from the wood and roses from the imposing vase standing in the centre of the table. The vase looked vaguely oriental. She had no doubt it would be Ming.

'My wife will be down shortly,' said Mr Ford-Hughes from the drawing room, and Erin quickened her pace to join him, feeling like a schoolchild loitering behind the group on a museum trip. 'Meanwhile, I've asked Paola to serve coffee.'

Joshua shot Erin a look that plainly said 'Butler!' which she did her best to ignore.

They were invited to sit on any of the large number of plump sofas and armchairs arranged around the fireplace. It is always tricky when visiting people to know which chair to avoid. There is always one favourite that it is unwise to take, especially when the person who may or may not have a preference is out of the room but is expected momentarily. Mr Ford-Hughes offered no assistance, so Erin perched at one end of a vast sofa and tried to look as temporary as possible in case she had to leap up. David and Joshua took an armchair each, Joshua sinking into the cushions and looking instantly at home, while David remained vigilant and upright.

Mr Ford-Hughes continued to stand. Perhaps he had read all the psychological research showing how aggressive body language can turn a social interaction to your advantage. Perhaps he was merely waiting for Paola with the coffee? She duly appeared bearing a large tray with cups, saucers and all the paraphernalia of spoons, cafetière, milk jug and sugar bowl, accompanied by the tinkling of small crockery towers. She carefully laid the tray on a low table and silently retreated.

Mr Ford-Hughes did not thank her, nor did he step forward to pour coffee for his guests. He walked towards the group of chairs, glared at Joshua (it was unclear whether it was Joshua's relaxed posture or his choice of seat which irked him), and lowered himself into another armchair. Although not in the same league as either his wife or Oscar, Mr Ford-Hughes was not a slim man. His stomach came to rest a moment after he had and they both occupied their chair in silence. After a moment, David cleared his throat.

'As I said, Mr Ford-Hughes, thank you very much for letting us visit you this morning.'

'My wife will be down shortly,' he replied, looking at the open double doors. 'Her injuries make it difficult for her. Things take longer.' He turned back to David pointedly, making it quite clear he knew whom to blame for his wife's injuries. His eyes moved to the coffee pot. 'My wife usually pours…' he said, looking vaguely at Erin as the sole female representative in the room. She took the hint. The coffee aroma was tickling all their nostrils.

'Shall I?' she asked, rather too brightly.

'Hmm, yes. I suppose you'll have to.'

Ignoring his sexism and lack of awareness of even the basic rules of politeness, Erin was in the middle of sorting cream and sugar (both, four lumps) for Mr Ford-Hughes, when the sound of footsteps in the hall announced the arrival of Mrs Ford-Hughes. Both her husband and David immediately stood up and, after a moment of head-jerking from Erin, so did Joshua. She wasn't sure if she was expected to, but found she was so swept up in the feeling of inferiority she rose too, quelling the impulse to curtsey.

Mrs Ford-Hughes's bosom drifted into the room first. She was wearing a tunic over wide trousers: the kind of floaty garment favoured by substantial women for its slimming properties. It had failed her. Her right arm was held in a sling, and she kept her left fluttering over it protectively as she walked. Erin reminded herself that it had only been two weeks since Oscar had died on top of her, and that Mrs Ford-Hughes was probably still in a considerable amount of pain. Also that she was not responsible for the manners of her husband. She smiled, preparing herself to deliver her charm onslaught and hoping it would be well-received.

Within thirty seconds Erin saw her envisaged plan was not going to work.

Mrs Ford-Hughes sailed past David and Joshua without greeting them, smiled at her husband, then stared at Erin holding the coffee pot.

'I was just – pouring?' Erin heard her voice rise like a transplanted Australian. 'Would you like some?'

'I'll pour,' she snapped. To Erin's surprise, her voice betrayed the melted caramel edges of a southern American accent. Erin was about to guess Texas, but realised that was probably because she didn't know many other states.

She surrendered the pot and they settled back in their seats. It took a long time to distribute the coffee, owing to the one-armed nature of the pourer, but eventually five cups steamed on the table and it was clear that the meeting had begun.

'Well?' asked Mr Ford-Hughes. 'You wanted to see us.'

'Yes,' said David. 'Firstly, I'd like to say again how sorry we are for what happened at the concert. I'm glad to see you out of hospital, Mrs Ford-Hughes.'

She softened a little and accepted his good wishes with a small nod of her head.

'Get to the point,' said Mr Ford-Hughes, drinking his coffee with sharp sips, like a bird pecking for food. 'My wife tires easily at present, and I would prefer not to engender a setback at this stage.' His eyes swept around his guests as if machine gunning all three of them.

'Of course,' said David, with only a slight rattle of the cup on his saucer. 'Well, we were discussing the forthcoming orchestral programme, and Erin here came up with a terrific suggestion, which I thought you might like to hear.'

Erin smiled at this description, smoothing her hands over her knees to get the crinkles out of her mind before she started. Mrs Ford-Hughes tried to turn her head to watch her, but winced as her collarbone protested at the attempted flex.

'Yes, well, we all thought it would be lovely to play some Bach at Christmas. Who doesn't? And, well – um – Joshua here was suggesting some oratorios we could include in the programme...'

Joshua nodded enthusiastically at both Mr and Mrs Ford-Hughes, relieved that he didn't have to talk yet. Erin carried on.

'...and then someone mentioned you were an accomplished singer.' She turned to Mrs Ford-Hughes, who looked surprised and pleased, and remained facing forwards. 'We wondered if you might like to take a solo? I don't know if you have any favourites? We were thinking maybe the *Magnificat*? I'm afraid,' she laughed a very small, self-deprecating laugh, 'I don't even know if you are a soprano, mezzo or alto. Sorry.'

Joshua looked at Erin quickly. This was going a bit off-piste. He didn't think he'd agreed to hand over the actual choice of Bach piece.

Husband and wife looked at each other for a moment.

'Well, darling,' said Mr Ford-Hughes, looking slightly taken aback for the benefit of his audience. 'This is a surprise.'

She looked thoughtful. She and her husband had talked about what would be put on the table during what was clearly a last-ditch attempt at buying back their favour. The clock on the mantelpiece ticked steadily as nobody spoke and each individual cup of coffee silently and steadily obeyed the second law of thermodynamics. Joshua's stomach chose that moment to broadcast to the room that it had not received sufficient breakfast and would not be fobbed off with a single coffee. It was ignored: all attention was on Mrs Ford-Hughes.

Mr and Mrs Ford-Hughes had not achieved all they had to date by passive acceptance of whatever situation in which they found themselves. He had created wealth with a great number of businesses in his empire. She had crossed the Atlantic for him and exuded determination. Together, they were a formidable team. 'Take what you're dealt and deal it right back' had been her father's motto, who was a man who had started with a couple of thousand acres of Arkansas ranch and, by the time he died, influenced business decisions across the United States and worldwide. Some of those decisions had been transformed into Ming porcelain and antique rugs from the best Arab weavers.

Joshua, Erin and David were in no way prepared for what was about to happen.

'I think it's a very interesting proposal,' she said, looking at her perfectly manicured nails as she spoke. 'I don't know who your source is, but they got me on the singing.'

There was an echo of Dolly Parton in the way she said it. That alone made Joshua nervous.

'Would you be interested in doing this?' asked her husband. 'Do you think your collarbone will be healed properly?'

'Oh yes, I think so,' she said. 'In fact, this puts me in mind of a pet project I've had for many years now.'

Joshua shifted around in his chair, worried now.

'It has long been an ambition of mine to do Strauss's *Four Last Songs*.'

'So it has, my dear,' agreed Mr Ford-Hughes, covering smoothly over sudden and palpable rising panic from David, Joshua and Erin.

'Now wouldn't it just be peachy if we could get those into a concert as well?' she asked, eyes wide with an innocence nobody believed in. 'How about the *Magnificat* to start with, then the Strauss, and then maybe a nice concerto or something in the second half?'

David swallowed. 'I'm – er – not sure that—'

Mr Ford-Hughes was quick to interrupt.

'I'm sure you appreciate that if my wife were to be generous-hearted enough to lay to rest the memory of her horrific ordeal, then perhaps we could reconsider our financial arrangement?'

He left that hanging. Joshua was looking at Erin with alarm. David, however, was more pragmatic. He had spent longer than either of the other two in Rafael's company and knew just how essential bringing the Ford-Hugheses back on board was.

'Absolutely,' he said. 'Gosh, would you really be prepared to think about that in return for, I mean, alongside Mrs Ford-Hughes's musical contribution?'

Mr Ford-Hughes almost smiled. 'I would, David.'

'How marvellous,' said his wife, drinking her coffee with the satisfied air of a successful meeting concluded. 'Thank you so much for coming.'

They all rose except Mrs Ford-Hughes, who smiled and waved them away in quite a regal manner. Mr Ford-Hughes showed them to the front door, in a much better mood than he had invited them in, and smoothly herded them out onto his pristine gravel and shut the door.

They crunched their way back onto the street.

'What the frigging fuck have we just agreed to?' hissed Joshua eventually.

'I think you'll find we've just saved the finances of the orchestra and amended the programme of a single concert,' said David.

'You're being very calm about this. You don't have to bloody conduct her! And do you think she'll stop at one?'

'Now don't go getting any ideas about being ill for two concerts in a row,' warned David. 'Look what happened last time. I know nobody blames you, but it has to be said that if an element of blame were to be apportioned, some could, in all honesty, fall on you.'

'Now wait a minute,' Joshua's voice rose.

'He has a point, Joshua,' said Erin, who was carrying her own share of that guilt. 'It's just one concert. We're just going to have to bite the bullet.'

They trudged away from the house. Behind them, the curtain moved at the bay window, where Mr Ford-Hughes was watching their retreating backs and interpreting their conversation quite accurately. He correctly divined grudging acceptance in the droop of their shoulders as they reached the end of the road and he turned from the window with a smile of calm triumph.

Chapter 11

Erin and Joshua left David at Battersea Park station and turned north again to cross the river.

'Do you have time for lunch?' asked Erin. She was always aware of Joshua's wife: the third party in any infidelity. She also knew that 'lunch' seldom meant just lunch but, as the relationship underling, didn't feel able to specify exactly what she wanted. Sometimes she wondered if it was because Joshua kept her giddy so she wouldn't notice. Sometimes she thought she was getting paranoid and over-analytical. Her views oscillated on the continuum of these opinions depending on the elapsed time since he had last kissed her. We are never in as much control as we like to think.

Erin had chosen not to assign herself guilt, since Joshua had pursued *her*, but the longer it went on the more she realised that her position was untenable. The moment an affair tries to turn into a relationship is the moment it ceases to exist solely in the present tense. To admit elements of the past or envisage some sort of future is to take the confection of transient pleasure out of its paper case and to set it more solidly into your life. Erin found it increasingly difficult to go along with Joshua's easy acceptance of how things were.

Her instinct to connect tried to slow her as surely as Joshua's fluid finessing buoyed her up as they swept through the weeks. A river has many serpentine twists and hidden sandbanks to ground the unwary.

'Oh, no, I can't do lunch today, honey,' said Joshua, kissing her hand briefly before letting it drop. 'It was hard enough getting out this morning – gotta do a thing later on. Sorry.'

Erin felt his vagueness grate. Somewhere, very muffled at the back of her brain, a tiny alarm bell blinked into life with a single note. A warning. Not a continuous din. The first.

'Fine.' She heard her voice hide the warning with a breezy insouciance.

'Sorry – I'd much rather spend the afternoon with you,' he said into her ear as they approached Albert Bridge, his hand sliding over her hip. 'You know that.'

Erin heard the alarm again and realised, as clearly as if a filter had been snapped over her vision, that she was being played. That kind of realisation is one-way only. Once it drops, you can never claw back how you felt. Over the course of half a dozen steps all the elements of their affair had been coloured with this new knowledge, and she almost said the 'oh' of realisation out loud. Instead, she merely laughed.

'Of course I know that. I was just asking, you know, on the off-chance.'

They walked over the bridge, out of step.

* * *

Erin got back to her flat, took off her coat, dumped her bag and keys on the table and sat down with the whole afternoon stretching away from her. Her cello case stood in the far corner. There had been a time when all she had wanted to do was play: before the tedium of getting an education or earning a living had encroached. Seized with a sudden feeling of 'Why not?', she walked over and opened the case.

It was not a Stradivari. It was a perfectly serviceable nine-teenth century German model, better than a lot of others. She pulled the velcro strap securing the bow and started tight-ening the bow hair, feeling as always the tickle of old rosin rising as the strands of some unknown horse's tail aligned themselves and straightened their kinks. Her left hand felt, blind, into the inner velvet pocket at the top of the case and emerged with her sellotaped rosin box cupped in its palm like an egg. Deftly balancing the rosin lid on the top clip of her cello case, she rubbed the hard amber along her bow: short, stubby strokes at each end and longer, smoother ones as she worked her way along the length.

The first leaves of autumn were blowing down to her base-ment front door. Erin stared through the window, noted idly that it needed cleaning again and watched the crisp leaves tick their way down her stone steps. She had a powerful sense of the turning of the season. This was just the planet leaning away from our star once more, only the latest change in the rhythm that would go on beyond her and the tiny affairs and manipulations of the minutiae of our lives. There was now. There was what had been.

There was now. And there was Bach.

She laid the bow on a chair and returned the old rosin box to its pocket, feeling the spare strings coiled in their flat enve-lopes against the case wall. She unbuckled the leather strap around the cello's neck and pulled it forward, out of the case, and walked over to the chair. Sitting down, she swung the cello up onto her knees and felt down with her right hand for the spike, undoing the screw and pulling it out from where it had been retracted in the hollow belly of the cello. She tightened the screw again, giving it one last jerk to stop it slipping back when the weight of the cello was resting on it. She settled the end of the spike on the carpet, grateful she wasn't still in the Ford-Hughes's house and had to worry about spearing an expensive rug, and reached behind her for the bow. As she did, the fingers of her left hand bounced delicately over the strings – just enough to set them vibrating to let her know if it was still in tune – before she started to bow the open strings, listening in the double-stopping for that perfect fifth.

A fifth (the distance between the first and fifth note of a scale) has a wavelength ratio of 2:3. This is particularly pleasing to a human ear, and is reflected in our use of the golden ratio across arts as diverse as music, architecture and paintings. It is innate. Leaving all that aside, when Erin's ear heard her strings approach a perfect fifth, it set up additional harmonics that she wasn't even aware she was hearing. It suddenly just sounded right, like the sun coming out from behind a cloud or myopia cured with a lens. Mathematics and music have been entwined for centuries, and have not needed words to know it.

Erin settled the cello into its comfortable place on her ribs and looked out at the leaves again. Her left hand felt around the neck of the cello, oriented itself without her looking and she waited.

Her hand knew what she needed to play, and settled itself ready to start the *Sarabande* of Bach's second Suite. This piece was one of her oldest friends: a shape she knew as well as her own body, that could be both question and answer, whatever mood she found herself in. The first triple-stopped chord set its two open string lower notes ringing while she made the top note live on its own. Only Bach could produce music with such deftness and lightness of touch. He understood harmony in his bones. He knew how to suggest more complex parts than those available to one player with four strings at their disposal. The dance slowly wound itself around the cello and Erin together. She sometimes forgot to breathe until a note had changed and then her bow was joined by an involuntary exhalation as her body took over to ensure enough oxygen was in her blood to let her play the next phrase. Sometimes she was able to sit in the sweet spot of a note and it seemed to encase her in a bubble far away from the fumes of her London street, the sirens and shouts of too many people living too close to each other.

As the last ringing open G died away, she was still staring at the leaves, drifting to the corners of the flight of four steps leading down to her front door. Her left thumb pressed itself to each of the fingers on her left hand in turn, feeling the blood return under thickened skin. Her fingers had never been the same since she started playing cello: their sensitivity was gone. She often wondered how blind cellists ever read Braille: she certainly couldn't feel the subtlety of materials with her left that she could with her right hand. There were advantages. Holding a cup of scalding coffee was a commonplace one that impressed others. Very short nails were not usually admired in the same way, and she had often been accused of being a nail-biter by more glamorous women with perfect manicures. It was merely a question of mechanics: if you try to press as hard as you need to on a cello string with a long nail, either you break the nail or the note won't speak properly. Erin had always preferred music to looking like a fashion model.

She stretched out her arms, pulling tension from her shoulders that shouldn't have been there in the first place. She was out of practice. She frowned, looking at her left hand. Compared to a non-cellist, her finger pads were stiff and hard. But she knew that lack of practice had softened them, and if she were to play on for two more hours they would be red and sore. Orchestra once a week was not a substitute for the practice she used to do.

She balanced her cello on its side, laid the bow on top and walked over to her tall bookshelf. Climbing a stool, she reached up and lifted a large stack of music from the very top, above the books. She wondered if she had put it there deliberately out of reach. Sitting on the stool, she expertly flicked each booklet up from the pile on her lap and caught it at the vertical under her chin, until she found the one she wanted. The pile went on the floor. She found her music stand, extended all the complicated bits of metal that had to be opened in exactly the right order for it not to be knotted up like some sort of tedious steel puzzle and tightened the nuts. She smoothed the music onto the stand, settled with her cello once more and started her warm up exercises of daily studies. One cycle of them took forty minutes and, when she was in practice, this would be an automatic start before she did any serious work on a piece. It was time to relearn.

Chapter 12

Joshua had indeed planned 'a thing to do later on'. Before he had even left his house that morning, he had called Fenella and arranged to meet, offering himself as some kind of musical expert when she went to collect her Strad. After all, she had never heard his opinion of her playing, and he wasn't going to let an old, hasty opinion get between him and a piece of musical history. His wife, equally impressed by the thought of a Stradivari furthering her husband's conducting career, had simply encouraged him. Joshua was aware how fortunate he was in his choice of wife.

Fenella had informed him she was to be accompanied by 'Mummy' for the actual collection, but agreed to give him a cup of tea back at her flat when she returned. Thus it was nearly three o'clock when Joshua pushed the bell of Fenella's apartment in Hammersmith.

'Oh, hi, Joshua,' she said, her face framed on the video intercom. 'I'll buzz you in. Come up.'

Her apartment building was somewhere on the upper part of the scale between Erin's flat and the Ford-Hughes house. Joshua smelled window polish and high-class carpet shampoo as he crossed the lobby to the lift which, even he noticed, was spectacularly clean. He slipped a piece of spearmint chewing gum into his mouth on the way up, as a chameleon will copy the most important aspects of his surroundings. He was not going to distract Fenella in her own habitat with a second-hand aroma of salt and vinegar crisps.

She opened the door wide as he approached.

'Well! This is nice!' she said, kissing each of his cheeks when he was close enough to aim at. Already the chewing gum had paid dividends. Joshua was slightly shocked: her greetings at orchestral rehearsals were much more informal. And distanced. He felt some of her transferred moisturiser evaporate off his cheek and fought the urge to wipe the rest, refusing to look like an eight-year-old. He could get used to this, now he was apparently her friend rather than merely her conductor. And actually, her moisturiser smelled good.

'Hi,' he said, walking into the open-plan flat. 'Wow – that's quite a view.'

Two walls of Fenella's flat were entirely glass and, from the fifth floor perspective, he could see the Thames rolling past.

'Isn't it marvellous?' she agreed. 'That's the main reason I chose this flat. Gets a bit hectic round here on boat race day though!'

They both laughed in the way people do to share non-aggression rather than agreeing there had been anything amusing said.

'So,' she continued, 'would you like some tea? Or are you itching to see it?'

'Um – both? Is that possible? Is that it?'

Joshua was looking towards a second cello case standing by the grand piano, alongside Fenella's familiar usual one.

It was the usual size and a dull brown colour. Nothing suggested the cello inside was in any way out of the ordinary.

'Yes,' called Fenella from behind her open plan kitchen island, where she was filling the kettle.

'It looks so ordinary.'

'It does, doesn't it? Mummy was quite disappointed, I think, when she saw it this morning. I think she was expecting a gold-plated case or something.'

Another joint laugh. The kettle started to accompany it, and Fenella reached into cupboards for tea and cups.

'So, was it complicated?' said Joshua. 'To collect, I mean? Did you have to have an armed guard or anything?'

'Ha! No, nothing like that.' She flicked her hair over one shoulder to get it out of the way of spooning tea into the pot. 'We just showed all my ID and proof of ownership and stuff, and then off we went.'

She brought a tray with a teapot, two china cups and saucers round the kitchen island, set it on a table and walked to the cello case. Each of the five catches flipped back with a creak as the tension was loosened, then a metallic rattle as the tarnished loop fell to one side. As she opened the case, Joshua caught his breath at the sight of the cello. Its varnish – the famous Stradivari red varnish – seemed to glow, illuminating the grain of the wood underneath. It is said that this secret varnish recipe is what gave his instruments such an extraordinary tone and depth. Nobody else had matched it, at the time or since. Fenella held it carefully round the neck and lifted it out of the case. The light touch of her hand on the strings set a couple of them softly ringing.

She gave it to Joshua to hold while she got the bow from the case.

'Are you sure?' he said. He wasn't a cellist, and had never been in charge of any instrument worth this amount of money before.

'I trust you,' she said, turning for the bow with a smile.

'Did that bow come as part of the package?' he asked.

'Yep. It's probably worth more than a lot of cellos itself. Scary really.'

Joshua plucked the strings one by one, listening to the sound decay in awe. Even plucked, the sound of this cello was different: richer with fewer tinny overtones than on a modern instrument.

Fenella held her hand out for it when she'd tightened the bow, and took it over to her practice chair by the piano.

'I'm not used to it yet – I've only played it once, when I got it home this morning.'

'Oh, let's just hear some!'

'It needs playing. It's been stuck in that bank for years. It'll take weeks to play it in properly.'

'What do you mean?'

'String instruments need playing. They go sort of stiff when they're not. A bit like us being out of practice. When you play it for hours every day it loosens up: it makes a huge difference to how it sounds.'

'Oh. I'd heard about that. Suppose I never really thought about it, though.' One of many things Joshua was discovering he was not an expert in.

'And these strings need changing too – God knows how long they've been on. I need to get the whole thing looked at properly.'

She checked the tuning, and the resonant fifths bounced off the walls and windows. Then she played a few scales at random, feeling the range of the cello stretch from sturdiness in the bass notes up to a supple top register. She let a few *arpeggios* arc under her bow, then seamlessly went into the first few bars of Elgar's Concerto, which is what all cellists do when they try out a new instrument in front of other people. In a few short bars you can play impressive quadruple-stopped chords and then slide off into a sinuous melody that everyone can hum. She stopped after a bit and tried some of the Brahms *E Minor Sonata*, which starts with a lush tune rising up the C string: the bottom string of a cello, usually kept for bass lines, not the main melody. Brahms knew how to tempt sexiness out of that string, and Fenella played it, as usual with her eyes closed. Since she was playing completely solo, her idiosyncratic grasp of rhythm was not so obvious.

Joshua watched her with close attention. He had never heard Fenella sound so good. Well – not as irritatingly bad as usual – anyway. He was not, as has been noted, a cellist himself. He was primarily a pianist before deciding to be a conductor, and had picked up enough of the technical stuff about most instruments to be able to hold a conversation in an orchestral rehearsal without seeming too ignorant. He lacked the apprentice years playing in orchestras as a child, which an orchestra can sense and exploit. He sometimes had the glib brittleness of a management consultant flown in to fix structural problems. However, even he could hear the tone of the Stradivari ringing out under Fenella's fingers.

He poured tea for them both, then walked round to the piano keyboard as she played and sat on the stool there to watch from a different angle, sipping his tea. He saw the piano part of the Brahms lying on top of a stack of music piled on the piano lid and reached for it.

The next time Fenella stopped, he said, 'Shall we run through this?'

Always happy to play, she agreed, and hunted through her own stack of music at the other end of the piano. Their tea, his – half-drunk and hers – untouched, went cold.

A sonata is a musical conversation between two people, and Brahms was an expert at writing them. Playing chamber music with someone lets you get to know sides of them more quickly than talking: it's like a dance. There is an ebb and flow between the piano and cello just as there is when we talk, with questions answered and suggestions made. By the end of the first movement, Joshua was aware of most of Fenella's weaknesses as a musician, but knew a lot of them were being covered up by the instrument she was playing, as well as his split-second adjustments to his accompaniment as she miscounted a tie or set off too eagerly on a quaver run. He wondered if she had ever played the Brahms to a teacher and, if so, if any of her errors had been pointed out. Maybe they had and maybe Fenella simply forgot or ignored advice?

By the end of the fourth movement, he started to form a plan that would make Machiavelli proud.

Fenella finished the Brahms on her quadruple-stopped chord with a flourish, lifting her bow off the strings, bringing her hand up and round in a circle and letting the sound of the Strad ring out. Joshua, with the sheet music of Elgar's Concerto flat in front of him on the piano, started to nibble gently around his idea.

'Did you know that the chord you just played is exactly the same as the final one of the Elgar? Isn't it funny how composers can't think of any other way to end a cello piece in E minor. It's the second chord Elgar starts with, too.'

Fenella put her head on one side, looked at the end of the Brahms and felt around the neck of her cello with her left hand for the position of the chord. She then hooked her bow into the palm of her right hand, strummed with her right thumb the first few chords of the Elgar Concerto and smiled at him.

'I never noticed that before!'

Joshua marvelled at how a tiny coincidence could be given preternatural weight merely by connecting it in a sentence. Joshua was not a mystic. He had, however, a good photographic memory (great for learning scores quickly) and a pianist's ability to recognise the shape of a chord under his fingers, as a proficient reader will know the word being read with a glance at its shape without having to sound out the letters.

And now Fenella was absorbing the idea that his powers of observation were both keen and directed solely at herself.

He picked up the Elgar music, seeing the idiosyncratic Novello typeface making Elgar's melody look perkier than it would have in any other printing. Anyone who has played or sung Elgar knows what a Novello score looks like, with the 'o's of each crotchet and quaver eagerly making their slanty way into the next note. It is as if they are all leaning up and forward, hurrying along. The Brahms, in contrast, in its stolid Breitkopf edition, positively reeked of Germanic heaviness and four-square metronomic rhythms. Its crotchet heads were round and fat. Even the identical chords which finished each piece looked very different. Fonts insinuate themselves into the mood of a book. Printed music influences the way people play the notes. Perhaps that explains why Jacqueline du Pré looked so irritatingly buoyant: she spent too much time with her Novello notes.

Joshua hadn't finished with Fenella.

'I'd love to hear some more. Have you ever done the Elgar? Would you be up for a bit more, or are you all E minored out?'

Fenella laughed, as Joshua had intended her to. And agreed. He smiled, handing her the cello part of the Elgar.

'What about some more tea first? We don't seem to have got very far with the first cup. Sorry.' He was far from sorry.

As Fenella laid the Strad carefully on its side by her chair and rose to fill the kettle, Joshua carried on smiling, embracing the ease of it all.

Chapter 13

David telephoned Rafael, and later Pearl, on Saturday afternoon after their visit to Mr and Mrs Ford-Hughes. He knew Pearl wouldn't mind what happened as long as she could see the problem being sorted out and the result allowing her to continue doing the things she loved: playing in her orchestra and feeling indispensable running it. Before putting the call through to Rafael, though, David was apprehensive. Rafael had made it very clear how grave he thought the financial situation was, but David wondered if anyone not present in that room while Mr and Mrs Ford-Hughes operated their slick pincer movement operation would quite appreciate the absolute snowball's chance in hell they had of getting out without agreeing.

David allowed himself a small tomato juice before dialling. He sharpened a pencil and made a bullet point list on an old water bill envelope, to keep him focused during the call. Sitting at his kitchen table with the smell of lunch's bacon wafting out of the open window, he took a deep breath and picked up the phone.

'Hello?' Rafael's clipped voice suited the tinny quality of electromagnetic transfer of sound. He had a Mozart piano concerto on in the background, which did not survive the transfer quite so well.

'Rafael? David. Hi.'

'Ah. How did it go? I've been expecting your call.'

'Well, they agreed to see us. Mrs Ford-Hughes seems very well recovered. Considering.'

There was a pause.

'And?'

'Well, yes. Erin was very useful. She buttered them up marvellously. Even Mr Ford-Hughes seemed to like her, in the end.'

'Indeed?' Rafael's voice was edging towards incredulity. 'What happened? Is she singing some Bach and are we getting their money back?'

'Ah, well. Yes, she is singing. Seemed to think it was a great idea, and contributed a few ideas too.'

'And the money?'

'Well, that's not quite finalised yet. We did get him to agree to revisit his decision, but by the end of the meeting they were really both sounding quite positive about the whole relationship again.'

'That's great news. Well done.'

David swallowed some tomato juice, to lubricate his dry mouth for the next bit.

'Mrs Ford-Hughes was incredibly keen, actually. Who knew she was such a strong amateur singer?'

'Oh?' Rafael didn't like the sound of the way this conversation was going.

'Yes, she not only suggested some Bach – liked the idea of the *Magnificat* actually – but also mentioned that she had always wanted to do the *Four Last Songs*.'

Rafael's blink was almost audible.

'Strauss?'

'Er, yes.'

'Richard Strauss? Those *Four Last Songs*?'

'Yes.'

'Bloody hell.'

'Well, Joshua wasn't too keen either at first—'

'I'm not surprised!'

'But he came around in the end. As Erin said, it's just one concert, and if it means we'll get their financial support again, surely it's worth it.'

'If,' said Rafael, with dark cynicism in his voice. 'Do you think they will?'

'We just need to rejig the programme a bit for this term. What would you say to keeping *Fingal's Cave*, plus maybe excerpts from the *Magnificat*, then instead of the symphony we were planning how about Mrs Ford-Hughes's Strauss and maybe a concerto or something in the second half?'

David pencilled small ticks on the list in front of him while Rafael digested these suggestions in silence. Mozart changed from *adagio* to *allegro* with a flourish from the pianist.

'Has anyone actually heard her sing?'

'Ah.' David had been hoping Rafael wasn't going to ask that, but gamely underlined his next bullet point and carried on. 'Nobody that I know. Don't think Ann has – she'd just heard she was a singer. But if you think about it, they are bound to swell the audience to the concert with a substantial number of their friends and family. If it is, to a certain extent, a vanity project, we can at least expect them to help sell tickets.'

'Mmm. I suppose in that case their friends won't hold it against us if it's complete rubbish.'

'Exactly.' This was going better than David had hoped.

'Well, there's nothing we can do, is there? If Joshua is on board with it, then I suppose we'll just have to knuckle down and get through it. If we're doing a Bach thing, can we use that local choral society we had a couple of years ago for Beethoven 9? Do you think they can do it at such short notice?' Rafael's analytical brain was already motoring through the practical issues with a reinvented concert three short months away.

'Well, we can try,' said David. 'It may be some of them can – we won't need their full strength anyway, for Bach. I'll have a word with Joshua and see what he thinks about choral rehearsals.'

'We know what Joshua thinks about choral rehearsals. Let's just hope he can keep a lid on it.'

David ended their conversation with a much lighter heart than when he started. Now all he had to do, he realised, as he ticked the last of his bullet points, was to sell it to the orchestra without anyone leaving or having a hissy fit. He restrained himself from adding vodka to his tomato juice. It was early. And he had promised he wouldn't do that anymore. And despite all the misgivings about Mrs Ford-Hughes's abilities as a soprano, he loved the Strauss songs and hadn't yet had a chance to play them. All horn players know the beautiful and terrifying four bars of solo at the end of the second song, *September*: so exposed, just when the soprano finishes singing, conveying the weight of Richard Strauss's regret and acceptance of death. David was already looking forward to playing them, even from his low fourth horn vantage point. The nerves of the solo would be at the other end of the line.

He drained his tomato juice and wandered out into the garden to kick a football about with his ten-year-old.

He was surprised later that afternoon to have a call from Joshua, who also wanted to talk about the next concert. It took less than five minutes for Joshua to convince David of the benefits of having a Stradivari cello headlining the evening, not least among which was the fact that Fenella would not need paying as she was keen enough just to get solo exposure. She would gain publicity and could invite press and agents along to hear her. The orchestra would get a free concerto on a priceless instrument. And Mr and Mrs Ford-Hughes would be associated with a piece of history. David couldn't see any flaws, apart from the musical ones.

So, by Monday's rehearsal, Joshua had accepted he was going to have to conduct the untried Mrs Ford-Hughes in Strauss. On the other hand, he had the *Elgar Cello Concerto* on a Strad. This was what professional conductors dealt with all the time. He could massage the enormous Ford-Hughes ego and attempt to get through four pretty tricky songs without them falling apart. He could hope Fenella's counting didn't go too AWOL during the Elgar or, if it did, hope that the orchestra for once in its amateur life could watch him and stay with it. But to conduct a Strad! That would get the critics in. Then at last he'd get some exposure and reviews, and start to move on.

He had forgotten, of course, that the programme was also to include some Bach and the interminable *Fingal's Cave*. And that the Bach would necessitate a chorus. He had forgotten that right up until Monday's rehearsal, and was unpacking his baton while everyone else was getting out their instruments when David stood up at the front and raised his hand to get their attention.

'Good evening, everyone. Er, I'd just like to update you on our meeting with Mr and Mrs Ford-Hughes at the weekend.'

Erin turned round while rosining her bow to get a look at the reaction David was going to get. She had had a few days to get used to the Strauss idea, and wondered how David was going to spin it for the orchestra. Joshua was on the other side of the hall and gave her a quick smile. She hadn't seen him since the meeting and hadn't heard from him either.

Charlie was standing next to her, also getting his cello ready to play.

'Did you work your feminine magic, then?' he whispered, as the other players stopped talking for David. 'Are we getting a fat, wobbly Bach aria?'

Erin looked at Charlie apologetically. 'It's a bit more than that. I'll let him explain.'

Charlie raised his eyebrows and looked over at David.

'As you know,' he was saying, 'Joshua, Erin and I visited Mr and Mrs Ford-Hughes last Saturday to see if we could come to some sort of… arrangement regarding our forthcoming programme and, um, their forthcoming funding.'

A laugh rippled round the orchestra. David was encouraged.

'You'll all be pleased to hear Mrs Ford-Hughes is making a good recovery from her broken collarbone. She would be delighted to join us for a bit of Bach's *Magnificat* before Christmas.'

There were murmurs of congratulation, during which Fenella walked in and put her cello case down near Erin and Charlie. They looked at it. It wasn't her normal one.

'Bloody hell,' said Charlie. 'Is that what I think it is?'

Fenella nodded, a tight grin of excitement around her face.

'Really?' asked Erin. 'You brought it on the tube?'

'No!' said Fenella. 'Came in the car. Thought I'd better, for now. Has David said about the concert yet?'

'He's just getting to it,' said Charlie, with only half an ear on David now that Fenella was about to open her case. 'Come on, let's have a look then.'

'It's great news, isn't it?' said Fenella. 'What an opportunity!'

Charlie and Erin both thought Mrs Ford-Hughes's singing couldn't quite be classed as an 'opportunity', but were too distracted by the thought of standing next to a multi-million pound Strad to take much notice.

David continued to speak, clearing his throat for the next bit.

'She also suggested we could do Strauss's *Four Last Songs* together, perhaps with a concerto to round the whole thing off.'

Joshua looked over at Erin and grimaced in a 'we're all in it together' kind of way.

'Why, does her husband play something as well?' came the heckle from a trumpeter. 'It could be a Ford-Hughes double act.'

'It's OK, we could do Cage's *4'33"*,' quipped someone else.

There were guffaws from the players, thinking that scenario was far-removed from actual events, until someone else remembered why the Ford-Hughes were being involved at all.

'Hang on. I thought we were broke. How can we afford a soloist for a concerto?'

'Ah – that's where we are fortunate indeed!' said David, quickening up now he could sense the end of his speech. 'Fenella has kindly offered to play the Elgar Concerto with us on her newly-acquired cello.'

Several faces turned to Fenella in silence, including Erin's. Fenella herself was extracting her cello from its case and looked up at that moment and across to Joshua. Erin followed her eyes and froze.

'What?' said Marco, from the violins. He was not the only one.

Joshua was not looking at Erin. He was looking at Fenella, with that warm, open smile that Erin knew very well indeed. He caught Erin's gaze then and she saw the flicker of self-awareness over his face that answered all her half-asked questions of that week. She had clearly been dumped by a man who did not belong to her anyway, for a ditzy airhead and a better cello. Even Erin at that moment could appreciate Joshua was moving on for the dual attractions, not just for the hair flicking allure of Fenella alone. Fenella with an ordinary cello was an annoying, basic player who couldn't count and never watched the conductor. But Fenella with a Strad was a magnet for attention, and she knew Joshua couldn't resist that pull.

She turned back to her case to replace her rosin in the top pocket. Charlie did the same with his, having observed the triangle of glances going on underneath David's speech.

'Oh,' he said softly next to Erin's ear.

'I didn't know about that bit,' she said, just as softly.

'Or the other bit, by the looks of things.'

Erin shut her case, holding her cello and bow in one hand. 'No.'

'You can't compete with what she's got.'

'No shit, Sherlock.'

There was a rising noise from the others in the hall, which David tried to dampen down with flattening motions of his hands, to little effect. Joshua peeled himself off the edge of the stage and walked over to his stand.

'You may be interested to hear that Fenella has recently inherited a very fine cello, and we thought it would be a perfect outing for them both.'

'Oh yeah?' sneered someone.

'Well,' said Joshua calmly, 'it's not every day you get to hear a Stradivari play the Elgar right next to you, is it?'

A gasp travelled around the players as if Joshua had discharged some sort of electrical energy with this fact. Fenella picked up her cello and went over to her usual place at the front of the section.

Ann, who had been unpacking her cello close to Erin and Charlie, stepped closer to them.

'Ah. That hasn't gone exactly as I'd hoped,' she said, with a dry sort of smile.

'Just look at her!' said Charlie. 'Instant princess. She's going to be even more insufferable now.'

'I hope the meeting wasn't too awful?' Ann asked Erin. 'I did feel a bit guilty as soon as I saw you'd been press-ganged into going as well.'

'Oh, it was fine. We didn't cover this new development, though,' said Erin.

'No.'

'It's alright for you,' said Charlie. 'I'm the one who's got to sit next to her!'

'Well, look on the bright side,' said Ann. 'You'll be leading the cellos when she's up at the front playing Elgar. Your moment of glory…'

Charlie laughed at Ann despite himself, appreciating for the first time how fun she sounded.

'Oh, you'll be fine,' said Erin. 'I might even come and sit next to you, if we're all moving up one, like Mad Hatters.'

'You're taking... all this,' he hesitated, gesturing to encompass the Fenella adoration going on in front of them as well as what he had seen of Joshua's behaviour, 'very well, considering.'

'Aren't I?' she agreed.

'Good,' said Ann. 'So you'll both come for a drink afterwards then?'

They nodded. One has to have a goal.

Chapter 14

Erin and Ann found themselves a table away from the rest of the players drinking after the rehearsal. Charlie had instructed them to seek one out while he got the first round, and Erin turned her back on the sight of Fenella and Joshua holding court near the bar, both clearly over-excited about their current project. Ann manoeuvred herself to the far side, so their courtship display would be in her sightline, not Erin's. Charlie was not the only one who had picked up on all the evening's layers of developments.

'You're a better cellist than her, you know,' said Ann, nodding to where Fenella was perched, once again, on her favourite bar stool, crossing her legs and giggling more than usual. The Strad case was stowed safely against the wall next to her. Going to a pub as a cello section has its disadvantages: those players who travelled by public transport and therefore couldn't lock them in the boot of a car had to bring them in. This pub was used to them, and staff thought nothing of making a short voyage round a cello case archipelago protruding from the end of the bar. Ann and Erin had tucked theirs beside their table. Ann watched as Charlie made his serpentine way over to them with his case slung on one shoulder and their three drinks cradled between his two hands out in front. Pub carpet is very forgiving.

'Cheers!' said Erin, as her pint came into view over her shoulder. She helped Charlie deposit the glasses, mostly full, onto the table, leaving his hands free to settle his case next to theirs.

'Here's to the next concert, which will be bloody awful!' said Charlie happily, and downed a quarter of his pint.

'Thanks,' said Ann, starting her bottle of lager, and looking back at Erin. 'I meant it. You're better. Don't be put off. The music world isn't run on purely artistic lines: don't expect it to be. It's as corrupt as any other industry.'

'What's this?' asked Charlie.

'I'm trying to tell Erin that she can play rings round Fenella – even Fenella on a Strad.'

Erin laughed, grateful for Ann's support.

'Well, don't just laugh it off, you stupid cow,' said Charlie.

'Ever the charmer,' said Ann.

'You know what I mean. If we don't bash her over the head with it, she's not going to remember any compliment we give her. She's the kind of woman who only takes away the negative comments and erases the good bits. How you girls do it is beyond me.'

There was a silence as Charlie's uncharacteristic emotional astuteness blinded them for a moment.

'It's inbred, I guess,' said Erin.

Ann looked at her without speaking. Erin was thirty years her junior, with none of Ann's grey hair or lined face. Ann had a practical short hairstyle and a slightly whiskery chin. She wore no make up. She had reached the age where she no longer worried about how she looked, she merely wanted to be the right temperature. Some women, more than men, never achieve this state of self-confidence and happiness with their achievements: it is a complicated web of gender assumptions and a drip-feed of behavioural expectations. Her children had left home, save for the occasional weekend visit, and a few years earlier her husband had professed himself to be bored with her bewhiskered chin and buggered off in a cliché of mid-life crisis with a girl about Erin's age. Ann, on the whole, had felt a slight relief at his departure. She taught cello, qualified by the certificates she had from the Royal Academy of Music and her years as a professional cellist before she had become a mother. Full-time work as a classical musician, with its working hours geared to providing entertainment for others in their leisure time, was never going to be child-friendly. She had scaled her ambitions to a more domestic field.

So, for twenty years she had made her living teaching cello. Her reputation and background filtered out the daft ones, the no-hopers and those to whom music would always and forever be an unlearned foreign language. She nurtured the seriously talented – those who would get into the Academy or College or Guildhall and wanted to put in the ten thousand hours of practice it takes to be proficient. She came along to Monday evening rehearsals to keep her hand in and discovered the absolute delight in sitting at the back of the section with nothing to prove – feeling useful merely by being the most musically reliable cellist there. Of course she should have been leading the section, but Ann much preferred it where she was. She could share a joke with the double basses or swap library recommendations with the trombones. She wore sensible shoes and was happier in her fifties than she ever remembered being before.

'When did you last do any practice?' she asked Erin.

'What, apart from every Monday evening, you mean?' said Erin, buying herself time before she had to answer the question for real. Before she'd opened her case that last Saturday afternoon, the answer was a longer time than she ever admitted to herself.

'Do any of us have time these days?' said Charlie. 'We're not at school anymore. We've got jobs. And lives.'

'Try children one day, if you're feeling busy now,' said Ann, with a dry look at Charlie, and then turned back to Erin. 'Come on. How long has it been?'

Erin looked down at her fingers. The tips of her left hand were still a bit bludgeoned from her session at the weekend, now recovering after the secondary pummelling that evening. She ran her thumb over them absentmindedly as she answered.

'Funnily enough, I sat down last Saturday and did four hours straight, after I'd got in from the Ford-Hugheses'. I don't know why, really. Before that, it's been – God – years. Probably eight years. Since I left school I suppose.'

She looked halfway between appalled and resigned at this maths. At what point, she wondered, should one stop calling oneself a cellist if you don't really do it anymore?

Ann was suddenly brisk, and took a gulp from her bottle.

'You should come to me some time. I'd love to help you.'

Charlie and Erin stared at her. The group of musicians around Fenella on the other side of the bar laughed, probably at something Joshua was saying, and Erin felt the sound break on her back like the shock wave from an explosion. She saw Ann's eyes flinch with her, and knew she absolutely understood. She flashed Erin a look of sympathy.

'You'd teach me?' Erin asked in amazement.

Charlie was grinning. 'You'd have to do some bloody work, you know. Ann's not going to put up with you slacking about and wasting her time. You know the calibre of pupil she usually has – they're queuing up!'

'Yes, I would,' said Ann, frowning at Charlie. 'Teach you, I mean. I'm serious – you can stop taking the piss, Charlie. You're going to waste, Erin. I don't like to see that. I can help.'

'Remind us,' said Charlie. 'How many orchestras did you play in?'

'Oh, sometime in the last century I must have played in most of the London ones,' Ann smiled. 'I'm old enough to have seen a lot of players come and go.' She laughed then, a rich, throaty laugh that was dirty and infectious at once. It sounded as if she had spent most of the last fifty years on forty a day. 'So, what do you think? I bet you could play the Elgar too, with a bit of practice.'

Erin laughed into her pint.

'I *almost* could, years ago. But then again, on Sunday I could hardly move my hand after all that practice on Saturday. Are you sure you want to take me on? It's been years since I had lessons.'

'I'm not suggesting once a week. We're both too old for that!'

Charlie was fiddling with a beer mat on the table in front of him, crimping its beer-dampened edges with his thumbnail like a piecrust. It crossed his mind that he could be feeling left out, but he took himself by surprise when he realised he wasn't. After the punches Erin had taken that evening, he couldn't begrudge her any of this.

'Well, then… yes please! I'd love it.'

Ann grinned at her.

'Great. I was hoping you'd say that.'

'Here's to the next Yo-Yo Ma,' said Charlie, absurdly pleased at this result even though it did not affect him at all. Somehow he felt it was important. He drained his glass.

'Absolutely!' said Erin. 'Here's to it!'

Ann raised her glass to Erin's, and the chink of their connection slotted their plan from prospective to definite.

'And now it's my round,' said Ann. 'Same again?'

She took the empty glasses back to the bar, leaving Charlie looking at Erin and Erin gazing at the pads on her left hand fingers.

'They'll harden up no problem,' he said. 'Your days as a hand model are numbered.'

Erin looked back at him quickly. 'It's amazing. She's amazing. Why do you think she's doing it?'

'Are you fishing for compliments?'

'Sorry. No, not really. I just wasn't expecting it.'

'Well, I think the answer is that, even without Fenella's clear advantages in shampoo advert slow motion, you're worth it.'

She threw a beer mat at him, and they were happily regressing to teenage behaviour when Ann returned with more drinks. They spent the rest of the evening getting pissed and teasing out of Ann some vitriolic and bitchy anecdotes about her racy younger days as a professional cellist.

Ann drank them under the table, of course. That is the true qualification for a professional musician.

Chapter 15

The next morning, Erin woke early with a hangover. Cursing her lack of foresight at not drinking a pint of water with a couple of prophylactic Nurofen the night before, she walked to the kitchen with her face screwed up in a half-pain-half-asleep grimace. Pills and much cold water successfully swallowed, she staggered back to bed and lay there, propped up on pillows with a stomach feeling like a water-filled spacehopper, waiting for the drugs to kick in. She brought her phone in with her and laid it on the bed next to her head. If her head stopped pounding she could check Twitter. Just as soon as looking at a screen wouldn't make her feel sick.

She felt balanced on the dead centre of a see-saw. Perhaps she should have taken Joshua's clear and abrupt rejection harder than she had. Lying in bed, with her only companion a noisy headache, she made a dehydrated attempt at introspection to find her reasons for not crumpling in a defeated heap. It had been barely three weeks since she thought Joshua had died. She tried to remember how that had nearly broken her. Whether she had grown stronger or his pull had weakened she didn't know, but that emotional bond was truly alien to her now. Had she really fainted at the rehearsal? God. Her toes curled under her duvet as she remembered.

And now, to counterbalance what could have been dragging her under, there was Ann. Erin felt herself chuckle again as she remembered the sound of Ann's deep laugh from the pub, but stopped as she set up sympathetic waves within the water in her distended stomach. Even Charlie hadn't been able to keep a straight face when he heard it. She was excited about playing again. She couldn't remember when she had last felt like this. Nobody had believed in her that way for years. Even she saw the irony that in all her time of searching for someone or something to be just that rock of encouragement and inspiration, it wasn't until she hadn't been looking for it at all that it appeared to have found her anyway. Maybe that was the rule.

She dozed a bit, then found herself in a sweet sleep just when the alarm went off at 6.15. Giddy with sleep haze, but thankfully no more headache, she stumbled to the shower and got ready for work.

Friday journeys to work were always less hassle, as people increasingly started to 'work from home' on Fridays (nobody ever admitted to using the quotation marks). Either that or the employees who really embraced the weekend culture started early. Whatever it was, Friday mornings were always Erin's favourite. She stopped at her usual Caffè Nero and, as usual, beat up her inner activist about not seeking out a small independent coffee roaster of character. Her inner activist was always talked over loudly by her inner pragmatist, who pointed out that there was no such place within walking distance, and if she chose the organic Fairtrade stuff there really wasn't all that much to get annoyed about. Still bickering with herself, she didn't notice she was behind the same two women in the queue who had been talking about Oscar's death. They were locked in a new discussion involving the wife of a Premier League footballer and a deformed chihuahua saved from a rescue home. The existence of the dog was being hotly disputed, as well it might have been, since it had only been summoned into existence to join the conversation a couple of minutes earlier, to counteract detailed knowledge of the wife's beauty regime secrets. They were still arguing as they left, and Erin ordered her coffee and exchanged bemused head shakes with the smiling barista. She walked the last couple of hundred yards to her office slowly, enjoying the early autumn sun on her face.

There were the usual calls of 'Morning!' as she went through the open plan office to get to her desk, on the far side with a view of the car park. She put her coffee down, switched on her screen and pulled the in tray towards her as the computer took an age to decide it was ready to do some work. Her boss, Craig, saw her through the glass wall of his office and stuck his head out of the door.

'Hi, Erin. Morning. Could I have a word – when you've got a moment?'

'Yep, just firing the computer up now,' said Erin. 'Be with you in a tick.'

Craig retreated and shut the door. Erin frowned. He wasn't usually in that early. Craig had a personality profile that was more suited to using a stick rather than a carrot. Indeed, he would not have felt out of place as a senior officer in the First World War, stationed behind the front line and being safely thick. Erin was part of a team where morale was not high: if it threatened to rise above normal morose British phlegmatic grunting, Craig would assume they were being far too frivolous to be productive and would compose snide departmental emails about focus and drive. Craig was a medium-sized cog in a very large and complex organisation, and regarded most of his staff as grit which would impede his ability to turn efficiently.

He was not loved, but you don't have to be loved if you work in finance. Erin was only still there by mistake: she had fallen into it while temping. Craig had discovered she had a flair for database design and found his department worked more efficiently after her arrival, so she stayed. She wasn't sure why, sometimes.

Clicking her email open, she sighed at the eighty-something new messages in her inbox that had arrived since she had left the office the previous evening. They were mostly from the company's New York office, being sent during their afternoon to ambush her on her arrival the next day. If she hadn't dealt with them by lunchtime she knew they would start to telephone, with their super confident voices asking whether she was 'good' and informing her that they were 'good' in return. All their emails were flagged as urgent. It was a state of mind in the US.

Turning her back on the screen, she decided that even Craig's irritating requests would be preferable to 'delivering the optimum outcomes' for her delightful State-side colleagues. She picked up her coffee, tapped on Craig's door and went in.

'Ah, yes, come in,' he said, clearing a small space on the edge of his desk for her coffee. He looked grumpier than usual, if that were possible. Perhaps it was an effect of getting into work uncharacteristically early. He sat on the other side of the desk and swivelled his chair to face Erin. 'I won't beat about the bush, Erin. We've had some bad stats in from the US last week, and the call has come from on high to make some savings across the board.'

Erin wondered if back-to-back clichés made delivering this speech easier for him. She had a feeling she knew what was coming next. She sat back in her seat and sipped her coffee in silence. There was no way she was going to make this easy for him.

Craig moved two pens from their place at the top of his pad of paper to the right hand edge, lining them up carefully with the direction of the paper. One was red, the other green.

'Your post is earmarked for reintegration into the team.'

He pushed the red pen a little bit further up his desk.

'Which means, as I'm sure you're aware, that I'm going to have to give you notice.'

'Ah,' said Erin, sipping more coffee. Suddenly the eighty emails didn't seem so daunting. She wondered if she was experiencing something medically defined, such was her detachment to events around her. First Joshua, now this. Unemployment seemed preferable at that moment to Craig's bluster or insurmountable database problems that she could have been entitled to say were out of her pay grade. Good luck, she thought, at finding a way through without someone doing my job.

'So, I've had a look at your HR file,' Craig was saying, pulling out a folder with her name printed on the top corner, 'and it looks like you have a four week notice period, with fifteen days' annual leave still owed.'

Erin smiled. Her salary just about covered living, but no frills. There had been no holiday on a beach for her for a while. It was a rueful smile.

Craig was warming up to his task. 'So that neatly leaves one week for you to tidy the ends up and hand over to the appropriate staff. I can draw up a list...'

Erin was looking out of the window but, at this, turned to face Craig squarely through the steam of her coffee cup.

'List?'

'Of staff you can brief on the various sectors. I think a week is enough time to incorporate up-to-date stats in your reports.'

Erin laughed. 'You want me to work my arse off all next week so you can save yours?'

Craig looked shocked. Erin had never given the impression that she could dish it out like that. He wondered, too late, if his departmental cull had fallen on the wrong victim.

Erin stood up, giving him a pitying look.

'I think you'll find, Craig, that you can whistle for your sodding reports. I'll set my emails up to forward to you automatically – there are already a few there from New York that need attention.'

'No,' he said, his voice rising as he also stood up. 'I specifically informed Group Heads that you'd be handing over smoothly—'

'Did you?' said Erin, opening the door and walking towards her desk. 'Oh.'

She quickly leaned over her keyboard and typed swiftly, setting up an out-of-office message informing anyone looking for her to direct themselves to Craig, who would be more than happy to help. Hitting 'apply', she closed down and turned back to Craig.

'I'm sure HR can sort out a week's unpaid leave in lieu of working out my notice period,' she said cheerily. 'Go and talk to them. It's a lovely morning. I'm off.'

Waving to a number of open-mouthed colleagues who had overhead this exchange, Erin sauntered out of the building, still carrying her coffee, feeling unaccountably light-headed. Surely being sacked wasn't supposed to make her feel this happy? Maybe it was the giddiness before the reality of rent and food muscled in. She stepped onto the pavement, tipped her face up to the sunshine, and smiled. Whatever she had to do in the next few days to sort out the hole in her life, there was the here and now of warmth on her face: that lingering touch of an October sun made all the more precious by knowing it could be the last of the year. We are creatures evolved for the elements, no matter how cerebral our focus. Erin lifted her skin to the sun like a flower, absorbing the last of the season's vitamin D to stockpile her through the winter darkness.

Flexing the fingers on her left hand, she turned for home. After all, she had the rest of the day to practise now.

Chapter 16

Ann opened her front door wide and beamed at Erin.

'Fantastic! Come in.' She stepped back to let Erin and the hunchback shape of her cello case past into the hall. 'I've been looking forward to this.'

Erin had called her as she made her way home from the office, newly unemployed. Although they both knew Erin would only have a couple of days to prepare, Ann had invited her over that very Sunday morning for their first session together, keen to get started on reversing Erin's musical decay.

She lived in a Victorian semi-detached villa near the Oval and had done for so many years that the eye-watering property price rises had grown around her like a verdant rainforest, leaving her sprawling house adding noughts to her theoretical wealth which never manifested themselves into her bank account. The house sagged comfortably into its foundations, happy in its haphazard arrangements of levels and different styles of window. It was the house in which Ann had brought up two children and waved off a husband; a house she had kept while he had walked off with most of the money. In a world of transient opportunity, Ann gathered things to her that she could touch and love for their durability.

Erin stood in a hall cluttered with an untidy coat stand and a table spilling post and newspapers onto the floor. A fern in a china pot on the table added to the squash. It was a vibrant collage though, not a dissolute entropy. The house was living with a busy purpose, not falling into itself through lack of use.

She followed Ann through to the music room, which opened up across the front of the house with a spacious bay window, a fireplace, a grand piano and a rug on polished floorboards. She heard the acoustics change from the muffled bumps of the carpeted hallway to more resonant knocks in this room, with her footsteps bouncing off bare walls and the hard edges of the floor. This was where Ann worked and where she loved to be. Where she could hear with clarity.

Ann's cello lay on its side by one of the two chairs on the rug. Two music stands were already there, open and empty. Suddenly Erin felt nervous.

'Why don't you get your stuff out and I'll make a cuppa?' said Ann, leaving Erin to settle herself alone. 'Tea or coffee?'

'Coffee, thanks,' said Erin, and unlatched her cello case as she heard Ann fill the kettle in a distant kitchen and clink about with mugs. The house stood on a street away from the main road and was quiet, or as quiet as any London house can be. Outside the window a line of mature, gnarled plane trees were set into the pavement all the way along the road. They bore the scars of many pollards and stood as solid guardians. Erin could see why Ann loved being there.

She was just tuning up when Ann returned with mugs, finding spaces for them on small tables near each chair, which she carefully set back out of the way of a moving bow.

'What strings do you use?' she asked, sitting opposite Erin.

'Jargar dolce,' said Erin.

'Good. You might need a new set though – when did you last change them?'

'God – not for years. Probably not since I was at school.'

'Well, we can get to that in time. What about your bow?'

'It's a Paesold. Not very good, but better than my last one. I remember having to get this before being allowed to take my grade eight.'

Erin handed her bow to Ann, who felt the weight of it in her hand, turning it over and back. Erin felt embarrassed that she hadn't taken more care of it. There were short spikes of horsehair sticking out of the frog where she pulled away the broken ends of one every now and then.

'Hmm. Needs re-hairing, of course. You'll find, though, that a different bow can make an unbelievable difference to the sound you can make. Almost as much as a different cello. Here, try mine.'

She gave Erin her own bow, which had been balanced on the side of her cello on the floor.

Erin gulped. 'Really? Are you sure?'

'Don't be silly – go on. It's a Tourte.'

Erin took it gingerly, recognising the name of the eighteenth century French bow maker and hardly daring to think about how much it was worth. Her right hand fingered the blonde tortoiseshell frog, inlaid with a pearl eye with a gold ring round its edge. The wood itself was octagonal, running in an elegant curve away to the point, holding the hair at tension. The balance of it was extraordinary. She turned her hand over so her palm was upwards, flipping the bow over as she did, then brought it back over again, feeling the centre of gravity shift above her hand. It seemed to be light yet quivered with potential, much as a wand might feel in the hands of those who understand magic.

She drew it across her strings, just open strings at first, feeling the tone leap out of her cello in a way it had never done before. She hardly had to press through her index finger at all: her whole right hand relaxed when it realised it didn't have to do all the work. It was as if the note swam up the bow from the string itself, nothing to do with her arm. She began a slow, winding scale, unevenly exploring how the cello spoke in different registers, then ran up and down some chords and listened to them ring. She looked at Ann, excited.

'Wow. It's amazing.'

'It is a nice one, isn't it? It can give you power without feeling like you're hefting a ton of bricks around.'

'I've never played with one like this before.' Erin started some experimental *spiccato*, watching in awe as the bow bounced with lightness and control at the smallest guidance from her hand. She stopped suddenly. 'It's probably worth more than my cello, isn't it?'

Ann laughed. 'Well, I've had it a long time. Maybe eighty grand, or thereabouts. Who knows? I'm not selling!'

Erin took a more secure hold on the bow. It was indeed worth about eight times as much as her cello, which itself had seemed eye-wateringly expensive when her parents stretched their budget to buy it for her as a teenager. She resumed her quiet exploratory playing and realised that she had never heard her cello sound as good as this. She suddenly understood just what the real value of this stick was and what craftsmanship must have gone into making it.

Ann was hunting on the piano through piles of music, letting Erin get the feel of the new room, the new bow and a completely new dynamic between them. She could hear Erin adjusting her playing style as she felt her way around the alien balance of the bow and knew Erin's right hand was in a constant cycle of test and consolidate. For a musician, a lot of practice is simple physical repetition. Players will say that during a familiar piece their hands will know where to go without direction. They have ceded autonomy from their conscious brain to the unconscious and little understood hegemony of well-drilled motor and sensory nerves.

In less than five minutes, Erin had learned the feel of Ann's bow, and looked up again, smiling.

'It really is lovely. I suppose I should start looking for another one now. It's time I moved on from that,' she nodded at her old Paesold on Ann's chair.

'Well, it's cheaper than buying another cello – usually – and will give you an instant result,' said Ann. 'As you've just discovered.'

'Not the greatest time in my life to start splashing out, though.' For a moment, Erin looked worried. She had promised herself to put off the thought of unemployment until Monday and try to sneak a weekend in first before admitting that she would have to look for another job.

Ann was brisk.

'Well, we'll cross that bridge as and when the river is unfordable.' She put an open book on Erin's stand. 'Which of the Bach Suites do you know best? Why don't we start with one of those? Use my bow.'

Erin smiled, betraying her nerves. She decided on the second one, in D minor, falling into the familiar shapes while trying to forget that this was essentially her audition for lessons from Ann. The Tourte bow nosed its way among her strings as if they had suddenly become three dimensional instead of flat things to be skated over. Erin felt as if her right hand was able to dig into contours of sound rippling up as the bow pushed into the strings.

Ann stopped her before she had played more than a dozen bars.

'Try holding the bow more in a Baroque way, up away from the frog.'

Erin moved her hand up towards the centre of the bow, holding it on the stick about one quarter of the way up from the end, with her fingers entirely free of the ebony frog.

'That's right,' said Ann. 'I know it's not an actual Baroque bow – we can get on to that later if you want – but this way gives you the feel of the old balance without that heavy frog getting in the way. You'll find the string crossing passages will feel quite different like that. Have a go.' She smiled. 'It was nice, by the way. Sorry to interrupt.'

Erin started again, and felt herself having to relearn all over again as the balance of the bow had shifted behind her hand. As she went on, however, the semiquaver runs that crossed over three strings were easier to control with a light touch. Bach hadn't written these Suites for a modern bow: he was familiar with the more convex shape of the eight-eenth century bows, which could exert more friction over the strings than the modern, tight bows do. It doesn't help that a modern cello bridge is more curved than its ancestor, like a hump back bridge as opposed to a flat suspension bridge. It also doesn't help that modern strings are metal, not gut. All this means is that Erin, along with every other twenty-first century cellist who does not play on a Baroque cello with a Baroque bow, had to work harder and move her right arm more than Bach had intended his players to do. Holding her bow away from the frog was her first step back in time.

Ann listened all the way through the Prelude, hearing Erin's intentions break through every now and then from underneath the silt of years of lack of practice. She knew Erin's fingertips were sore: you can't build up a decent pad of hard skin after a week when you've let it go soft over many years. She knew her shoulder muscles were aching as she approached the final *arpeggios* across all four strings, hurting as she tried to make the bass notes ring out while she put the harmonies in at the top. Bach was a master of implied harmony, but it involves such precision of playing. Something that sounds perfectly straightforward, even easy, belies the technical skill required to make it sound like that. Bach can be singularly unforgiving like that.

Erin played the final D minor chord, stretching two octaves on all four strings, and relaxed back away from her cello, shaking the cramps out of her left hand. She grimaced at Ann, knowing all her failings as a player had been flashed as if they were neon signs above her head. She could hear them as well as Ann could. She had been a better player at school – hardly surprising, given the pull of box sets over hours of rigorous practice in recent years. Adulting was complex.

Ann saw Erin was being hard on herself before she had said a word. And, like all good teachers, she resolved to build up her pupil's confidence before adding to that burden of expected improvement. She could hear all of Erin's potential, both the lost skill which would need recovering with the patience of an archaeological dig and the untapped future which even Erin hadn't explored.

'It's not as hopeless as you think,' she smiled. 'Have some coffee. What did you think of the bow?'

Erin gulped down her, now lukewarm, coffee gratefully.

'My muscles are shot. Fingers too.'

'Nothing that hard work won't fix.'

'Your bow is amazing, though. Really responsive. I could pick out some of those runs that I just can't with mine.'

'It does make a difference, doesn't it?'

'There's a bounce in it, but from somewhere in the middle of the string, not just on the surface. That's the difference I can feel.'

Ann smiled again. 'Absolutely right.'

'So, you think we can get somewhere with this?'

'I do indeed. If you're willing to put the work in.'

'What else have I got to do at the moment?'

'Good. Well, let's look out some studies you could try, and then we can talk about what exactly we need to work on before next time. And, do you know what?' Ann's smile was now turned up to something officially classed as wicked.

'What?'

'I think we could take a look at the Elgar as well, don't you? Let's not let Fenella have all the fun with it.'

Erin laughed. 'OK, if you want. I did the first movement years ago, but not the rest.'

She left Ann's house a couple of hours later with raw fingers but a brain buzzing over the work she was going to have to do.

She also had a second bow in her cello case. Ann had loaned her one of her spares, which she hardly ever used. Not quite the Tourte, but still worth more than Erin's cello. She hadn't known quite how to react when Ann had gone over to a shelf on the other side of the music room and taken it down. To be worthy of that investment of Ann's trust and fearfully expensive bow was both a responsibility and an exhilaration. Erin walked away from the house, leaning away from the weight of the cello case on her shoulder, under plane trees that were striping the pavement with cooled cylinders of air. It was as if Erin's existence was flickering in and out of her current state of being, and readying itself to appear, quantum-like, in the next one.

Chapter 17

October was ageing, curling the green out of leaves and dropping brown husks onto pavements all over London. David was in the middle of negotiations with a choral society about when they would be free to come and rehearse some Bach with the orchestra. He had never had to organise a concert quite so quickly before, and a tic in his eye he thought he had conquered years earlier had surfaced again. He was determined not to subdue it with whisky this time.

The first problem was that the scarcity of rehearsal time before a December concert meant that the choir would have to learn their parts in their own rehearsals, on top of (or instead of, as David was trying to persuade their conductor) their existing repertoire. They were unwilling to set aside their own concert plans, so the uneasy truce David feared he would have to concede was that they would learn the *Magnificat* as well as their festive jollity, and come along for a rehearsal with the orchestra later on. He only hoped that the singers, some flakier than others at the best of times, would manage to grasp enough of the Bach for Joshua to whip them into some sort of shape in the final couple of rehearsals he would have.

Knowing these singers from experience, he rather doubted it but clung to the plan with dogged faith, remembering the future of the orchestra may well depend on the success of this concert and the funds it would unlock.

Rafael, ever-supportive of orchestral funding crises, had asked David if there was anything he could do to help. Short of taking sectional rehearsals with the chorus, they agreed it was all in the rather unstable lap of any god in which they cared to believe. So, before the delights of choral Bach rehearsals, and to give Fenella a couple more weeks to work on the Elgar, David admitted that the time had probably come to unleash the large force that was Mrs Ford-Hughes onto the orchestra.

It was, therefore, on the last Monday in October that she entered the hall where the orchestra was unpacking, cradling her copy of the *Four Last Songs* as a mother would a small baby. She had covered the book with heavy duty wrapping paper and plastic film, as if she had been a guest on *Blue Peter* in the more exuberant John Noakes days. Underneath there was the decidedly ordinary Boosey & Hawkes 1959 edition, which had a blurred picture of Richard Strauss on the cover staring moodily out over his preternaturally neat moustache. Mrs Ford-Hughes had decided she much preferred a bold floral print, and many years earlier had painstakingly used off-cuts of their dining room wallpaper to cover her copy. She did not see anything odd in the juxtaposition of singing about death from a jauntily-coloured tulip-patterned book. As soon as Joshua caught sight of it, he felt a flutter in his stomach. David also saw it, and one eye winked and twitched about with such a sudden increase in tempo that he had to press the heel of his hand against it in order to focus properly with the other.

Mrs Ford-Hughes's right shoulder was strapped up, but she didn't seem to be in any pain from her fracture. It was nearly a month since Oscar had used her to trampoline out of this life, and her collarbone was knitting smoothly in its cocoon of adipose tissue.

The tulips were carried, reverentially, across to Joshua, who recovered his poise in time to smile a welcome and extend his hand, which was shaken carefully in Mrs Ford-Hughes's left so as not to wrench her right shoulder again.

'Great you could make it.'

'A pleasure.'

'I hope your shoulder is not causing you any trouble singing?'

'No, no. It's fine, thank you.'

Mrs Ford-Hughes was gracious and almost regal, sweeping her gaze across the orchestra, still hugging the score to her ample bosom. One might almost think she had been a soloist for years, as indeed she had in her imagination. Now the reality was about to join with her projected personality, she was willing to extend every politeness to her fellow professionals. Joshua nodded at her score, trying not to look as if he was drawing attention to her bust.

'Er – which edition have you got there? Boosey & Hawkes?'

'Yes.' She lifted the red and yellow splodged book towards him. She noticed him looking intently at the flowers. 'I find those drab covers so functional, don't you?'

Joshua was saved from needing a reply by David walking up to them, trying to smile through a madly twitching side of his face. If the stress of organising all this gave David a stroke, Joshua realised nobody would be able to spot the warning signs. Meanwhile, the potential stroke victim was shaking Mrs Ford-Hughes's hand and echoing Joshua's professed delight in her attendance.

Erin and Ann chatted as they unpacked their cellos. Erin had brought Ann's bow, telling her, with joy, what a difference it was making. Fenella had already sat down at the front and was adjusting her spike, throwing glances up at Joshua from behind Mrs Ford-Hughes's back that started more than one person wondering how far their musical partnership had progressed.

'OK, everyone,' called Joshua. 'We have a lot of work to do and not much time, so can we make a start please?' He flashed a stern look at the trombone section, daring them to heckle then or – his frown implied – at any time during the evening. It didn't help that Carl, one of the trombonists, and Gwynneth, the oboe player, both knew how to sign, and regularly shared silent jokes during rehearsals. If they suddenly cracked up for no apparent reason, one of them was certain to have signed something obscene. Joshua slightly dreaded what they would communicate when Mrs Ford-Hughes opened the tulip-covered book of death.

Charlie stepped closer to Erin and Ann.

'What's going to happen, do you think?' he said quietly, propping the neck of his cello in the crook of his arm as he tightened his bow.

Ann was philosophical. 'I know she's been singing for years. Perhaps not this kind of solo work, though.'

'There was no way we could have stopped her,' said Erin, looking worried.

'It wasn't your fault,' said Charlie. 'At least this is cracking music. Maybe we can drown her out if it gets too bad? Don't we split into four in one of them?'

'Yep,' said Ann. 'Most of it's split. Really thickly scored.'

'Ah. Fenella's holding her own on the line, then. I'm sure she'll set us right!' said Charlie.

He went cheerfully off to sit next to Fenella, who was busy trying to sort out who should play which part in the four-way split. Cellos, like the other strings, are a herd animal. Any complicated divisi makes them nervous. Having Fenella in charge did not allay those fears.

Gwynneth sounded an A on her oboe, and the strings began to tune. As usual, the wind and brass tried to join in and, as usual, the leader had to wave his bow about and ask them to shut up so they could get their fifths right. While the rest of the brass were tripping up and down all the natural harmonics and adjusting little bits of plumbing to get them approaching Gwynneth's A, Mrs Ford-Hughes took little steps away from the orchestra and hummed to herself, starting as low as she could and stretching her voice up and over her high register and down again. This 'sirening' is beloved of singers, often marking out those who regard themselves as inhabiting the professional end of the spectrum regardless of whether or not they have ever had a paid gig. It is generally accompanied by intense and increasing irritation among those who are within earshot. Charlie turned round to share wide eyes with Erin, mouthing 'Marvellous' at her. He was settling in for a good evening's entertainment.

'OK,' Joshua said again, opening his score. 'We might as well start at the very beginning, as the great Julie Andrews would say. *Frühling*.'

Fenella turned round, hissing to the rest of the cello section, 'Normal divisi where it's in two. Where it's in four, front two desks split the first part, third and fourth desks split the bottom part.'

Ann, who sat on the fifth desk, usually alone, smiled at Erin.

'I'll just put my oar in where it's needed, then?' she asked, innocently.

Fenella shot her a cross sort of look and nodded, turning back quickly to ready herself for the start. Joshua was waiting pointedly for the cellos to sort themselves out.

'Everyone else clear about which part they're playing?' he asked to the world in general. 'Good. Now, we'll play through these in order: *Frühling*, *September*, *Beim Schlafengehen* and *Im Abendrot*. I know there's all sorts of academic waffle about the correct order, but let's not muck about with what's printed here, OK?'

There was a murmur of agreement. Joshua smiled at Mrs Ford-Hughes and raised his baton.

'Ready?'

She nodded, opened her score and revealed a page covered in so many pencil crossings-out and scribbled instructions the printed notes were virtually hidden.

For three bars it went quite well. Halfway through the fourth, Mrs Ford-Hughes came in. She had begun to fill her lungs at Joshua's first downbeat, increasing imaginary room in them by raising her eyebrows and tipping her head forwards, so by the time she sang her first note she was like a whale primed for a deep dive.

Her Arkansas vowels spiked through Hermann Hesse's text like stubble through a drag queen's foundation.

Strictly speaking, it was not her fault the phrase sported no fewer than three umlauts, but perhaps she could shoulder some blame for producing no sound approximating to any of them. Hesse's poem begins '*In dämmrigen Grüften träumte ich lang von deinen Bäumen und blauen Lüften*' which translates roughly as 'In dark tombs I dreamed long of your trees and blue skies'. Mrs Ford-Hughes managed to invoke a rawhide and sawdust twang to the whole thing, with the nasal delivery of a second-rate country singer. By the word '*Lüften*', which rises to a top A, her vibrato width would have rivalled Peter Pears's during his wobbliest later years.

Joshua tried to refocus during the eight bars before her next phrase, but soon she was approaching her top B on '*Wunder*', which frankly sounds better with the German pronunciation of 'voonder' rather than a more Doris Day approach of 'S'Wonderful'. Her approximation of the pitch seemed to loiter without the orchestra before she meandered down again, and no matter how energetically Joshua stirred the treacle oozing round his podium, he couldn't get her to quicken. She approached the end with the phrase '*deine selige Gegenwart*' ('your blissful presence'), but since '*Gegenwart*' stretched over five slow bars, when she reached the last syllable she had lost all recollection of what she was trying to pronounce, and ended up rolling her southern American diction around '*wart*' as if describing the protuberance on a witch's nose. Most of it became the 'r', much as REO Speedwagon's Kevin Cronin immortalised the line in 'Keep on Loving You' – 'Still I don't rememberrrrrr'. Her final 't' was lost in the desperately swelling strings that Joshua encouraged to drown her out.

He put down his baton and turned to Mrs Ford-Hughes, trying to smile. Just before his lips turned white, he unglued them and tried to think of something to say that wouldn't reveal his honest reaction to her performance.

She saved him the trouble.

'You're gonna have to take those strings down, y'know. I can hardly hear myself.'

Joshua's hands frantically signalled behind his back to prevent the trombones from saying anything too loudly, as he arranged his face into a pleasant, non-aggressive expression of respect.

'Oh? Did you feel—'

'Yeah, yeah. And the oboe was hurrying too.'

There were murmurings, passing across the orchestra like waves along a shore. When they threatened to become ugly, Joshua decided to press on, thinking that getting through the basic music before coffee would be preferable to any kind of serious rehearsal. He would deal with the fallout later.

He smiled once more at Mrs Ford-Hughes.

'Well, let's just block the music for now and get used to each other. We can fine-tune it later.'

'You'll have to lop a semitone off her vibrato each way then,' came bursting out from somewhere suspiciously close to Carl, but all the trombone players were suddenly terribly busy cleaning their slides or finding their mutes when Joshua turned and glared at them for him to be certain. Luckily, Mrs Ford-Hughes seemed not to have noticed.

'Right,' said Joshua, in a slightly higher pitch than usual. 'Let's press on. *September*, please.'

Charlie turned round to Erin, grinned and muttered, 'Keep up!' As the inside players on their desks, they were playing the same part when it split into four, and it had become clear that they were with Joshua's beat whereas Fenella was leading her team on the outside rather waywardly.

Joshua's baton was up and suddenly they were immersed in the slightly more optimistic-sounding second song, until the words revealed the music's lie and reminded the listener that everything is dropping off and dying.

When Mrs Ford-Hughes came to her line 'Golden tropft Blatt um Blatt' (describing how gold drips, leaf by leaf from the high acacia tree), it was as if she was channelling Lloyd Webber's setting of the words *Jesus Christ, Superstar*. He had so clearly stolen Strauss's phrase and rebooted it a tone higher. Mrs Ford-Hughes gave her interpretation such a jaunty swing that the whole orchestra was engulfed in a vision of 1970s white jumpsuits and cod gospel singing they almost forgot what they were supposed to be doing. Luckily there were no top Bs in this one, except the unofficial ones at the highest oscillation of her vibrato on a G, and Joshua managed to steer the whole thing safely to the pause before the double bar line with most notes intact. There was of course the pronunciation question of Mrs Ford-Hughes's last words, which were 'Augen zu' ('eyes close'). Instead of the open 'ow' vowel in 'Augen', and a crisp initial 'tz' on 'zu', she opted for a more relaxed recalling of a visit to a local zoo somewhere called 'Eye-gin'.

An *andante* semibreve, to Mrs Ford-Hughes, was four long beats of a strangled vowel. Not to be defeated, she took a breath just before her final note and held it on far longer than she should have, into the hallowed territory of the orchestra's last eight bars without her. It is hallowed because one of the most famous horn solos swells out from the orchestral texture just as the soprano finishes singing: as her note fades away, the first horn takes up the melody in a haunting remembrance of what life was and what one loses in death, in four bars of possibly the most beautiful melody Strauss ever wrote. Mrs Ford-Hughes's nasal buzz competed with Neema playing the horn solo for almost three bars of the four, despite Joshua's repeated gestures with his left hand that she should cease. The other three horn players, and some other players nearby, rubbed the soles of their shoes on the floor when Neema had finished, to show their appreciation of a solo well played, whatever the distractions.

Joshua was sweating slightly when he brought off the last string chord, and he nodded at Neema to indicate that she had played it beautifully despite Mrs Ford-Hughes's accompaniment. Fenella came off slightly later than everyone else, as she had her eyes closed to absorb the harmonious majesty of the moment. Charlie rolled his eyes at Erin, and Gwynneth could be seen to sign a very slow and emphasised 'Oh my fucking God' at Carl. Even those non-signers in the orchestra caught the drift of that one.

Pearl rested her viola on her knee, leaned forward (as if the six inches difference that made had a material effect on how far her sound travelled) and whispered to Joshua, 'Is it coffee time yet?'

Erin got the giggles. When musicians are trying to behave, sometimes all their efforts can be subverted by a release of tension, and soon everyone was stifling laughter. It rippled out around Pearl in small snorts and wheezes. Joshua shot them a pleading look, and most of them tried to wrestle control of their diaphragms. Erin leaned down behind her cello and glanced back at Ann, who winked, which just set her off again.

Joshua made haste to gloss over this and, with an increasing look of white about his eyes, turned to Mrs Ford-Hughes.

'Lovely.' He ignored the resurgence of snorting behind him in the strings. 'We can get our teeth into that later on – I'm just trying to get a feel for what our... parameters are at the moment. Just one tiny thing before we go on, though: your last note, your A on '*zu*' – do you think we could come off cleanly at the end of the bar so Neema can take over the line?'

He gestured to where Neema was emptying out some water from an obscure curl of her horn. She looked up and nodded gratefully. Mrs Ford-Hughes tucked her chins further into her chest with distaste at the sight of the watery mechanics of horn playing.

'But that note has a pause on it. I was holding it on especially.'

'Er, no...' Joshua checked his score quickly. 'No, you just have a normal semibreve.'

'But I have it marked here.'

Joshua looked at the graphite embellished page thrust under his nose. Amid the complicated drawings over the last note, decorated as it was with the happy faced suns that singers draw to remind them not to go flat, he thought he could see a black pause marking: a bracket turned like an umbrella over a dot. It looked as if Mrs Ford-Hughes had crayoned it in as if she were drawing on eye make-up. He cleared his throat.

'Well, yes, but it's not marked in the score, you see. I think Strauss needed the clean cut-off after four beats to let the horn solo take over.'

'I've always sung it like that.'

The first desks of violins saw Joshua's fingers tighten into white stripes round his baton.

'Well, perhaps we can discuss the finer interpretive details later. Shall we press on for now? I'd like to get everything played through at least once before coffee,' he nodded at Pearl, who beamed, 'and then we can pick it apart in the second half.'

Mrs Ford-Hughes frowned, but said nothing more. She took out her 6B pencil and made more markings around the accused note, but it was more along the lines of shading an already finished charcoal portrait rather than adding any new feature.

Joshua looked around the orchestra. Those who weren't still giggling were looking at him in a pleading, silent horror. He mouthed 'Sorry' at them which drew some wry smiles and a general acceptance of the unavoidable situation. There was a barely audible 'You owe us all a pint' from somewhere in the woodwind section which Joshua acknowledged with a small smile.

'Right, everybody. Let's crack on. *Beim Schlafengehn* please.'

He looked to his right over at the cellos and basses, who had the first entry, with a rising motif splitting off from the ground note in the basses, like a tendril unfurling from under-ground into the light. Mrs Ford-Hughes made it through her first phrase, finishing that section with '*Alle meine Sinne nun wollen sich in Schlummer senken*' ('All my senses now want to sink into slumber'). Luckily she didn't attempt to hold on to her last note longer than the printed quaver, because Strauss had added another flat to the key signature, marked the music *sehr ruhig* (very slow) and given the leader of the orchestra fourteen bars of a solo violin passage with which to hypnotise any listener into a state of altered consciousness. Richard, the leader, took the melody and played it with such musicality, keeping his eyes on Joshua so they synchronised their phrasing, it suddenly seemed as if the piece wouldn't be a total disaster. Strauss shone through at last.

Unfortunately, the fifteenth bar heralded a slow climb by Mrs Ford-Hughes to a top A flat. She seemed to hang there, or in its approximate region, forever, before toppling off and trying to work out which vowel on which to sing '*freien*'. She opted for the musical equivalent of an emergency vehicle going past, complete with Doppler effect. The most painful section, however, was when she sang a repeat of the same violin solo, nominally at the same pitch, to the word '*Flügen*'. It should have been an echo of floating beauty, reminding us how life repeats and changes, adapting yet returning to its inevitable end. She had ten separate notes to sing on the first syllable and managed (admirably, in some respects) to fit ten different pronunciation attempts at the umlauted 'u' on the way.

Joshua held the orchestra's last chord on way beyond the normal extension even a pause should have given it, almost as if he was delaying the moment he would have to speak to Mrs Ford-Hughes again about what had just happened. When he could see the strings were on their third bow change and poor old Brian on flute was turning purple, he brought them off with regret and turned to look at her.

She was still standing where she had been on her last note, clutching her music to her bosom as though it contained holy relics. Her eyes were closed, and her face was frozen into a picture of such piousness it would not have looked out of place as the marble death mask of a long-dead, saintly virgin. There was a startling similarity between her and Fenella, who was taking her time to come down from whatever high the last note had given her.

'Nicely done, Richard,' Joshua murmured. There was a whisper of 'Hear, hears' and general noises of agreement in the vicinity. Nobody could really understand why Richard played with the orchestra at all. He was another one at Ann's musical level: effortlessly note-perfect and unfailingly reliable. Whereas she had been a professional for a decade, Richard had kept his music as a hobby and pursued a far more lucrative profession in the City as something in mergers and acquisitions. Richard faced incomprehension in both of his two worlds: neither community understood the first thing about the other. They formed a completely non-intersecting Venn diagram. His colleagues at work watched him leave early on a Monday night with his violin case, accepting that he had winked out of their lives and would appear, like a new email, in the morning. Richard had long since known that mentioning banking to his musician friends caused a quick glazing of their eyes and a deft change of subject. He had learned to compartmentalise. He had wondered whether to invite some of his departmental colleagues to the Strauss concert, precisely because of his solo. They could finally hear what it was he did every Monday night. Having heard Mrs Ford-Hughes, however, he rapidly decided to wait for a more suitable concert programme.

Joshua nodded at Pearl and she sprang from her seat like a released greyhound, much preferring to prepare coffee than sit through any more of that rehearsal.

'OK, guys. Thank you,' Joshua said, carefully avoiding meeting anyone's eye directly. 'Coffee soon,' (a muffled cheer from the orchestra) 'but first, we just about have time to play through *Im Abendrot*.' (A not quite so muffled groan.)

An excited clanking of bangles to his left from Mrs Ford-Hughes attracted his attention, and he turned to see her waving and smiling at someone just coming into the hall. He looked along her sightline, and saw her husband nodding with satisfaction at the scene as he made his way over to a chair at the side of the hall. He settled into it with an exhalation as if he had been transported on hydraulics.

He raised his hand to Joshua in greeting, as if they were the best of friends.

'Don't mind me – you just carry on!'

'Thank you,' said Joshua, not really knowing why he needed permission. The tulip-covered book was more animated as Mrs Ford-Hughes flipped the pages back and forth and he realised, with a shock, that she was nervous.

He swallowed several swear words and turned back to the orchestra. The fat lady was about to sing. He wondered what kind of ear 'The Money' had.

'Give me a real attack on this first fortepiano, to kick us off. It's a long way in after that.'

As Joshua had requested, the strings pushed off like a huge ship leaving port, and the glorious horn chords seemed to fill their sails as they drifted out on their journey. The melody melted over the bar lines without pulse or rhythm, and the orchestra were just getting nicely into their stride when Mrs Ford-Hughes joined them.

One positive spin was that the soprano line didn't go up so high in this song as in the others, so she somehow seemed calmer and had therefore tamed her wayward vibrato. Either that or she was finding the presence of her husband in the room rather restricting. Positive spin aside, the lazy, dreamlike harmonic developments blurred any clear pulse of beat: Mrs Ford-Hughes and Fenella were like two moons independently orbiting the gravity of Joshua's baton. However, with the rest of the orchestra's frankly unexpected goodwill and attention, Joshua managed to steer them all through the vagaries of bizarre vowels and abrupt glottal stops towards the final line of '*Ist dies etwa der Tod?*' ('Can this perhaps be death?'). Then the violins, violas and cellos accompanied each other on a downward braided pattern, as if their heavy ship were slowly giving up its buoyancy, sinking deeper and deeper through an ocean, away from the sunlight and into everlasting dark. The last few solid chords were only broken by occasional birdlike chirruping trills from the flutes, reminding us of life continuing on the surface.

Mr Ford-Hughes broke into loud solo applause, which brought his wife out in fluttering giggles.

'Brava!' He was not one to waste an opportunity to dispense some grammatical correctness. 'Marvellous!'

He didn't seem aware he was the only person in the non-audience. Since he didn't stop clapping, Joshua motioned to the orchestra that they should get their coffee, a movement which brought Mr Ford-Hughes to his feet and over to his wife, who was simpering like a teenager. As he leaned forward to kiss her on the cheek, Joshua noticed the nub of an expensive, discreet hearing aid glint from one of his ears. He had perhaps stumbled on the true reason for Mr Ford-Hughes's devotion to his wife's singing.

Chapter 18

'I don't want to worry you,' said Charlie, passing back pints from the bar after the rehearsal, 'but you do realise we've only got three more weeks before we have to do all that in a concert?'

Erin and Ann tried to turn from the bar to get to a table without either spilling their drinks or kneecapping anyone else with their cello cases. Erin especially tried not to make any kind of contact with Joshua, who was in the crowd behind them waiting to be served. He was holding the Strad cello case for Fenella. Rather proprietarily, Erin thought, given that she had only discovered his transferred allegiance a week earlier. Fenella was swaying next to him like a pliant grass stem. She was never still, but blinked constantly and either swung or tossed her hair in one direction or another. She was deep in conversation with Joshua about the Elgar, and several times in the short wait to be served laid her hand on his arm, once even reaching up to brush some hair away from his eyes. Joshua's arms may have been pinned down with an unfamiliar cello case as well as his usual bag, but he acquiesced in this very public expression of intimacy with a staggering insouciance.

Erin took all this in with one sweep of her gaze as she tried to plot a course through the people without approaching either of them. Joshua seemed to be of the same mind, and organised a parting of the crowd through which she and the other two walked as if they were leaving Egypt.

'I don't know how we're going to get through it without laughing,' said Erin as she found an empty table. 'I'm hopeless. I'll get worse, not better, the more I hear it.'

'She has an idiosyncratic voice, I'll give her that,' said Ann.

Charlie laughed. 'It *is* more Tammy Wynette than Elisabeth Schwarzkopf. I keep expecting her to segue into "D-I-V-O-R-C-E".'

They all let that frightening scenario sink in as they drank.

* * *

Back in the hall, David and Rafael were sorting out the final three clear weeks of rehearsal time before the concert. As Charlie had noticed, there was precious little time before they had to perform four pieces, two of which they hadn't yet seen.

They had waved away the elated Mr and Mrs Ford-Hughes after the rehearsal. The second half of the rehearsal had highlighted many more issues in her performance meriting close attention but, after a rather strained conversation between Joshua and David in the break, the flow of Strauss's music had been allowed to continue for the most part uninhibited. Sometimes there was just no point: the horse had already died.

Mrs Ford-Hughes had flapped away her husband's attempts to carry her score, instead keeping it, at all times, pressed firmly to her chest. However, she did allow all his compliments to flow towards her, scooping them up with a beatific smile as if merely collecting what was due. Luckily, David and Rafael did not have to join in, as Mr Ford-Hughes barely stopped for breath between applauding her performance and ushering her out of the door like a movie star.

The men let his chattering fade as they watched them walk to the street, and then looked at each other wearily.

'Sometimes these things are necessary,' said Rafael, searching for something comforting to say.

David straightened his shoulders and nodded. 'Well, we know we can get through it. Whatever she comes up with.'

'Did you manage to have a word with Joshua in the break?'

'Yes – he's on board. I outlined the rehearsal timetable for the next three weeks. It's not ideal, but…' David shrugged. 'As you said, sometimes these things are necessary.'

'Absolutely,' agreed Rafael, who had already factored the prospective Ford-Hughes cash into his forward spreadsheet, and was briskly dismissive of the collective pain required to put it there. 'So – next week we have a stab at Fenella's Elgar?'

'Yes, plus a read-through of the Bach before the choir join us for one rehearsal the week before the concert. That leaves one rehearsal in the middle, when we can refresh *Fingal's Cave* and top and tail the Strauss and Elgar, if they need it. That's going to have to do. It's a bit seat-of-the-pants, but I think we'll be OK.'

Rafael frowned. 'Are the choir going to be alright with that, do you think? Just one rehearsal?'

'Well, theoretically they'll have learned the stuff beforehand, so—'

'Theoretically?'

'...they *should* be fine. And it's only a short piece.'

David sounded more confident than Rafael felt. But then Rafael remembered they didn't have to deal with the choral conductor they were used to. He had been hopeless and had retired (with a rather firm push) the previous summer. The rumour was that the choir had nabbed themselves an up and coming hotshot, who was potentially an even brighter star than Joshua wanted to be. The churn of conductors through amateur groups is unceasing and endless and, the more talented they are, the faster they pass through.

'What's their new conductor like? Who is it?'

'Eliot Yarrow. Yeah, sounded quite upbeat on the phone.'

David didn't relate the delicate negotiations he had undergone with Eliot and the choir's manager, which had been as finely balanced as last ditch union talks to avert a crippling strike. David had future orchestral accompaniments as a bargaining chip: always crucial for a choir. Eliot was an essential component in the plan that could return the Ford-Hughes's wealth to the orchestra. Each knew their power and had tried to get the other to compromise first without giving ground. They had eventually reached an agreement. What David didn't know was that Eliot was intrigued about the real reasons for this sudden change of programme and quite keen on satisfying his curiosity.

Rafael and David left the hall together, as they did every Monday evening. Pearl had already gone home. They seldom went to the pub with the other players. Each sketched an awkward wave at the other before separating: David to the tube, Rafael to his still-scratched Audi. Rafael glanced down the street in the direction of the pub but, sighing, unlocked the car door and got in. He was aware of the almost teacher/pupil divide he engendered with members of the orchestra, and sensed the dampening of conversations around him when he socialised. Most accountants will have experienced something similar: it could be seen to be an occupational hazard. The spark of the spreadsheet does not ignite us all equally.

***

Charlie was, at that moment, returning from the bar to Erin and Ann with the second round of drinks.

'Hey – Stradpants seems to have got her claws into Joshua right and proper.' He glanced at Erin, and saw her sudden flush. 'Sorry.'

Erin raised her chin and shrugged. 'Doesn't matter.'

'Yeah, well, I've just heard them talking.'

'Stradpants?' Ann repeated.

Charlie and Erin looked at her, fearing perhaps a sudden onset of uncharacteristic deference. They need not have worried.

'Like it,' she grinned, and took the first drink out of her second bottle of lager.

Charlie took a gulp of his pint too and continued, 'Apart from all the blatant touchy feely stuff that I'm not going to inflict on you, they were talking about next week. We can expect an Elgar outing next Monday.'

'Oh my Lord,' said Ann. She looked at Erin. 'Why can't you play it instead?'

'Because the performance is in a month's time! And because nobody's asked me.'

'And you don't happen to have a Stradivari between your legs,' said Charlie. 'It's so bloody obvious. Doesn't make it right, though.'

'You'd play it better than her, even by next week,' said Ann. 'I'm looking forward to hearing how you've got on with it anyway. You still on for a lesson this weekend?'

'Yep yep yippity yep.' Erin grinned. The second beer was kicking in.

'You could get up to speed. It's not as if you've got anything else to do,' said Charlie. 'How is the world of unemployment?'

'Actually, I'm quite enjoying it. It gives me time to practise, eat lots of cake and mope about the house. That's what people with broken hearts are supposed to do.'

'Until the food runs out,' Charlie pointed out.

'Point taken. But 'til then, I'm fine.'

Ann was brisk. 'Let's just call it a sabbatical. We all know you could walk into another job tomorrow if you wanted to. I think you're doing more useful work with your playing just now. Let's see how far we can get!'

'Did you know,' Erin said to Charlie and leaning in towards him conspiratorially, waving vaguely in Ann's direction, 'that she's not letting me pay for these lessons?'

Charlie grinned at Ann over Erin's head.

'I did not. You must think she's a deserving case.'

'Very,' said Ann, with emphasis. The subject seemed closed.

* * *

Eliot Yarrow went to the following week's choir rehearsal with a folded piece of paper he had received that morning.

David had sent through the publicity flyer for their joint concert, having cajoled the printer to hurry.

On the tube, Eliot pulled it out of his coat pocket and had another look. David had programmed *Fingal's Cave* first, then Mrs Ford-Hughes singing Strauss, then after the interval the choir with the *Magnificat* and finally Fenella doing the Elgar Concerto. There was a big splash about it being played on a Stradivarius. At least the audience wouldn't leave in the interval if they had a draw like that to hang on for. Eliot could see the logic of splitting up the Strauss and Elgar across the interval – otherwise all the solo stuff would be in the same half of the concert – but he wondered if David could be persuaded to change his mind. Eliot knew his choir, even though he had only just started conducting them. He knew how they thought, their concentration levels and their willpower. Given this was a fundraising concert, there would be wine in the interval. It was a strong choir that could resist the waft of alcohol under their noses, despite the threat of a performance minutes later.

On the whole, Eliot much preferred to get his Bach over with before the interval, so that he, and the choir, could either get pissed and/or bugger off, and either way it wouldn't matter.

He knew Joshua's name: conducting is a small world. He knew they were roughly the same age and were aiming for the same kind of future. Rivals, really, though classical musicians are far too eloquently catty to use that base term.

Chapter 19

As anyone with a passing knowledge of the Second World War will tell you, careless talk costs lives. Back then you never chatted at the back of the bus in case there was a German spy listening in, who would then cause Churchill's downfall because the shortage of nylons caused girls to draw up the back of their legs with a brow pencil. Now, we all know that loose chat in a pub can be heard by anyone. When the chat – and possibly the eavesdropper – is drunken, great disasters can occur.

When Fenella parked her car, for the next Monday evening rehearsal, she didn't notice two men get out of a battered Transit further down the street. She didn't see them come towards her in the gloom as she got out of the driver's door and walked round to get her cello out of the boot. It was only as she turned away from the car, pressing her key fob, that she saw the orange flashing of her lights as the car locked strobe their faces as they came in close. The first to reach her nodded at the cello case and said,

'Bit Al Capone, eh?'

The other one sniggered at the wit displayed by his friend, but that didn't stop him grabbing the cello case from Fenella, pulling it off her shoulder by the leather strap. Her hand was clenched around the carrying handle, but he ripped it from her fingers and sprinted away, bumping the case along the ground a few times before he hefted it into a higher grip.

Fenella screamed and tried to run after him, but the first man, who had stepped aside to let his colleague have a wide getaway channel, slammed into Fenella, spinning her around into the side of her car and tripping her so she fell on to the kerb.

'No you don't, darlin',' he growled, kicking her, as she lay trapped between the kerb and her front wheel. She moaned and tried to put her arm over her head to protect herself.

Seeing that she wasn't going to try to give chase again, the man turned and ran back to the Transit, which had its engine revving and its back door open. His accomplice had already jumped in with the cello, and he joined them with an agile leap, banged twice on the side with his fist and the van spun its tyres as it accelerated. An arm reached out from the dark interior and pulled the back door shut as it turned the corner, and the overworked engine noise faded into the city as the smell of scorched rubber drifted back towards Fenella.

The whole thing had taken less than a minute.

She tried to sit up, but stopped and squeaked as she realised she had hurt her arm when she fell. She was looking around hazily in the direction the van had taken when David appeared before her.

'Fenella? God, are you OK? Fenella?'

He knelt down and tried to help her up.

'Ow – don't, don't,' she said quickly. 'My arm.'

'What happened?' David asked. 'I saw that van drive off – was it them? At least you still have your bag.'

Fenella looked down at the pavement and saw that her handbag was indeed lying there. They hadn't touched it.

Other players were approaching from both directions. Pearl rushed up and knelt next to David.

'Oh you poor thing! What's happened?'

'Mugged,' said Fenella. 'Need to get up. Could you...?'

David and Pearl supported her as she gingerly pushed herself up into a sitting position with her right arm.

'You want to get that head seen to,' Pearl said, fishing a pack of tissues out of her handbag and dabbing at Fenella's forehead. The tissue came away stained a bright red, with a few bits of black gravel transferred from the kerbstone.

David was looking at the angle at which Fenella was holding her left arm, and he frowned.

'I think you need to get more than your head seen to.'

He pulled out his mobile, called for an ambulance and then turned briskly back to Fenella and the small crowd around her.

'Can you give us some space, please? Thanks. Now, Fenella, do you think you can stand up? Are your legs OK?'

Fenella nodded slightly, holding another of Pearl's tissues to her head.

'Great. Can I have some help please? Oh good. Richard? Carl? Can you help me get her into the hall? I've told the ambulance we'll keep her in there 'til they get here.'

Together they half-lifted Fenella into the hall and settled her onto a chair just inside. Pearl produced a blanket, which she tucked around Fenella's legs, and bustled off to make her a cup of panacea.

Joshua arrived to see her being cosseted by a number of people and hurried over.

'Oh my God! What happened? Are you OK?'

'Mugged…' Fenella whispered, looking increasingly pale.

'Ambulance on its way,' said David. 'But at least your bag's intact and your car's still locked. I checked.'

Fenella looked so miserable at that news, Joshua dreaded to hear what was coming next.

'And your cello?' he asked. Everyone went very quiet.

Fenella started to cry. 'That's what they wanted – they took it. Oh God…'

Joshua put his arm round her gingerly, not touching her left arm where it was cradled on her lap. By that time most of the orchestra were milling about around them and whispered versions of events were being passed back like ripples in a pond. Ann was wearing a very fine wool scarf, and came forward to tie it gently around Fenella's arm as a sling, to support the weight of her left forearm. She tucked the material gently around Fenella's wrist and hand, trying not to move it.

David took his mobile out of his pocket again, assuming command of a clearly tense and complicated situation.

'We have to phone the police as well. Shall I, Fenella?'

She nodded miserably. 'Yes, I suppose so. Oh heavens.'

The next ten minutes waiting for the ambulance were spent with David relaying his conversation with the police to Fenella, holding the phone to her ear when they needed specific information. He ended the call by briskly taking down all relevant telephone and crime numbers they would need.

By the pauses and repetitions of the six-million dollar value during the exchange, the onlookers were in no doubt that the police understood the seriousness of the crime.

When the ambulance crew arrived, Fenella was sipping a tea with four sugars and shivering. Rafael had tried to herd most of the orchestra to the rehearsal end of the hall, but Joshua, David, Erin, Charlie and Ann remained with Fenella. It was arranged that Charlie would drop Fenella's car back to her flat, followed by Ann, who could then give him a lift home. Ann had a car large enough to take both Charlie's cello and her own: always a consideration when lifts were being organised among the lower strings.

The police were going to meet Fenella at St Thomas' Hospital. Even David couldn't persuade them to send an officer out to the scene of the crime straight away. Fenella needed medical attention first and it had been a straightforward mugging, albeit with an expensive aim. There was no flying squad specifically for multi-million-pound instruments.

After the ambulance had gone, Joshua stood in front of the orchestra and shrugged.

'Well, what do you suggest we do now? We were going to run through the Elgar tonight.'

'We don't know if Fenella's arm is anything serious yet,' said Rafael from his seat in the bassoons. His mind had become a feverish, recalculating nested-spreadsheet ever since he'd arrived that evening, searching for alternatives that would allow the orchestra to survive.

'Even if it isn't,' said Charlie, 'surely the main point of the Elgar in this concert was to do it on the Strad? That was the whole thing, wasn't it?'

'Harsh…' murmured Erin, behind him.

'But it's true!'

Without Fenella there to hear, it seemed an accepted fact that she had been chosen to play *because* of her Strad. Joshua did his best to defend this choice with which he was inextricably linked.

'OK,' he said, patting the air around him with flat hands as if to calm an excited litter of puppies. 'We don't know what Fenella's done to her arm, so we don't know if she can play a concerto in three weeks' time. We don't know if the police will have found the Strad by then. My question is: is it worth playing through our bit tonight anyway, so we're prepared? David? Rafael? What do you think?'

Nobody expected him to ask Pearl's opinion, not even Pearl. Her position on the Committee was limited in scope and even more in perception.

David and Rafael looked at each other. In the last hour, an improbable financial survival plan had been jeopardised, and they both knew there was no 'Plan B'. Goodness knows, if there had been, Mrs Ford-Hughes would probably not have been torturing them with her musical interpretation and Strauss's winding sheets could have remained unknotted.

'As I said, we don't know if it's serious yet,' said Rafael. His hope was tenacious, if not exactly infectious. He was willing to test the efficacy of a mantra.

'We might find out tomorrow that Fenella is fine and her cello has been recovered,' added David. 'We don't have long till the concert. Why don't we prepare some Elgar anyway, if you agree, Joshua, and then maybe after coffee we can have a look at the Bach so we're ahead of the game when the choir comes along. We've only got one rehearsal with them, remember.'

There was sniggering and groaning among the players in equal measure, as they remembered previous rehearsals with that choir.

'Yep, OK,' said Joshua. 'Elgar till the break, then. And we don't have long, so let's get on with it.'

'Erin can mark it for us, if you like.' Ann's voice was raised over the sound of an orchestra finding their place in the new piece on their stands. 'It's always difficult to rehearse a concerto without the solo part.'

There was a general swivelling of heads towards her, including Erin's.

'What?' asked Joshua, looking confused.

'Quite,' said Erin, staring at Ann. 'What?' She also mouthed 'the fuck?', but not everybody saw that.

Ann smiled at Joshua. 'We've been working on it and I've got the cello part in my bag.' She looked at Erin. 'I was going to give it to you tonight. You were going to have a look at my markings.'

Joshua looked to David for guidance. David, already overburdened with the decisions and implications of the evening so far, merely shrugged, effectively delegating all responsibility. Joshua turned to Erin.

'Well, I suppose it would be a help, if you know it anyway,' he said. 'Would you mind?'

Erin looked behind her again at Ann, who nodded vigorously and dug in her bag for the part. Resigned, she got up to take it from her.

'Where shall I sit, then? Can I do it from here?' She indicated her usual orchestral seat in the second desk of the cellos.

'No, best to come out the front, I think,' said Joshua. 'It'll sound better.'

He was brisk, letting no hint of personal feeling leak around his words. Erin found that hard edge useful to lean on. She set her face in a mirror of his emotionless granite and moved her chair to where he had indicated. Someone put an extra stand in front of her, and she opened Ann's copy of the music, sat down and grimaced at Charlie. He merely nodded as if all was right with the world and everything had achieved its proper place. There was no time for nerves.

Those iconic first chords rang out – Erin had the whole hall to herself. The orchestra only joined in halfway through the third bar. She felt Ann's bow do its indefinable thing of finding an extra dimension to her strings, so she seemed able to make all four sustain notes at once. That is, of course, impossible on a modern cello with its curved bridge holding the strings at different heights. It makes it easier to play individual ones without touching the others, but more difficult to play chords, which must be teased out, bottom to top.

By the time Erin got to the famous two and a half octave semiquaver scale at the end of the first run of the theme, she had forgotten she was nervous. That was a good thing, as that scale starts on the top A string and just goes right on up, through stratospheric positions, higher than a cello should rightly play. It *starts* in the treble clef, which as any decent cellist knows is the clef of the devil and should be reserved for the violins or any particularly extrovert viola players. It ends on a top E, three ledger lines above the stave. Even sopranos don't usually go there unless they are Mozart's Queen of the Night. The cello is a bass instrument. At those heights, players can become dizzy. Those with shorter arms can't even reach. This scale is not for the faint-hearted.

Erin sailed up it as easily as a cat up a tree, every accidental dead in tune, and even managed to meet Joshua's eyes for the last few notes so they could coordinate the *ritardando* at the top. The whole orchestra swung in behind her, repeating the theme for a few bars and allowing Erin to shake the tension out of her left hand in time to pick it up again.

Ann grinned to herself at the back of the section.

Chapter 20

'Told you the Elgar would be alright,' said Ann, changing gear and following Fenella's car's brake lights as they turned left. 'Does Charlie know where he's going, do you think?'

Erin was in the passenger seat of Ann's car. They had decided such an eventful evening couldn't be allowed to pass without a significant debriefing, so Ann had managed to pack three cellos in her dented Volvo estate and she and Erin were following Charlie to Fenella's flat.

'He's got satnav – I guess so.'

'He's a bloke,' said Ann. 'He won't turn it on.'

Charlie took another left turn, then another and ended up on the same main road as they had just been driving along, only a few hundred feet back. He set off with increased purpose towards Hammersmith Broadway.

'Oh God, hang on,' said Ann. 'We could end up anywhere from here. It's like an inescapable vortex. Sometimes I come off this dressed as a bus.'

After a few red lights and lane jumps, Charlie led them towards the river and Fenella's apartment block. He drove the car through the electronic security gates into the underground car park and the red lights descended into the darkness. Ann turned her own car round and waited at the kerb for him to return.

Erin peered up at the wall of glass rising into the night. 'Swank.'

'I believe her mother bought it for her,' said Ann. 'The one at the top.'

'How do you know all this stuff?'

Ann rumbled a chuckle deep in her throat. 'Because I have lived longer than most people and am very inquisitive. If you hang around long enough with your ears flapping, you pick it up.'

There were no passing cars. Fenella's apartment was in a cul-de-sac which ran down to the river, ensuring the exclusivity that the residents had wanted to purchase. Five storeys up, Fenella was even immune to gawping pleasure-boat trippers, which was why her flat had cost considerably more than those on the ground floor.

A few early Bonfire Night fireworks flashed among the stars and were reflected off the glass of the building.

'For instance,' Ann continued, as if the pause had merely been her drawing breath for the next logical statement, 'I'm old enough to be nostalgic about November 5th being just one night of bangs and whizzes. These days it's about a fortnight. I can't keep my cat in for a fortnight. He'd go barmy. Well, a different sort of barmy from being chased by explosions.'

'Isn't it Diwali as well around now though? I never know when: I think it moves around like Easter.'

'Humph.'

The next shower of green sparks illuminated Charlie, who was climbing the slope from the subterranean car park.

He walked round the barrier and came towards them. Ann lowered her window.

'You're in the back, round the other side.'

'Shift forward, Erin,' he said, as he tried to fit his knees into the car. 'I have real men's legs. They are longer than you think.'

Erin obligingly slid her seat forward and felt the car's suspension dip as Charlie's weight fell in.

'That car park is like a motor museum,' he said, as he pulled his door shut. 'I'm not kidding. Aston Martins, Porsches, BMWs – there is some seriously expensive shit under there. And they're all so clean! Do you think they have staff?'

'Do you think she's not the only person in that building with a Strad, then?' asked Erin, smiling.

'Well, she doesn't have one right now, does she?' Ann pointed out, starting the engine. 'Where to? I've got wine at my place, which means I don't have to drive home. You guys can get cabs from mine, can't you?'

'Yep,' said Erin.

'Can't believe Fenella treks all the way over from here every week to slum it in Stockwell. There are loads of orchestras in the posh west for her.'

The car turned out of Fenella's cul-de-sac and made quick time through the evening's emptying west London streets, towards the Embankment and across the river to the Oval.

'Maybe there's too much competition,' said Charlie. 'Posh, West End girls all growing their hair long and flicking it in each other's faces.'

'Charlie!' Erin was laughing. 'Not like you to join in the bitching.'

'Can bitch with the best of them, darling,' he said, 'I've never been to your house, Ann. I'd like to see where you're performing this magic on Erin.'

Erin snorted. 'Shut up.'

'She's doing it all herself, as we all heard tonight,' said Ann. 'I merely give her two hours in a room and rant at her for a bit until she gets better.'

'And an expensive bow,' said Erin.

'Well, yes. For the moment.' Ann's eyes twinkled. 'I'm gonna want that back, you know.'

'Oh, I know,' said Erin, quickly. 'I didn't mean—'

Ann's giggle brought Erin's stress levels down from panic to teased in three seconds.

'You're so easy to wind up!'

'I'm just a bit… it's all happened a bit fast tonight. Do you think Fenella's OK?'

Charlie leaned forward and put his head between the two front seats to join in, angling awkwardly round the cello digging into his ribs.

'Her arm didn't look great when she got into the ambulance, did it? They're not supposed to have three wrist joints.'

'It was her left arm,' said Ann. 'I know some players who can carry on if they've bashed their right hands, or even come back before they should do after a broken finger on the right, but you're buggered if it's your left. There's nowhere to compensate.'

'Unless you're Django Reinhardt,' said Charlie.

There was a pause in the car to receive that information. Erin eventually turned her head and pointedly blinked at Charlie.

'OK. I'll bite. What's Django Reinhardt got to do with Fenella?'

'You're kidding? Django Reinhardt? Best gypsy guitarist ever? Duetted with Stéphane Grappelli?' He shook his head at their blank looks.

'I've heard of Stéphane Grappelli,' said Erin, rather defensively.

'Man alive, you girls need to spread your musical nets a bit wider. When he was eighteen his trailer caught fire, and the fourth and fifth fingers on his left hand were so badly burned there was hardly anything left of them. He had to re-learn how to play guitar. Fenella doesn't have the next few years to develop an alternative fingering system – we need her Strad played in three weeks.'

'We need her Strad found first,' said Ann. 'Unless it's been squirrelled underground for some agoraphobic nutter, it should turn up. You can't shift an instrument as easily identifiable as that on an open market without someone spotting it. And the theft will be flashed round to all the dealers so they'll be on the lookout.'

'You sound as if you know a little too much about this racket.' Charlie laughed. 'You're old enough to have had a murky past. Were you a fence for hot Strads?'

'You have an overactive imagination, young man,' she said. 'But we have to remember the essential point: assuming that all may yet turn out well with its recovery – you are correct, Charlie, we have three weeks.'

She parked, got out of the car and opened the back door to extract the back seat cello: always a tricky manoeuvre. Travel seems to wedge cellos deep into a car's chassis. They need to be dug out on arrival. Ann continued to talk as she struggled to loosen the seat's grip on her cello case.

'We need her *Strad* played in three weeks. We don't necessarily need *Fenella* playing it. It's the Strad that's going to be the concert draw, not the unknown latest owner.'

Charlie and Erin swung their own cellos out of the Volvo's boot and onto their shoulders.

'But, my dear Ann,' said Charlie, enjoying this game immensely, 'surely you're not suggesting a sneaky switch of player?'

'Uh-oh,' Erin muttered as she walked towards the front door.

'I am suggesting nothing,' said Ann, primly. 'But if it *were* to come to pass that Fenella's injuries were so severe as to preclude her playing the *Elgar Cello Concerto* in three weeks, I would be in a position to suggest a very promising pupil of mine in her place.'

'And she couldn't *not* lend her Strad for such a worthy cause,' added Charlie.

'I'm still here, you know,' called Erin, who was waiting at the top of the path for Ann to unlock the door. 'I *can* hear you.'

Ann grinned. 'I'm sure she wouldn't disappoint her latest paramour. And I'm equally sure that he won't want to give up the opportunity of conducting such a newsworthy concert which may well further his professional career.'

Charlie looked at Ann with open admiration.

'Remind me never to plot against you, won't you?'

'Hello?' called Erin again. 'Thirsty. Will you two stop taking over the world and open the bloody door. I'm freezing.'

Chapter 21

As Ann let Erin and Charlie into her house, and they stood their cellos in a trio while they opened wine and later, drunkenly, pizza boxes, Fenella was lying on a trolley in A&E. At the moment Ann poured claret into three glasses, a tired junior doctor filled three syringes of Fenella's blood from a vein in her right arm and sent them off to check that whatever they ended up doing to her wasn't going to make her more ill than she already was.

She had waited two hours with a swelling wrist and clotted head wound, as a stream of other people's wounds which had not knitted themselves were triaged in front of her. She could see the logic of this, but grew increasingly grey as the evening wore on. She had not had to wait alone, however. Soon after her arrival she had been joined by a young, uniformed policeman who asked her a lot of questions about the men who had taken her cello. At some point during her answers, another police officer poked his head round the curtain. He was older and wore no uniform. Both facts encouraged Fenella, who had been worried she had been speaking to a work experience student who had no idea of the value of what had been stolen.

'Miss Stroud?'

She nodded, then wished she hadn't as it kick-started the throbbing in her head again.

'I'm Noel Osmar. I'm heading up the team looking out for your cello and the men who bashed you. You OK for a few questions? I know my colleague here has been getting the basic facts from you already.'

Fenella looked at Noel wearily. Dried blood had encrusted the front part of her hair where it had oozed before Pearl's tissue caught it. She was still wearing Ann's scarf round her left arm, which she rested on her chest. She managed a weak approximation of a smile.

'Yes. Do you think we'll find it? You do know what it is, don't you?'

Noel didn't even look at a notebook before he answered. 'I believe we're looking for an early eighteenth century Stradivarius cello. Worth around six-million dollars, whatever that is in our money these days. Is that right?'

Fenella almost smiled for the second time in a minute. 'Yes.'

'I've spoken to your insurance company, thanks for passing on their details so quickly.'

'I've only recently inherited it. Are you going to find it?'

'Well, we're certainly going to try. Now, were you aware that a GPS device had been placed inside the case?'

Fenella's look of absolute incredulity was interrupted by a doctor twitching aside the aggressively pastel-blue curtain and bustling to Fenella's side. She felt gently around Fenella's head and arm, shone a torch in her eyes, took her pulse and ordered an X-ray. Noel waited until all this medical activity had finished before continuing his conversation.

'This is news to you? The GPS?'

Fenella nodded.

'It's not uncommon and, as you might imagine, it makes our job a lot easier. I've got guys looking at the CCTV from the street now to see if we can identify the attackers. We've already got a partial registration number for the van, although they'd tried to obscure that. Your insurance people are going to contact me with the GPS info, and then we can get cracking to recover the instrument.'

He spoke as if recovering a multi-million dollar, antique instrument were an everyday occurrence in his working day. Fenella was suddenly suffused with a feeling of rosy confidence, which could have been Noel's sense of purpose or the painkillers recently injected by the doctor.

The curtain moved again, and Joshua pushed his way through the gap. He saw the police uniform and nodded at it curtly, as you do if you are middle class and have an inbred borderline respect for or, depending on the wildness of your youth, a fear of, uniforms. He also nodded at Noel, but without the clothes to indicate how he should nuance his greeting, it was a more diffuse nod as if between peers. Class interaction in Britain is as vibrantly layered as it has ever been.

'Sorry, am I interrupting?' Joshua asked.

Fenella flapped her right hand in Noel's direction. 'He's looking for the Strad. He's a policeman.'

'Ah.' Joshua straightened and gave Noel the benefit of a second nod, this time imbued with appropriate levels of curt. 'I suppose it's too soon for any news?'

'We're working on it,' said Noel, seeing how Fenella's eyes kept darting to Joshua's the way lovers' do, but that Joshua had not rushed to her bedside to clasp her uninjured hand. 'And you are…?'

'Er – I'm a friend,' said Joshua, with a little too much haste before Fenella could answer. 'I conduct the orchestra. That Fenella plays in, I mean. We were rehearsing tonight when she got – when her cello was stolen.'

'Ah yes,' said Noel. 'Stockwell Park, isn't it? I attended the incident at your recent concert. But I don't believe you were conducting that.'

'Well,' said Joshua, nonplussed for a moment. 'No.'

Noel let Joshua's discomfiture swirl around the cubicle for a moment longer, then gathered up his underling and took his leave, promising to keep in touch with Fenella. Only when he'd left did Joshua walk up to the bed and take Fenella's hand.

'How are you feeling? It doesn't look like they've done anything yet. Shall I call someone?'

'No, it's fine. I'm going to X-ray soon, I think. How come you're here? Where have you said you are?'

'Oh, I just said there had been an accident and I had to check in before I came home.' He smiled down at her. 'Don't worry.'

He leaned down and tried to brush some of her hair out of her eye, but it was caught in part of the dried blood clump and refused to budge. Just as his hand was near Fenella's cheek, Noel poked his head round the curtain again, almost as if he had been waiting the other side for a suitably incriminating moment to interrupt. Joshua jumped back guiltily. Noel looked directly at Fenella and did not acknowledge anything had happened at all.

'Sorry. I omitted to leave you my number, in case you need to get in touch with me.'

He put a business card on the bed near Fenella's right hand, and with a valedictory nod, left again.

Joshua frowned at the swinging curtain before turning back to Fenella. 'That said, I can't stay long,' he said quietly, half-expecting Noel to leap into view again and accuse them of having an illegal affair. The stress of the evening was showing. 'I just came to see you were being looked after. Did you call your mother? When is she going to get here?'

'I don't know what the time is now. She was at home, so it'll take a while, especially the last bit of the journey. She hates driving in London.'

Joshua stayed a few minutes longer, then kissed Fenella gently on her cheek and left the hospital. They had not discussed the Elgar, or whether Fenella had broken her wrist, or whether the Strad would turn up again. Joshua had not told her that Erin had played through the Elgar that evening and, despite not expecting to do it, had been impressive. Joshua even caught himself fleetingly wondering why he hadn't played anything with Erin while they had been lovers, forgetting that she had no piano and he had never been able to ask her to his home so he could play his.

Joshua, if he was learning at all, was learning too late.

As he left the hospital, he held the door open for a woman coming in from the street. Mrs Stroud nodded her thanks and looked for the signs to A&E. Joshua peeled himself out of one of his life's many compartments and into the November night, then drove home to his wife.

Chapter 22

By the next day, everyone in the orchestra who was on Twitter knew that Fenella had broken her wrist in such a complicated way that she had had to be fitted with external metal pins as well as a plaster cast. The exact words of the doctor were not used outside the hospital. Even 280 characters precludes a full description of a dorsally displaced fracture of the distal radius, with external fixation to prevent late collapse and malunion, and the hope that any pin-track infection would be minimal.

By being mugged on a Monday evening, Fenella neatly slipped into the hospital weekday queuing system, not buckled by weekend drunks and no consultants. On Tuesday morning she was in theatre having her wrist set, and was safely on a ward before pub closing time that evening.

That Tuesday morning, while Fenella was under general anaesthetic and a surgeon carefully pinned her bones together in straight lines, Erin made a large mug of coffee and sat at her kitchen table with Ann's copy of the Elgar in front of her. Her phone lay flat next to it. She had spent the last half an hour confirming Fenella's injuries which left no doubt that Fenella was not going to be able to play in three weeks' time. Indeed, there was doubt that she would ever be able to play properly again. Charlie's thoughts on that were characteristically brusque, but at least he had the subtlety to direct message them to Erin so Fenella wouldn't see. Joshua had also relayed to the orchestra Noel's judgement that the police would recover the Strad very soon.

Erin blew steam off the top of her mug and looked out of the window. She had three weeks to learn a concerto to performance standard, and possibly get used to a different cello on which to do so – one that was worth more money than she had ever seen concentrated together in physical form before in her life. If that didn't make her nervous, she didn't know what would. She caught Ann's voice in her head, telling her not to be daft, it was made of wood and metal and gut just like any other. She needed to concentrate. To work. Like she had never worked before. Sod the unemployment situation. There wasn't time to do this and look for a job as well. This: this would be her life for the next three weeks. Erin was not immune to a small feeling of satisfaction – schadenfreude almost – at what Joshua must be feeling that morning. To cheat on your wife is one thing, but to dump the other woman and go for another other woman, only to find that the alluring pull had defaulted back to the first other woman must smart. As the hot caffeine began to seep into her blood, Erin's self-awareness managed to loop around ahead of her idling speed, and she congratulated herself on the first step of healing. Her heart had been broken. Now her brain was bored with that hormone mix. It was time to move on.

She decided to work on the third movement: the slow one. Elgar had written the concerto during the summer of 1919, in his Sussex cottage. From there, the year before, he had heard the First World War artillery shells explode just across the channel and knew that the sound meant millions of men and boys being blown to pieces. After recovering from anaesthetic to remove an infected tonsil – something a man in his sixties could well have died from – he started to write this concerto, and it turned out to be a very different thing from his previous gung-ho, patriotic foot-tappers. He could not go back to that world.

He made the cello sing about death and the futility of war. This third movement especially captures his anger, bound up in regret for such a catastrophic waste of life. Its *adagio* quaver beats have a pulse of less than one per second, and the cello seems to sigh from one phrase to the next as if lamenting all those millions of souls lost in the mud.

To play that melody takes a phenomenal control of arm muscles. Erin felt the first few phrases whisper their questions as she lifted them up, as a voice will lift when asking for something. When the answer seemed to be that there was no redemption and no reason for the slaughter, she reached for those octave leaps as if doubling the wavelength could bring some understanding unknown in the undergrowth of solid ground. The whole movement undulates up and down the cello's register, holding notes at the crest of each hill over to the next bar so there is no feeling of pulse, no feeling of making a path of sense through the 'why's of those left behind by sons, husbands, fathers and brothers who did not come home. Wilfred Owen once said that the poetry was in the pity. Elgar wove pity through that movement, wrapping it hard into the stave with each rising and falling phrase. Some are so cloaked in accidentals you no longer know which key to feel at home in, so it wanders, rudderless, in the no man's land of shifting harmony, until it tries to come home again, and just when you thought the melody had come safely into harbour with a B flat, it turns in on itself and falls down a fourth to an F instead. It leaves you wrong-footed, feeling unfinished.

Erin felt the vibrations from her cello pass into her breastbone. They were strong when, nearly at the end of the movement, she played lower, as the music was finally written back in the bass clef it had started in, after its stratospheric wanderings through the tenor clef and even into the treble clef on its last pause on a top D which seems to hang forever, *pianissimo*, but with all the control of a juggernaut of grief waiting to give it impetus to return down again. She was *en pointe*, holding up the world. The cello buzzed against her bones, as if it had its own life and she was just cradling it in her arms to hear it singing.

The fingertips on her left hand were toughening up, but sliding up and down a wire for the ten inches or so it takes to move an octave up the A string is harsh. There were grooves in the pads of her fingers where she had run them repeatedly along the strings, training her arm to know when to slow, when to increase the pressure and when to stop at the precise point to make a perfectly tuned note without the listener noticing the break from the previous one. Some of these leaps were slurred, so Erin had to slide without even stopping the bow in her right hand making a sound. She was training blind: the muscles in her left arm had to learn how much to stretch and contract, what angles were needed for which note, how far up the fingerboard each note was in the two and a half octave range up the A string. There were around thirty different potential positions her left hand had to find, unerringly and without her looking, in any order, with a microscopic shift in position, without sounding out of tune.

Erin's fingers learned those leaps, and the nanometre accuracy they required, by repetition. She slid between two notes that were causing her trouble twenty – thirty – times, until she could feel her fingers learn where they needed to be. She carried on until the pads on her left hand were sore, red, and prickled when she took them off the fingerboard. She knew they would harden up, with callouses appearing like those that feet develop in well-used walking boots. She knew the end result would be unnaturally strong fingers with ends so tough it dulled her sense of touch for everyday things. Press them on the wire of a cello string, however, and the nerves would be able to think their way inside it to coax just the right frequency, to roll over the string to release enough vibrato for the note to live on its own. It was like a drug – to be able to get into the cello and play it from the inside.

Chapter 23

Noel Osmar was also drinking a large cup of coffee that Tuesday morning. He took careful sips of the scalding liquid while he looked at the download on his iPad screen slowly filling clockwise. The Stradivari insurers had been busy overnight, and had sent Noel their software to track the location device they had inserted in the cello case.

The lines around his eyes appeared and faded like a time-lapse sequence of a plant growing, as he squinted through the steam to the progress on screen. There were too many lines there for them all to be from laughing: they were evidence of some of the things he had witnessed, and of missed sleep. He was a small man who moved like an off-duty acrobat. He had tired eyes and grey temples. He sipped his coffee.

When the welcome dialogue box of the search software finally unfolded, he typed in the unique identification code they had given him for Fenella's cello, and pressed enter. The box winked out in the centre of the screen and he was left staring at an hourglass tumbling over and over in its place. There was no indication of how long it would take to find the signal. Noel didn't even know if the thieves knew of the transmitter's existence and, therefore, had either destroyed it or dumped the case somewhere. He'd heard of a police van blue-lighting it towards what they thought was a stolen violin on its way out of London only to close in on a loaded skip lorry heading up the A1 which was carrying the empty case.

Noel's young uniformed colleague, who had been with him at the hospital with Fenella, was sitting at a nearby computer cross-checking their partial number plate with Transit van registrations. There wasn't much to go on so it was a long job. Frank was scrolling down the list marking possible matches and absentmindedly picking his nose at the same time.

Noel glanced over. 'Have we got anywhere with the CCTV footage yet?'

Frank jumped, and snatched his hand away from his face. 'Still working on it. Never got a shot of the driver and the other two had their caps pulled down all the time. We've got a better one of the bloke that hit the girl, when he turned round to stop her following and knocked her over. Still looking.'

Noel nodded, still staring at his hourglass. At that moment, it stopped spinning, turned green and unfolded into a world map. A world map which had a flag with the ID number on it blinking over the UK. Noel zoomed in, and again, as the map realigned itself over Europe, Britain, London. The Thames grew across the screen until Noel was looking at an arrow pointing to a cul-de-sac in Petersham, an exclusive location just outside Richmond to the west of London.

'Hello,' he breathed to the screen.

Frank turned at the sound and came up behind Noel to look at the signal.

'Where the fuck's that?'

'That, my young friend, is somewhere you'll never afford to live. Petersham. Elvis's daughter rented a converted church there. Woody Allen filmed a thing in a house on that street.' He pointed at the screen with a pencil. 'The local garden centre café got a Michelin star. Richard E. Grant lives there. Quite your cultural enclave.'

'And you know all this how?' asked Frank, half in awe of Noel and half disbelieving.

'Working. Working. Always working. Come on.' Noel stood up, put on his coat and picked up his iPad. 'You drive.'

They approached Petersham from the south side of the river, through Richmond Park. The last oak leaves were clinging to gnarled branches, with drifts of leaves silting up against fallen logs. Frank drove at the requisite twenty miles per hour with a look of a city boy on safari, as if he half expected to see an elephant loom into view over the horizon.

'This is proper wild countryside, innit?'

Noel raised his eyes briefly from his screen. 'Well, it beats Streatham High Road. But wild? No, not really. You know they can't let the deer out of the park, so every year they have to shoot a load of them so they don't all starve.' He glanced down to check that his blinking flag was still blinking in the same place, and caught something of Frank's disappointment. He tried to make amends. 'Wouldn't be without it, though. Lungs of London and all that. Next left, out of the park.'

They wound round a few more twists in a road that seemed still to regard itself as a country lane rather than a main road leading into a capital city. History is all very well, but it doesn't mix with a double decker on its way to Richmond Station trying to negotiate a chicken run with a cement mixer bound for Kingston. The old brick walls of houses that were built hard by the road were pockmarked and gouged with the errors of previous drivers.

'In here,' said Noel suddenly. 'We can park up behind the houses and walk round.'

'What, just you and me?' Frank looked nervous.

'Yes, Frank. Just you and me. We're just a couple of chaps out for a walk, enjoying the fragrant riverside air. What we are most definitely not are two rozzers, so put my anorak on and turn off your squawkbox.'

Frank still looked dubious. Noel sighed.

'If I had a very expensive stolen item in my house, I'd be a bit nervous. Nervous might turn to something altogether more worrying if a uniformed police officer just happened to stroll past my windows and look interested.'

Frank leaned forward against the steering wheel and shrugged out of his uniform jacket, while Noel emailed the locator software to his phone and brought the map up on the small screen.

'Sorted,' he said with satisfaction. 'Now we can fit right in. Walking together, but I'll look like I'm too busy checking Twitter to be bothered to talk to you.'

They got out of the car and doubled back down the main road for a while before turning off, leaving the choked traffic surprisingly quickly for what passed for a quiet lane. This is what residents of Petersham paid for. Frank did his best to stroll nonchalantly in an anorak with sleeves stopping short of his wrists, and ended up shoving his hands into his pockets to disguise it.

Noel walked up a gravel track between two houses, twitching his head for Frank to follow. The centre of the gravel was matted with straggly grasses, and they both instinctively walked on that so the crunching didn't announce their arrival to anyone who might have been listening for it. Behind the houses the track turned and opened up in front of a line of garages. Noel scanned the back windows of the houses, but saw no twitching curtains or watching face. His eyes flicked to the corners of the buildings, the flat roof of the garages, the telegraph poles. No cameras. No movement sensors.

'Double bluff or audacity?' he wondered under his breath, walking along the line of garage doors with the scale of his map as large as he could, watching as the flag's arrow followed him like a compass around a pole. He walked back one door, and it steadied at him horizontally.

All the doors were locked with varying sizes of padlock, and the one next to Noel was rusted at the corners, leaning into the once-white and peeling paint in companionable dilapidation.

'Hold this,' he said to Frank, handing him the phone.

'What? I thought this was just a recce?' Frank was back to his original level of worry. 'What're you gonna do?'

'If we phone through and get a warrant and backup and all that malarky, chances are they'll move it and all we'll be able to do is follow. There's no one about. Let's have a look.'

'But—'

'Frank. Shut up and give me the bolt cutters out of my coat pocket.'

'That's what that is... been wondering what the hell you'd got in there.'

Noel efficiently cut through the old metal of the padlock, which gave up with a small thunk as it landed on the gravel. He pocketed it, handed the cutters back to Frank and pulled the door open just enough so he and Frank could slip inside. He pulled it shut behind them.

It was easy to spot in the gloom, once Noel's torch had done its first lighthouse sweep of the garage. Leaning against a pile of flat boxes wrapped in tarpaulins, the cello case looked as if it had been waiting for them. There were scuff marks along the bottom, when it had been bounced along the pavement on its journey to the Transit van. Noel walked quickly over to it, stood it upright and undid the clips, holding his torch in his mouth. The deep red gleam of the cello shone out of the case when he opened it, and he froze for a moment. The colour was so unexpected in this dark junk heap, appearing to have its own luminescence. He almost understood what the early California gold rush prospectors would have felt, picking pure gold out of the gravel rivers: the glint of promise, of a rich future, of something so refined that it was alien to its current landscape. Noel had never seen a Stradivari before. He would never forget his first.

Quickly, he clipped the case shut and swung the leather strap over his shoulder, almost staggering with surprise as he hefted the weight of it on his back. Frank was staring at him.

'What, we just walk out with it?'

Noel walked over to the door. 'Yeah. Let's give it a go, shall we? And, at the risk of sounding like Dixon of Dock Green, keep your eyes peeled. Doubt I've got much of a turn of speed carrying this thing.'

He pulled the door open a crack and scanned the driveway, as far as he could.

'Come on.'

They left the garage, and Frank pulled the old door closed and fixed the hasp over the loop that had held the padlock.

Unless you were actively looking for disturbance, the line of doors seemed untouched.

Noel started for the road with the hunched gait of the seasoned cellist, leaning away from the weight he carried. Frank strode next to him, fearing any moment there would be a shout from behind and several angry, and quite possibly armed men, would be after them. He still held Noel's phone in his hand and glanced down at it as they walked along. The flag's arrow remained pointing steadily at Noel, and was keeping pace with them along the street. Noel's voice interrupted his admiration for the technology.

'Car keys out, please. Let's not dawdle unnecessarily.'

They turned onto the main road and quickened their pace towards the car. It was impossible to hear any footsteps above the traffic, which was crawling more slowly than they were walking and pumping out choking exhaust fumes.

After the longest hundred yards Frank had ever known, they turned into the street where they had parked and he lengthened his stride to reach the car before Noel and open the boot. Noel slid the cello in gently while Frank started the engine. By the time Noel had closed his door the car was already moving.

'Where to now?' asked Frank.

'Straight down to the end here. We can do a loop. Let's just keep going.' Noel was breathing hard. He glanced over to Frank, whose face had the sheen of recent sweat. He chuckled. Frank exhaled with his lower lip jutting out, trying to direct the breeze up over his face to cool him off. By the time they had turned onto the main road again, they were both laughing. They drove past the road where the garage was, and both looked to see if there were any people running about, but the place was as quiet as it had ever been.

'Bloody hell,' said Frank.

'Yep,' agreed Noel. 'Bloody buggering hell. Well done, by the way. Top sidekicking.' He smiled. 'I'm going to phone that address in. It looked like an Aladdin's cave of top-end stolen goods. I bet those tarps the cello was leaning on were covering paintings. And the rest of the stuff was in interesting packaging. Definitely deserves a look. Hand us the phone, would you?'

Frank dug in the pocket of Noel's jacket and passed it over, and while they made their way back east in the rush hour, Noel dictated the address of the lock-up (now not so locked up) and arranged for an armed raid to visit it at their earliest convenience.

His next call was to his contact in the Strad's insurance company, to notify him of the cello's recovery, and to congratulate him on some superb software. Finally, just as Frank was drawing into the police station, he called Fenella and told her voicemail the good news, warning that he hadn't checked it for damage but that he had seen the marks at the bottom of the case. She was, at that time, anaesthetised and unable to take the call.

Chapter 24

Fenella was only reunited with her belongings when she moved from the recovery room to a ward. They had been packed into a transparent plastic bag by nursing staff while she was still in A&E. It managed to remain with her during her various incarnations as surgical patient, post-operative zombie and upper floor denizen, like a soul cleaving to a favourite body through different stages of reincarnation.

Mrs Stroud found the bag in Fenella's bedside locker when she was searching in there for no reason other than a mother's nosiness about her daughter's surroundings.

'Oh look, darling, your things are here!' she said brightly. She had spent most of that Friday saying things brightly, to convey a positive attitude to Fenella and, along with the grapes she had brought, aid recovery. Fenella was still feeling groggy from the anaesthetic. She had failed to eat much of the pale lunch proffered by hospital staff, and was beginning to suffer throbbing pain from her newly pinned wrist. She turned her head listlessly towards her mother's bag rustling.

'Here's your phone. Did you want it? I don't think we're allowed to switch it on here, though.'

An increasingly insistent feeling occurred to Fenella that she needed to check it. After all, Noel had taken her number and promised to get any news of the Strad to her. She hardly dared hope that it had been found, but discovered it was impossible to think of anything else unless she knew for certain.

'Oh, Mummy, do you think you could take it outside or wherever we're allowed to switch it on and check if there are any messages on it? The police might have news...' She tailed off, suddenly certain that they couldn't have found it so soon. The next second though, she was looking back at her mother with pleading eyes, on a see-saw of hope and fear.

'Darling, I don't know how to work it. I'd get out to the car park and wouldn't know which buttons to press.'

'Look, I can show you,' Fenella started, but was interrupted by the sight of Noel walking towards her bed from the other end of the ward.

He nodded at the phone in her mother's hand and said, 'Was wondering if you'd managed to pick up your messages. I left you one this morning.'

He could see by Fenella's blank face that she hadn't and smiled kindly at her. He knew how broken bones felt. He turned to Mrs Stroud and extended his hand.

'Good afternoon. I'm Noel Osmar, heading the police team on this case.'

Mrs Stroud tried to convey her usual absolute delight in meeting anyone new, but failed to achieve critical energy. She shook his hand rather more limply than her usual crisp clasping of new acquaintances. 'Hello. I'm Fenella's mother.'

Noel smiled at her, accurately reading her level of fatigue. He turned to Fenella.

'Good news. Your cello was recovered this morning.'

He watched the news sink into her face, setting off a smile which spread over her tiredness and almost won. Mrs Stroud was first.

'Oh, that's marvellous. Did you hear that, Fenella?' She raised her voice slightly, to its usual loud, bright tone. 'They've found your cello.' She sounded brittle herself: spending a sleepless night at the hospital had taken its toll.

Noel heard it too, and decided to indulge in a spot of stage management.

'I wonder, Mrs Stroud, if you know where the nearest coffee machine is? I am parched.'

She picked up her cue as a true hostess of her class is trained to do, and immediately offered to fetch one for him. After what seemed like an hour of fussing over his preferences, she walked off the ward, her skirt swishing against her petticoat with every step. One can never wear absolutely silent clothes if properly dressed.

Noel sat down by Fenella's bed.

'We picked it up early this morning. We think it's OK, although the case has taken some knocks and scratches on its base. I've had the insurers round having a look at it. They wanted to take it away to their expert, but since you weren't available to give your permission for that I said I'd hang on to it for the time being.'

Fenella nodded, speechless.

'How are you feeling?'

She grimaced, nodding at her wrist, which was suspended in front of her in its plaster cast and scaffolding of interlocking metal spikes. 'It's beginning to hurt quite a lot, actually. And I've got a bit of a headache.'

There was a neat rectangular dressing on her forehead, though there was still some dried blood in her hair. Disinfecting only spread so far from the actual wound before it became grooming, and therefore not a nursing remit.

She looked back at him. 'Did you catch the men who stole it?'

Noel allowed himself a small smile. 'Well, after the recovery of your cello we revisited the lock-up garage and surrounding area.' He left the actual order of legal proceedings in the obfuscation of omission. 'Not only did we find a large number of stolen items, but also the Transit van used to steal your cello and therefore the address of its owner. We've been busy this morning, paying visits of one kind and another, and our holding cells are becoming quite populated.' He smiled at Fenella again. 'I think I can safely say that yes, we've caught them.'

She rested her head back on the pillows. 'Good.'

'What's good?' called Mrs Stroud, returning from her coffee run and handing Noel a paper cup of brown liquid. He accepted with outer gratitude and inner resignation. Institutional coffee was the same, no matter what the institution.

'We've recovered the cello and caught the people who stole it,' said Noel succinctly. Sometimes it was best to paraphrase. He sipped his coffee, and belatedly rose from the sole bedside chair with an apology and gestured for Mrs Stroud to sit in it herself. She obliged demurely, crossing her legs and managing to flutter her eyelashes at him while drinking her own unidentified brown liquid. Noel remembered the previous evening and how the ghost of just the same eyelash flutter had tried to surface from Fenella when Joshua had arrived. He caught a strong gust of inherited body language and folded it away for future use. He imagined Fenella cross-ing her legs like that. He was a very good detective.

'So where is the cello now?' asked Fenella.

'Well, without your explicit consent to move it anywhere, I've kept it at the station,' said Noel, 'in the safest place I could think of. In a locked holding cell with strict instruc-tions left with the duty officer not to open it under any circumstances.'

Even Fenella smiled at that. Noel enjoyed the knowledge that the men who stole it were currently sitting in adjacent cells within feet of it, without any idea of their proximity to it or, indeed, how he had found it. The insurers were under-standably keen to keep any knowledge of their tracers on a strict need-to-know basis.

As Noel was taking his leave from Mrs Stroud and Fenella, another visitor arrived at her bedside. David had brought an enormous bouquet of flowers, which almost entirely obscured his face and body as he approached, giving the impression of the flowers conveying themselves to where they were required entirely under their own steam on a pair of extremely long and skinny legs.

Noel saw Fenella's exhaustion creep across her face, and on his way out, having exchanged pleasantries with David, he had a word with a nurse and suggested that Fenella's vis-itors might be encouraged to leave sooner rather than later. He used his full title of Detective Chief Inspector when introducing himself, which had the desired effect. He almost never mentioned it, saving it up to expedite situations of immediate need. It was a useful shorthand.

David had balanced the flowers on their stems in the gold-fish bowl bag of water in which they were tied, and they swayed a bit on top of Fenella's bedside cabinet wafting scent over the antiseptic hand-gel aroma hanging round the ward. He gestured to them with an awkward hand.

'They're from all of us really. I said I'd pop them round here, to see how… to say hello. You know…' He trailed off, turning his genial smile towards Mrs Stroud so he didn't have to look at the Eiffel Tower climbing out of the wrist of someone who was due to play a cello concerto in three weeks' time.

'Thank you,' said Fenella. 'They're lovely.'

'Any news on your cello?' David asked. 'Though it's probably too soon…?'

Mrs Stroud bustled into the conversation, eager to be of help.

'Oh yes – you just missed the policeman. He was just here. Oh, you must have passed him just now. Lovely man. He came in to say that they've found it and caught the men who stole it, so it's all looking very much better now.'

She stopped, stretching up towards David's height from her seat at the bedside chair, her spine leaning like an etiolated seedling growing towards the light. The pull her eyebrows were exerting on the skin of her face would have made any plastic surgeon proud, but from David's vantage point it only accentuated the dark circles under her eyes. He didn't need any nurse telling him not to overstay his welcome. He cleared his throat, knowing what he had to achieve before he ended the conversation, and wondering quite how to do that without causing any more heartache. He still had an orchestra to save.

'That's marvellous news. They may be looking younger all the time but clearly they can still do the job.'

'We don't know if the cello's OK yet,' said Fenella. 'He said there were some scratch marks on the case, so it might be damaged. I know they ran off pretty fast with it, and I think I remember hearing it get bashed on the pavement.'

'Better it than you,' said her mother automatically, and only when she had finished realised that both her daughter and the cello had been bashed. She cleared her throat and sipped coffee, blowing the steam in little puffs away from her glasses.

'And you?' said David, trying to wrench the conversation round to the direction he needed without sounding too callous. 'What have they said about your arm?'

Fenella shrugged, at least on the side away from her plastered wrist.

'Broken. In a couple of places, I think. They've stuck all this in it to get it back in the right place. But I don't know…' Her eyes sheened over with tears. 'They haven't exactly said how long. But they were talking weeks. And it will be ages once the plaster comes off to get all the motion back. If it ever does.' One eye overfilled before the other and a couple of tears fell down one side of her face. 'I'm not going to be able to play the Elgar.'

'Nonsense,' her mother said, back to her brisk normality. 'You'll be playing again before you know it.'

'No, Mummy. Not in three weeks. Maybe later, but not in three weeks.'

'I'm sorry,' said David, but grateful that Fenella had said out loud what had been obvious to him as soon as he'd emerged from behind the flowers.

'But Joshua was so looking forward to doing it.'

'Well, I'm not going to lie to you. We were all looking forward to hearing that Stradivari played. I'm sure I can include our audience in that too.' David smiled at Mrs Stroud to make it a more general statement of cultural anticipation, in case that had gone too close to the bone for Fenella. It was one thing to separate the attractions of a Strad and her playing ability; quite another to cleave them so clinically in front of her. He glanced over to the desk at the end of the ward, where the nurse was still sitting. He knew he didn't have much longer, and turned back.

'I wonder – and I stress I haven't talked this over with Joshua yet – I wonder – and I'm thinking on the hoof here – if you would consider… loaning your Strad to another performer for the concert?' His voice drifted upwards as if he were a born Australian, shimmering away from any possible offence caused by such a stark request. It did indeed sound as if the thought had just occurred to him, and not turned over and over repeatedly in his head during his many hours of financial worry-induced insomnia the night before.

Fenella stared at him. He went a little further with a lever he was counting on to bring results.

'I know Joshua had great plans to make this the first introductory concert for this cello. I think he has a season of them in mind: a sort of miniature festival, if you will. He really has been giving it a lot of thought.'

He stopped, worrying he'd been laying it on too thickly. He had not bargained on Mrs Stroud, however.

'A season! My! Did you hear that, darling? That would mean it wouldn't matter quite so much for the first one, what do you think? I think it's a marvellous idea.'

She would have continued to gush, had David not pointedly turned to Fenella and waited for her response. He had seen the nurse get to her feet and walk around the desk into the ward.

'Has he said that? A season of concerts?' She looked doubtful and hopeful at once.

David took the view that confidence at this stage outweighed definitive accuracy. 'The committee was very impressed with his ideas.'

The quiet squeak of rubber-soled shoes approached, and the nurse smiled at all three of them.

'I think a bit of a rest is called for, don't you?' she said to Fenella, before turning to David and Mrs Stroud. 'Perhaps you could come back again later on?'

David turned back to Fenella. 'Of course. I'm sorry, you must be tired. Er, what would you like me to tell Joshua?'

'Oh, alright. If we can sort the insurance out. It might not be playable anyway. Nobody's looked at it yet.'

David let about half his pleasure and relief spill out in the form of a smile, keeping the rest of it until later when it wouldn't be quite so obvious. It was still a broad grin that he bestowed on Fenella and her mother in equal measure.

'Of course. We can sort all those details later on. Thank you.'

'Come on, please,' said the nurse, opening her arms to usher them out as if she were gently shooing hens.

Mrs Stroud kissed Fenella on the cheek. 'See you later, darling. Get some sleep.'

David held the doors open for Mrs Stroud as they made their way out through the hospital, thankful Fenella hadn't got around to asking just who it was that was going to play her cello. It was obvious to the whole orchestra that there was no warm, loving team spirit between Fenella and the rest of the cello section, so the later she could find out that Erin would have the job the better, in David's view. He sighed as he left Mrs Stroud trying to remember where she had parked. Horn players were so much more straightforward than cellists.

Chapter 25

November threw fireworks above London every night over the next week, as people celebrated the torture and execution of a political dissident or the light of the unknowable, depending on which religion you took to. After a few days Fenella was allowed home, with her mother coming to stay to help her.

Eliot Yarrow had already told his choir that they were to sing Bach's *Magnificat*, and there was the usual mix of choral reaction. Some grumbled about having to learn something new in such a short time but, in fact, it is such a well-known piece there were very few of them who had never sung it before. A frisson rippled around their ranks like a small electrical Mexican wave as some members of the choir realised the potential for solos. There are always people who sing in choirs such as the Stockwell Singers who feel, rather like Joshua felt about conducting an amateur orchestra, that it is beneath them and merely a stepping stone to their great career as a professional. What Eliot hadn't told them was that one soprano solo aria was already taken by Mrs Ford-Hughes and that because they were doing a reduced version he was not doing some of the other solo stuff. He had not decided himself just which solos were staying in: he was going to hear them all through, see who volunteered and take it from there.

Eliot was at the more relaxed end of the conducting spectrum, often perching on his high stool on one buttock with all the jumper-wearing charm of a younger Val Doonican. He had the hair that comes from formative years at public school or a parsimonious attitude to hairdressing trips.

Two weeks before the concert, the Stockwell Singers gathered for their regular rehearsal in a further education college hall less than a mile from the school where the orchestra met. There was the usual chatting and milling about that happens before any music starts, just like orchestras, but with added aromas of Vocalzones and menthol inhalers. It was, after all, winter, and there are no people so ready to guard their voices against the tyranny of germs as singers. The serious ones carried water bottles, which they placed with care by their feet when they sat down. From there they could take sips every few minutes to keep their throat lubricated, drawing irritated glances from their more down-to-earth neighbours who had just come along for a nice sing and didn't fanny about with professional tactics like water bottles. The water-bottlers tended to congregate at the front of their respective sections, to spearhead the sound as it projected forwards to Eliot and out to the wider beyond and an imagined adoring public.

From his vantage point, facing the singers from the front, Eliot could accurately determine what most of them had eaten for lunch that day, and how many of them were currently sucking intense vocal lozenges. He had learned, by then, to take a couple of steps back when a truly committed chorus attempted Bach or anything else in German or Hungarian:

things tended to get a little damp around the consonants. A conductor's relationship with a choir can sometimes be more intimate than either of them would wish for.

'So,' he said, smiling at them all, sweeping his eyes around quickly and catching those people actually looking at him momentarily as he did so. Some conductors focus on the water-bottlers in the front row and ignore the rest of a choir, which leads to distraction and (in the case of tenors and basses) singing flat. The good conductors manage to make every singer feel that he had looked them straight in the eye every time he said something. For that kind of attention, a singer will sit up straight and take their eyes off their copy. They will focus. They will sing better. There were those, of course, who had their faces permanently drooped into their music, and had learned how to come in a nanosecond after everyone else from years of practice. They were the unreachables. No sane conductor goes after them: they are the collateral damage of a decent performance.

'Everyone got a copy of the *Magnificat*?'

Eliot smiled, sat back and fished out his phone while he waited for the inevitable confusion as people realised they had walked straight past the open box with the large notice saying 'TAKE A COPY', stood up, squeezed past their neighbours, apologised, got to the box, thought belatedly about who else in their section might have forgotten, called out, remembered a number to pick up, forgot to add themselves to it, returned and finally sat down again only slightly out of breath to relate their entire arduous journey to their next-door neighbour. Choirs can faff better than any other group of musicians. Eliot re-pocketed his phone and smiled brightly again, as if the last five minutes had been erased from his and everyone else's memory and they were there, keen as the proverbial mustard, to learn notes.

'OK. We've got the Peters edition. If any of you brought your own copies, I hope to God they are Peters as well, otherwise you're on your own. I'm not doing duplicate page numbers. There are spares here at the front if you want to change your mind?'

He knew they wouldn't. Several members of the choir had been singing for decades and had built up quite a library of their own vocal scores of the more commonly performed works like Brahms, Verdi and Mozart's requiems and the big Bach sings like the *St Matthew Passion*. They had spent years carefully marking in their own part all the different things different conductors had told them over the years – sometimes diametrically opposed instructions – and they were as welded to their own comfortable copy as moss to a north face. What they did when they reached a section marked in black underlining as *forte* and simultaneously (and equally black) as *piano*, nobody knew. Luckily, it was coincidentally exactly these singers who made less noise than the rest, so Eliot wasn't unduly worried. There was nothing he could do about it anyway. Contrary to some conductors' opinions, they are only mortal and cannot change human nature with a flick of their white baton.

'Right,' he said, opening his own score. 'Who hasn't sung this before?'

A few hands went up. There was a blooming of smug faces among the rest of them that made Eliot wary. A choir full of very experienced singers who thought they knew a piece backwards made for a conducting experience much like steering a large, fully-loaded cargo ship: not the most responsive vessel and a bugger to stop or turn once it had achieved a rolling momentum.

'We're not doing the whole thing.' He talked over the rising hubbub comprising two opposing halves: one expressing relief that their Christmas schedule was not going to be put out too much, and the other voicing disappointment from the Bach-loving solo-chasers. 'We just don't have time, people!' He raised his hands and slowly the noise restricted itself to a few mutterings. 'We'll be doing most of the choruses and a few of the solo arias. I'm not sure if the news has filtered through to you yet that the reason we've been asked at such short notice is that the Stockwell Park Orchestra is trying to put together a special concert to showcase a couple of people, for different reasons.'

The murmuring settled down like a cat turning around and around before finally flopping down to sleep. Eliot waited for the noise level to drop completely before speaking again.

'I suggest we simply sing though all the choruses now and see where we end up. Sopranos split. You clear who's singing what? Good. I'm not sure yet which solo numbers we'll be doing. I've heard there is a soprano lined up already, but haven't been told if she's a first or a second, so we'll just have to wing those next week, OK?'

He turned to Nick, who played the piano accompaniment for their rehearsals and had been sitting quietly at the keyboard listening to all the pre-sing faffing. Nick nodded, having already opened the score to the first page, keen to start the very black staves of semiquavers of the orchestral reduction. It takes a fine pianist to accompany choirs well, since a lot of the time they are playing an entire orchestral score with just two hands on a piano. The *Magnificat* opens with thirty bars of introduction before the singers come in, and Nick already had his hands hovering over the piano keys. Eliot looked at him enquiringly.

'You want to do the whole intro?'

'Yes, fine,' said Nick, mild indifference failing to cover up his eagerness. 'If you like.'

Eliot smiled and turned to the singers. 'Nick is going to go from the top. Hang on to your hats. Count! Here we go.' He turned to Nick, giving him a pulse and upbeat to set him going, knowing the thirty bars would both lull the choir into a Bach trance (some even closed their eyes and had a dreamy half-smile on their faces) and would pass much quicker than they were prepared for. As Nick's fingers flashed through the notes and approached the choral entry, Eliot grew more animated, trying to attract the attention of the singers, especially the sopranos, who had the first entry. As some of them still had their eyes closed, he resorted to calling 'Watch!' three bars ahead, which caught some of them, but then they were a page behind and, while they were trying to turn to the right one, the rest of the sopranos did their best.

Nick, with many years choral accompaniment behind him, gamely banged out their notes louder than the rest of the score as each part came in or sounded ropey. The first, full-on chorus was over almost before the choir had got into their stride, and their final '*Dominum*' just about fell into the right cadence as Nick once again wound his fingers around the running semiquavers, ready to carry on for the fifteen bars to the end of the movement. Eliot reckoned that since he had been allowed to have so much fun with the introduction, there was no harm in letting him run to the end. It was like taking an energetic dog for a walk: better behaviour overall is achieved by giving lots of time to run about where there was space to do it. Eliot was not going to sweat over a few minutes of rehearsal time for a concert that wasn't even his.

He sat down on his stool and let Nick come effortlessly to the end, with a subtle *ritardando* into the last chord. He quietly removed his hands from the keyboard and folded them in his lap, as if he had just played a grade one scale satisfactorily rather than a note perfect Bach score that had outwitted many pianists before him. Nick was a shy, thin man, and never looked so much like a turtle as when he played piano, with his scrawny, tendon-roped neck leaning forward out of his shirt collars that always seemed a size too big, wearing glasses that slipped down his bony nose.

There was spontaneous applause from the singers, who recognised a tour de force when they heard one. Nick blinked at them happily through his specs.

'Great stuff, Nick,' said Eliot. 'Well, we've got a few corners to look at on that one, but let's press on. We have a Sop. two solo for *Et exultavit*, then a Sop. one for the *Quia respexit* next...' He flipped over the pages in his score, pretending not to notice the front row of sopranos shifting around, some straightening their backs and trying to catch Eliot's eye, some deliberately looking at the floor. A solo is a solo, no matter what.

'Right, the *Quia respexit* runs straight into number four: *Omnes generationes*. Can you mark in your parts to look at me in the previous couple of bars, so we're ready?'

Pencils, traded within choirs like cigarettes in prison, went up and down the rows with whispered thanks and tutting respectively. Eliot watched all this with a benign patience he had cultivated during his first weeks as a choral conductor.

'Great. Nick, can you give us from bar twenty-one? Choir, that means we have four bars of Nick's brilliance before we come in. Sarah?'

A soprano jerked her head up towards him in surprise at hearing her name called. She was one of the water-bottlers, but managed not to make a feature out of it.

'Yes?'

'Sung this before?' She nodded. 'Can you give us the last couple of bars of number three to lead us in?'

Sarah nodded again, trying to ignore the immediate shifting of energy among her soprano neighbours. It was mostly envy, instantly layered with sisterly support and team spirit. Eliot didn't give it any time to fester, and merely made sure Nick and Sarah were both ready before he brought Nick in at the beginning of the bar, helping Sarah come in with her phrase a couple of beats later.

Sarah's voice rose above the piano in a slow arc, beautifully controlled as she let a long *adagio* minim blossom before tucking it into semiquavers to fit with Nick's playing. Eliot smiled at her before taking his attention to the chorus for the bar before they came in, making exaggerated beats so they knew what to watch for. The slow *adagio* tempo of the solo movement had to dock seamlessly into the quicker feel of the choral section: the dreamy smoothness of the soprano solo overdubbed with the basses and altos getting all energetic with their '*Omnes, omnes, generationes*'. There was a trick to making that switch without it sounding as though there were suddenly morris dancers jumping about all over Bach's beautiful melody. They didn't quite make it, but Eliot gathered them, shook up the reins, blew a quick kiss at Sarah and pressed on.

They read through the rest of it, for the most part reasonably competently, with Eliot letting whoever wanted to have a go at the solos sing. It wasn't really fair to expect choral singers to sight-read a solo without any notice, but in every section there were people keen to take on the challenge. Eliot had a good idea what they all sounded like, having worked with them for a year by then. When there was more than one volunteer for any particular bit, he weighed up the relevant factors in his split-second decision: one bass might have a lovely tone and lightness of touch, another might have perfect pitch and could rattle off acres of semiquavers without breaking a sweat or ever coming in on the wrong note.

There is an unfortunate amateur tradition of singing Bach where a soloist sounds uncannily like they have been inspired by 'The Laughing Policeman'. There are often many notes to sing on one syllable and, if a diaphragm isn't up to bouncy cling film tautness, then it can sound as if there is an 'h' in between every note. The bass aria, *Quia fecit mihi magna*, is one of those you really don't want a huffer to sing. In only the second phrase, he has to sing twenty-eight separate notes to the sound 'po', which can get a little wearing if you have to banish images of ruddy cheeks and a policeman's helmet as he goes past.

In the right throat, these Bach runs sound as effortless as a chirpy mountain stream tinkling over stones. There are few such throats in the world, and the Stockwell Singers had only their fair share of them and no more.

By the end of the rehearsal, Eliot knew which of the arias he was going to have to cut. What he hadn't yet heard was Mrs Ford-Hughes.

Chapter 26

Exactly a fortnight before the concert, Fenella invited Erin to her flat to collect the Strad. Rather than having to speak to her directly, she sent a curt text, which had the defiance of a gauntlet being thrown down prior to a duel. For all David's flattering and sugar-coating, Fenella found the news that someone else was to play her cello gnawing at the peripheral vision of her consciousness, always there like the dancing spots heralding a migraine. David had asked Joshua to inform her, as delicately as he could, that it was to be Erin, warning him with the sternest of looks that anything that upset Fenella should be strenuously avoided. This concert was turning out to be the most taxing he had ever organised. He found himself yearning for the new year, when he could talk to people normally without fear of them removing something really, really expensive from his grasp that he really, really needed. Joshua took this to include not confessing to Fenella that he had been sleeping with Erin right up until the moment he found out Fenella had inherited a Strad. Subtle he was not, but he could be relied upon to grasp most of a big picture.

Fenella clung to him, both metaphorically and with her good arm whenever she could. She asked him to be there that Saturday morning when Erin was due, and he, helplessly, constructed another lie to his wife and said that he would be.

Erin also felt the need for a 'second' after she read the adversarial tone of Fenella's text, to bear witness to anything that could happen. Ann understood absolutely. And so, the two of them stood together as Erin rang the bell at Fenella's apartment building at eleven o'clock and waited for the videophone to crackle into life, exchanging glances of excitement and apprehension. Erin's nose was dripping from the cold wind off the river, and she dug in her coat pocket for a tissue. Her fingers were freezing too, and she blew warm air onto fingertips sticking out of her fingerless gloves. She didn't want her first go on a Strad to be spoiled because of numb hands.

'Hello, Erin.' Fenella's voice was tinny and loud in the quiet street, with the electronic speaker transmitting faithfully her complete absence of welcome. 'Come up. Fifth floor.' She disconnected without seeing Ann standing there too.

The door buzzed and Erin leaned on the polished rail to push it inwards, welcoming the blanket of warm air that started to prickle her cheeks as she walked to the lift.

'All a bit glossy, isn't it?' said Ann. 'Bet this was just a marshy field when my house was built.'

Erin smiled, and stepped into the lift. As the box rose smoothly up five floors, she frowned, and sniffed. Quite apart from her runny nose, she thought she caught the trace of Joshua's aftershave in the enclosed space, and groaned. Ann looked at her.

'What?'

'I think we may be a cosy foursome.'

'Huh?'

'Could be wrong… but it smells as if Joshua's been in here recently.'

Ann laughed. 'My God! Are you part bloodhound or something? I can't smell anything. You have an overactive imagination, my girl.'

She looked more closely at Erin's face, and the deepening creases around her mouth.

'Really?'

Erin nodded, sighed, and shrugged, blowing her nose again. 'Sod him, right? We've come to get the cello.'

'Abso-bloody-lutely. Sod both of 'em. Come on.'

Ann strode out of the lift towards Fenella's door, which opened with disconcerting punctuality as she approached and lifted her hand to knock.

Fenella stood there with her arm in a sling, arranged carefully over the pins and connecting rods sticking out of the plaster.

'Oh. Ann. Hello.' She tried to smile and almost made it. 'I didn't know you were coming too.'

She stepped backwards around the door and ushered them in with a nod.

Erin followed Ann through the door and again smelled the familiar and now expected whiff of Joshua, stronger since the skin from which it was emanating was standing a few feet away. Not for the first time, Erin was thankful for acute olfactory nerve endings. Those few seconds of warning had enabled her to prepare to smile civilly at the shit who had dumped her for an expensive cello, and enjoy watching him watch it being given to her and then having to see both of them walk out of the door. It was all she could do to stop herself humming 'I Will Survive'.

Ann took her seconding duties quite seriously and gave a brisk smile to Joshua which left absolutely no room for doubt about what she thought of him.

'Oh, hello, Joshua,' she said, as if it was perfectly normal to find the married conductor of your orchestra in the lead cellist's flat on a Saturday morning. 'How nice to see you.'

Erin stepped right up beside her and joined in, feeling quite jaunty. 'What a surprise.'

Fenella had shut the door and reappeared by Joshua's side, turning awkwardly like a robot with no twisting capacity in its torso. Erin saw the discomfort on her face and resolved to try to be a bit more generous towards her, at least until her wrist had healed.

'How are you feeling? Is it mending well – do you know?'

Fenella smiled, a small, tight smile, acknowledging Erin's attempt at sympathy.

'It's still sore. I'm sure it will improve. Would you like some coffee? We've just made a pot.'

'Look, let me do that,' said Joshua, eager to be of use and to get himself out of the laser pincer movement going on between Ann and Erin's sight lines. He walked to the kitchen island and began collecting four mugs with such a familiarity with his surroundings that Ann raised her eyebrows to Erin.

Fenella gestured to the armchairs and the sofa arranged around a coffee table, and they followed her over. There was a single sheet of paper lying on the table, which Fenella picked up and gave to Erin.

'There's just this to sign for the insurance people,' she said, reaching down again to the table to pick up a pen. 'I've cleared it with them and all they need is your signature on this and it'll all be fine. You can't leave it in a car, though.'

'I wasn't thinking of leaving it anywhere, don't worry,' said Erin, reading through the paper. It was dense legalese, but seemed to make sense. She started to let go of the worry that she might end up owing six-million dollars of money she didn't have if something awful happened.

She sat on the sofa, leaned the paper on the table and signed. Meanwhile, Joshua brought the coffee mugs over and put one by Erin's hand and another in front of Fenella.

'How do you take yours, Ann?' he asked, and the bright syllables fell into the air around Fenella's head and seemed to sparkle at Erin and Ann. Either the painkillers or lack of sleep since her injury cocooned Fenella from noticing any of it. She leaned over and took the paper Erin had signed, folded it once carefully, and stood up to put it in her bureau on the other side of the room.

Ann looked at Erin with a level gaze as she replied to Joshua. 'Just milk. Thanks.'

He returned to the kitchen area to pour milk into her mug and stir, while Erin sipped her coffee.

Ann couldn't resist another dig. 'How's yours, Erin? Sugar in there OK for you?'

Erin gave a wry smile. 'It's fine, thanks.'

As Fenella came back to the armchair to drink hers, Joshua brought his own and Ann's, and perched on another armchair, looking outnumbered and justifiably scared.

Ann leaned back comfortably on the sofa next to Erin, crossed her legs and sighed, as if relaxing in a bath with a favourite book. She was enjoying herself enormously. It wasn't every day that she got to sit in the same room as a

Stradivari and make fun of a pompous conductor all at once. This appealed to her on many levels. It wasn't bad coffee either. She decided to take charge of the situation.

'So, now the legal stuff is out of the way, is it OK for Erin to touch the cello? How is it, by the way? Did it get damaged at all when it was stolen?'

Fenella managed a half-hearted flick of hair behind her shoulder, with her uninjured hand.

'It's basically fine. The case is badly scratched, but the cello was so well padded inside it doesn't seem to have come to any harm. We've had to replace the case, of course.'

She had been advised by her insurers not to say anything about the GPS tracking device, which was now sewn into the lining of the new case with invisible stitches. The thought of invalidating her insurance and losing six-million dollars was so upsetting she shut it away in the same place she put the idea of Joshua's wife and the stage of decomposition of Oscar's body.

'Great,' said Ann.

Erin tried to ease the situation with a bit of old-fashioned courtesy.

'We're – well, *I* am too – incredibly grateful to you for the loan of your cello,' she started, trying to nuance her tone between excitement about playing it and sympathy for the situation that caused it. 'I know you didn't have to. I'll try to do it justice.'

Fenella nodded with her lips pressed into a thin line. It wasn't a smile. It was the muscle movements made by someone who knew she should smile but didn't have the stamina resources or reserves of generosity to go through with the actual electrical nerve impulses.

They all sipped at their coffees and an awkward silence fell around them. Erin wasn't clear whether she should try to play the Strad at Fenella's flat, or just take it home to work on it there. Joshua looked at her with open admiration, mistaking her indecision for a sangfroid he found very attractive. Fenella flicked her eyes at him over the rim of her mug, looking like a pale, trapped bird.

Ann, the arch-observer, recrossed her legs the other way around, took a gulp of coffee and set it down on the table in front of her with a clatter.

'Is Erin allowed to try it before she takes it away with her?' she asked, noting another glance of Joshua's towards Erin. 'So we can hear what it sounds like properly.' She stopped, remembering that Fenella had been bringing it to the orchestra rehearsals for a couple of weeks already. 'Without all the rest of us sawing away, I mean…' She turned a wide smile on to Fenella, to forestall any correct interpretation of her former statement.

The minefield which underlies all communication between musicians coalesced into focus before Ann's eyes like the blueprint of a developing film, with white dotted lines clearly indicating the relationship between truth, flattery, obsequiousness and evasion. She had seen, heard and deflected all this – and worse – in her professional life for decades. She was finding this quartet, in a private apartment, a piece of cake to orchestrate.

'Oh, yes. If she wants to?' Fenella's inbred manners took over and her conscious thought was ambushed.

Ann turned to Erin and jerked her head over to the cello case.

'Go on. Just get the feel of it,' she said. 'I'd like to hear it close up.'

'Should be you doing it then,' Erin said, but put her coffee down and got to her feet anyway. 'Come to think of it, why *aren't* you doing the concerto? You'd be miles better than me. Why has that only just occurred to me?'

'Oh, I'm far too old to do that amount of practice,' said Ann, rolling one of her chuckles around the room. 'I plead incipient arthritis. Much more fun helping someone else along the way. Triumph of youth, and all that.'

Joshua kept his eyes on Erin as she walked over to the cello case and unhooked the clips. The red sheen of the wood leaped out as she pulled the front open, and she found herself almost gasping just as Noel had done when he first saw it. Feeling overwhelmed, she tightened the bow, taking a good look at the frog as she did so.

'What bow is this? Is it one that came with the Strad?'

'Yes. Mine is still in my other case.'

'Maybe you could borrow that as well, and try out both properly when you get home,' said Ann. 'See which goes better. You can't know until you try them next to each other.' She looked at Fenella, and added, 'If that's OK? Would that be covered by your insurance too?'

'Oh, yes,' said Fenella, with the air of ennui of someone who has come out the far side of caring and just wants the current situation to end as soon as possible. 'It's all covered. Help yourself.'

Joshua leaned over and squeezed her hand quickly, retracting his arm just as swiftly and replacing it in exactly the same position so as to disguise the fact that it had just moved, like the tongue of a toad catching a fly and snapping back to leave the toad munching silently after killing in midair. Ann didn't move her head at all.

Erin settled herself on a chair by the piano, leaned the cello on its back over her left knee and undid the spike.

'Is this OK on your carpet?' she asked.

'Yes, it's fine,' said Fenella.

So Erin upended the cello into its playing position and shifted it to lean on her chest, gently plucking the strings with her left hand as she did to see if it was in tune. It was. It had, of course, been tuned since being recovered and the jolting it had received when it was stolen didn't seem to have had any lasting effect on its ability to hold its tuning. Cellos are tougher than a lot of people give them credit for.

Erin drew the bow around the open strings first, just to check the tuning but also to disguise how nervous she felt. Even the plain open strings set up a vibration in her breastbone that made her feel as if she were leaning on another living thing. She slowly started to let her left hand feel its way around the fingerboard, and the notes swam up to her as if breaking the surface of a deep pond of clear water. There was no end to the depth of tone. With mass-produced instruments you can feel, from the moment you set a string vibrating, that you are standing in a bare, functional, square room, probably painted magnolia, and the echoes and reflections you get are only those off the four-square walls. It is characterless. Predictable. Limited. Erin had the immediate knowledge, as if someone had opened a vein and poured this pure understanding into her, that she had stepped into the hallway of a richly furnished palace, with a maze of rooms yet to explore, hiding behind tapestries. If she pushed the bow, the wave it created seemed to ripple through the very walls of the room she was in, to make it seem as if the everyday ordinariness of things shimmered away to reveal the intricate complications of what this cello represented.

After just a few minutes of stretching some *arpeggios* up and down its range, she met Ann's eyes. Ann nodded imperceptibly: more a lowering of her eyelids and letting the tip of her nose dip a couple of millimetres. They both just wanted to get started.

Erin stopped playing, and looked at Fenella.

'Wow.'

'Sounding good!' said Joshua, forgetting that a moment earlier his hand had pressed Fenella's with something like sympathy.

'Thanks,' said Erin. 'But I think we all know it's the cello sounding that fabulous, not me. Thank you, Fenella. I'll look after it.'

She put it away while Joshua floundered about trying to re-ingratiate himself with Fenella, watched by Ann with open contempt. She stood up as Erin stooped to lean into the cello's weight to pick it up, and they went to the front door and waited for Fenella to open it for them. Somehow, Ann felt that to march straight out while Fenella was still sitting on the sofa would feel too close to stealing it. At least if Fenella had opened the door with her own hand she couldn't legitimately blame them for taking it. Emotionally and psychologically, perhaps, but not logically.

Erin turned once she was out in the hallway.

'Thanks again. I know I keep saying it, but I do appreciate it.'

Fenella gave her a small nod, and shut the door.

'Joshua had better be good at buttering her up,' said Ann, calling the lift. 'And may I say,' she turned to face Erin, with an expression that for once was free of cynicism or sarcasm, 'that you are well out of that. He's a snake. Don't think that much of him as a conductor, to be honest, but I think even less of him as a person.'

Erin snorted her agreement. 'I got taken in by the chameleon, that's all. Grown up now. Thanks, mum.'

Ann aimed a slap at her head as they got into the lift, and they fell five floors in a controlled fashion.

'Do you want some help today, or do you want to try it out on your own first?'

Erin looked at her eagerly. 'Have you time today? That would be great.'

'Right, my place then?'

Erin nodded. Up on the fifth floor, Joshua was rinsing out the coffee cups trying to work out when he too could leave.

Chapter 27

Erin began to feel nervous for most of the time she was awake and, as the days passed, for a good deal of the time when she should have been asleep. By the week before the concert, she had evolved a timetable that she could survive and would also produce a decent performance: up at six-thirty, practising by seven-thirty with a pint mug of tea by her chair, coffee mid-morning, more playing until a break for a sandwich and then wind down. Another three hours or so in the afternoon, and then her hands were complaining too much for her to do any more. She found it impossible to switch off in the evenings, often clicking around the TV channels, roaming in search of something that would crowd Elgar out of her head briefly. Ann knew exactly what she was going through, so made a point of phoning her every evening to check she was still sane.

She was almost relieved when Monday came around. David had called and explained the remaining rehearsal timetable, saying that it was going to be Bach and Strauss that week, with a final top and tail of *Fingal's Cave*, leaving the last Monday before the concert to do the Elgar with her and anything else that looked too ragged the previous week. The pressure off, Erin set off for Stockwell with her ordinary cello, making sure with OCD emphasis that her windows were locked, the security grille was fixed and her front door was secured with both Banhams double locked. It was like leaving a baby in her flat. She just hoped nobody had been watching her exhibit this uncharacteristic behaviour and had decided to break in to see what all the fuss was about.

Inside, the GPS tracker silently bleeped its location to its watching satellites every couple of seconds, showing up on a corner of Noel's laptop screen. He had done his homework on the orchestra, and was intrigued by the cello. He knew nothing of Erin, but saw that the promotional literature was still advertising the Elgar concerto, and could see from the winking flag on his map that the cello wasn't in Fenella's flat. It had remained roughly where it was for days. He was like an unsuspected guardian angel, ready to swoop in if the cello needed rescuing again. He planned to go to the concert, hoping to hear the instrument played that had so caught his imagination when he had seen it in the Petersham lock-up. Frank had no idea that his boss was so taken with this unfamiliar world. Frank would never be tempted away from his beloved American Grunge.

When Erin arrived at the rehearsal it was already busier than usual, though she was fifteen minutes early. Pearl, David and Rafael were in a huddle just inside the door. Pearl was looking concerned about something under discussion: that is, at greater wattage than her normal level of concern. Erin walked past them to stand her cello case in the usual place by the wall, next to Charlie, who was already rosining his bow. He nodded over at Pearl.

'I think there's a logistical issue,' he whispered. 'Pearl's worried her decent coffee might run out if she's expected to provide for the choir too, and then we'll all be on the "Maxwell House Powder of Doom". Either that or she's trying to save the custard creams for the orchestra and give that lot all the broken rich teas.'

'How many of them are there? Shouldn't be an army. It's Bach, not *Carmina Burana*.'

'They aren't The Sixteen. They need safety in numbers.' He looked over at the singers. 'And – judging by the look of some of them – bulk.'

Erin giggled as she got her cello out, despite a background worry that she was encouraging Charlie's body-shaming tendencies. She was having much more fun at rehearsals since she had started sitting next to him on the front desk. The cellos had done a Mad Hatter's tea party shuffle up the seats to fill in Fenella's gap, which had thrown each desk partner together with someone new.

The relationship of string players at a desk is a complex one, that is a mystery to those lucky brass and wind players who play their own part and have their own music stand to themselves every time. String players – those herbivores grazing on the flat orchestral savannah between the raked mountains of brass, wind and percussion – are, as previously noted, a herd species. They have evolved to be this because of a number of factors: there are twenty or more of them (in the case of violins) playing the same part, meaning there is never a time when one player is the only one playing. Occasionally the leader might get a solo – and we need not at this stage mention the occasional blooper dropped into a rest – but in general it is *tutti*. Along with all the other orchestral nuances any player must learn, like blending the sound their instrument is making into the noise of the section as a whole, there is one specific to the string player: bowing.

The hot topic of bowing has probably caused more arguments and filibustering than any other stylistic discussion in orchestral rehearsals. You can just hear the collective sigh of the brass when someone near the back of the violins or violas raises their hand when the conductor is trying to explain his way round a knotty corner of the score, and does their best to distract the leader of their section away from that important, driver-seat discussion, to one about whether a particular note should be a down or an up bow.

There are many, many books that have been written about bowing and another universe full of those that could yet be. However, one fact scorches out of all the miles of text written on this subject. That fact is that bowing is, like a tossed coin, a binary question. Either heads or tails. Either up or down. Orchestral peripheral vision is legendary. Being able to read one's own part (with all the extraneous markings), following the body language of the leader of your section, having a laugh with someone in a different section and also keep the conductor in view at all times means that we are not far off developing a hybrid species of orchestral human with compound eyes. More than one player has failed their driving test because the tiny flicker of their eyelid was not enough to convince the examiner that they were actually looking in the rear-view mirror many times a minute. Sometimes being subtle does not pay.

You have to get a string section to use the same bowing at the same time, partly because it looks so much neater from the audience with all those pointy sticks going up and down at the same time like synchronised hedgehog spines, and partly so they don't spend all the concert bumping into each others' elbows.

Of course, orchestral parts are printed ready-made with what someone has thought is the correct bowing, and if all string players stuck to what was written there would not be an issue. String players are not like that, perhaps trying to break out of the herd animal stereotype. If you have ten violinists in the room, you would probably have a dozen or more opinions on how to play a particular phrase, bowing-wise. All orchestral string parts, if they are not pristine and virginal from the printers, will either be covered in pencil markings contradicting or 'enhancing' the printed bowing, or have bald patches in the paper where some poor underling has had to remove all previous markings with a rubber. If anyone has ever used a pencil harder than a 3B it is practically impossible to remove bowing marks without rubbing a hole first through the printed notes underneath and eventually through the paper itself.

A lot of string parts end up looking a bit like Mrs Ford-Hughes's Strauss score, through no fault of the hapless foot soldiers further back in the ranks. Sitting next to a desk partner who consistently ignores bowing marks, either those printed originally or marked in pencil afterwards, is one of the most irritating things about playing in an orchestra.

This behaviour by the strings is, of course, regarded with scorn by the rest of the players. They all have their own part, they are the only instrument playing that part, and that's the end of the story. They might have drawn a pair of spectacles to remind them to watch the conductor carefully at one point. There might be an indication to take an extra big breath because the phrase to come is long and exposed. If there is a bit which features the section playing as a whole, there might be a discussion about breathing together at certain points, but nothing more than that. A snatched breath is not so obvious to the audience as a lone string player on the wrong bow, when all their colleagues are going the other way. Bowing is like teenager's acne, the knowledge your child has nits or the Tena pants you wear. People would rather you didn't talk about it, especially on their time.

Pearl seemed to be placated as Erin and Charlie wandered to their seats, and she bustled over to her viola case with renewed purpose. Joshua had joined David and Rafael. Then the door opened to admit a group of singers and Eliot. Joshua turned. Eliot nodded at him, and started walking to him.

The atmosphere was suddenly an 1860s western frontier town, when the stranger rode into town and pushed through the saloon doors with his gang behind him. The airborne testosterone level jumped.

'What's Eliot doing here?' Joshua asked David quietly, smiling through it and making it sound as if he should have a ventriloquist's dummy on one arm. He was not as adept as some of his players for carrying on unnoticed conversations. 'Aren't *I* doing the Bach? God help me.'

'Probably just giving his choir moral support,' said David.

'I'll just go and get my bassoon out,' said Rafael, anxious to avoid any tension he could legitimately skip. He melted away into the throng of players getting their instruments ready.

Eliot completed his final few strides and held out his hand. 'Hi, Joshua. Good to see you.' He turned to David. 'And David – hello.'

As they all shook hands, the incoming choral singers started to mill about between the door and the orchestra, like a nervous tide rising up an unknown beach.

'Eliot.' Joshua couldn't think of anything else to say. A curt 'Why are you here?' seemed too stark, even if it was what he was thinking.

David stepped in. 'Hello, Eliot. Nice to see you. Sorry – we were just about to get your chairs set up but we're not quite there yet. Are you giving your troops moral support?'

Eliot laughed. 'That and checking out the opposition, you mean?' His eyes flicked over at Joshua with a merry sort of twinkle, which had the underlying current of something absolutely adamantine about it. 'No, not really. I want to hear how they get on, and I actually thought I'd sit in with the tenors just for now, as we're a couple down with this flu-thing going round. You know we're never exactly flush with tenors at the best of times.' He looked at David and then back at Joshua quickly. 'If you don't mind, of course?'

Joshua smiled straight back at him as if aiming a gun. 'Of course not. The more the merrier. Especially in the tenors!'

Eliot looked delighted and nodded. 'Where do you want us? Shall we grab some chairs and go round the back?'

Joshua looked vaguely behind the players, where there was a strip of available floor space. 'Er – yeah. Can do. I'll see what the balance is like when we start singing and we can get you round the front if we need to in the concert.'

'Right-o,' said Eliot cheerfully, and strode off to gather his singers after him and lead them around the orchestra to collect chairs and set them out in rows at the back.

Joshua cupped his hands around his mouth and tried to shout to the brass and wind at the back of the orchestra over the rising level of a choir settling themselves into an unfamiliar situation: never a silent manoeuvre. 'You might want to get your cases out of the way. The choir is coming through!'

The singers picked their way over and around horn cases that were splayed open like clam shells on a beach. Some cases had entrails of duster flopping out, inside them were the usual postcards wedged into a corner of the case, small pots of valve oil and slide grease, pencils and unidentifiable detritus from years of orchestral playing. The horn players gathered their cases closer to them, for no matter how careful a choir thinks they are being around instruments, someone will always stumble, put a foot in the wrong place, and break something. The whole effect was rather like a curling team sweeping a clear path so their stone can glide effortlessly towards its target. There was then more milling around until every singer had a seat in roughly the right line, and sat on it looking triumphant, leaning first to one neighbour and then the other to exchange stories about how they had come to be in this new position. Eliot took his place in the back row between the tenors and basses, from where he could give support to either part if they got lost, and tried to settle his excitable brood so Joshua could get on with the rehearsal.

'OK, people... could we get started?' Joshua called, as the last of the singers managed to scrape their chair into a position from which they could see the conductor (if they were one of those who looked for direction) or not (if they were one of those who never did). He looked around the room and behind him towards the door. 'Do we have Mrs Ford-Hughes...?'

Rising from a chair near the door as if raised on pulleys, the impressive figure of Mrs Ford-Hughes drifted across towards Joshua, bearing a copy of Bach's *Magnificat* in much the same reverent way she had carried her Strauss. Her husband remained in his seat, looking at her progress approvingly, as a preacher will watch the words of his sermon float over his congregation, taking with them joy to the world and the key to an enriched life. What Joshua saw advancing was more like a silk-clad armoured vehicle, filled to capacity with ill-pronounced German words. He smiled through his apprehension.

'Hello. Great. Would you like to stand with the singers for the choral numbers?'

Mrs Ford-Hughes leaned to one side to see around Joshua to where the singers were sitting, and retracted back to the vertical.

'I wasn't planning on singing through the whole thing,' she said, her tone implying that one of her stature should not be expected to sit with the plebs, much less sing with them. 'Save the pipes, you know?' She tapped her throat lightly with two fingers to indicate she had meant her vocal chords rather than some unspecified plumbing problem.

Joshua on the whole was relieved at this news and anyway, he wanted to start the rehearsal, since all the unscheduled choir faffing and Pearl's coffee worrying had delayed it already.

'Fine, fine,' he said. 'Why don't you sit at the side then, and we'll get you up for the numbers you're in.'

Mrs Ford-Hughes nodded graciously as if granting a wish, and billowed over to an empty chair by the violins, engulfing the unfortunate Marco in her perfume envelope. He coughed several times, but couldn't ease himself away since he had Maureen on his other side, who didn't give ground for anyone or anything. He shrank into his seat miserably, and mopped his nose with a crinkled hanky.

'Let's go from the top, everyone,' called Joshua. 'Choir – hello!' There was a general 'hello'-ing back. 'Good. Welcome along. Let's start with the first chorus and see how it goes. Sopranos, will you be ready to come straight in at your entry when we get there?'

Joshua took in the various mumbled 'yesses' and non-committal grunts, and realised he would have to restart when they failed to make it, but smiled at them brightly and raised his arms to ready the orchestra.

The eternally uplifting sounds of Bach filled the hallway, as reliably jaunty as a well-tuned engine. Any person who can remain perfectly still while listening to Bach is probably embalmed, or at least not worth getting to know. Joshua jigged up and down as the violins, trumpets and flutes took turns with the semiquaver runs, and a few bars before the sopranos were due to sing he started trying to catch the eye of some of them in preparation. A couple of people knew where they were and were counting; the rest were absorbed in the unfamiliar experience of being right behind an orchestra. They had a quaver rest at the beginning of their bar, then had to catch the offbeat and set off with a semiquaver run before the rest of the chorus came in. Those two singers who locked eyes with Joshua started with all good intent, but when they realised they were essentially singing a solo their throats quickly closed up with terror and their chorus-trained brains told them they must have miscounted and had probably just come in embarrassingly wrongly. All singing ceased despite Joshua's preternaturally wide eyes and almost rictus grimace to instil confidence in their entry. Choral meltdown goes viral in nanoseconds, and the tenors and altos were scuppered before they opened their mouths despite Eliot's confident, *forte* contributions. They never reached the bass entry. Joshua stopped beating and gave in to the inevitable.

The orchestra fell away quickly, and soon the only sound in the hall was the hushed recriminations being whispered between singers and protestations of their ability to count.

Joshua raised both his hands, trying to calm them down. 'OK, OK, don't worry. We'll pick it up from bar twenty-eight: that's three bars before your entry, sopranos. OK? Got it?'

There were a few nods from the front row, while some others were taking the first swigs of water from their bottles. Clearly, almost singing three semiquavers was enough to strain their voices and leave them needing lubrication.

Musicians betray a lot of unfiltered information about themselves while they are concentrating on music, like the main product of a jet engine being noise rather than the required thrust. The chorus chugged through the first movement in the perfunctory way many choirs sing Bach: four-square, neither quiet nor overly loud, as though adhering themselves faithfully to the dull underbelly of, what can be, the most uplifting music in the world will prolong their lives by not exposing them to any wide variance of emotional palette. They ended in style with their final '*Dominum*', which had about twenty different 'm' sounds as each member of the choir decided that they would instinctively feel where to put their last consonant at a time of their own choosing in a bar containing twelve semiquavers of orchestral accompaniment, rather than look at Joshua who quite clearly asked them to put it directly after the first crotchet. Thus began the final sixteen bars of the movement, during which the valiant attempts of the players to inject a bit of enthusiasm and verve into the music were increasingly obscured by the rising hubbub of singers' chat. Trying to convince singers to sit still and quietly during their bars' rest is as effective as encouraging toddlers to do the same. Joshua threw several stern looks in their direction and Eliot repeatedly tried to shush his neighbours but, by the time the orchestra played their last note, the choir barely registered that the music had stopped.

Joshua just stood there looking at them, in the manner of a disappointed primary school teacher and, eventually, one by one, they noticed and stopped talking. Some looked sheepish. Some seemed aggrieved that Joshua had interrupted their conversations. When all was silent, he said, 'It would be nice if you didn't try to compete with the orchestra when you've stopped singing.'

There were a few embarrassed buttock shifts.

'Still have a lot of work to do on our light and shade, but let's press on for now.' He licked his finger and flipped over a few pages of his score. 'We're not doing *Et Exsultavit*, so… now we're on to number three, *Quia Respexit*. Mrs Ford-Hughes?'

He turned towards her and invited her to stand. She wafted a super-charged perfume draught across Marco as she rose, walked towards Joshua and came to a halt, leaving Marco blowing his nose repeatedly and dabbing at his streaming eyes.

'OK, great,' said Joshua, smiling at her and turning to the oboes. 'Who's doing this? Gwynneth?'

Gwynneth nodded, twisting her oboe d'amore reed into place. The third movement is essentially a duet between the oboe d'amore and the soprano, with the pitch of the d'amore being lower than an ordinary, familiar oboe but higher than a cor anglais. Versatile oboe players can usually play all three instruments, although not all own all three, as standard. Gwynneth happened to own an oboe d'amore, and had played this movement many times before. She was not the only person dreading what was about to come out of Mrs Ford-Hughes's mouth. Carl signed something extremely rude from his place in the bored, Bach-redundant trombones, so Gwynneth had to fiddle around with her reed for a bit longer than strictly necessary so she could stop her lips twitching.

Joshua flicked the pages of his score forward and spoke to the choir.

'Now listen, you know we go straight into number four at the end of this? *Attacca*. Everybody except the first sopranos needs to be watching me like hawks. It goes off at a real lick straight away. Are we clear?' There were nods. 'Hmmm. I'll show you. All you have to do is watch.'

Joshua turned back to the beginning of number three and started the slow *adagio* pulse. Gwynneth's sad melody twined around Charlie's continuo cello solo, filled with all the accidentals and malleability of key that the masterful Bach could pack in. Bach was as adept at manipulation as any modern film score composer who will send in the soaring strings to pull tears from his audience.

Mrs Ford-Hughes prepared to sing the Latin words '*Quia respexit humilitatem ancillae suae, ecce enim ex hoc beatam me dicent*', that translated, in the familiar words of the *Magnificat*, as 'For he hath regarded the lowliness of His handmaiden. Behold, from henceforth, all generations shall call me blessed.' From her expression, it was doubtful that she had any idea what the words she was singing meant. She did her usual diving-whale-breathing routine while Gwynneth played with a musicality, a quiet insistence and nuance-perfect phrasing that she completely missed with her vocal performance. Mrs Ford-Hughes broke into what had been a spellbinding ensemble with a loud 'KERWEE', mistaking the diction of a singer who can emphasise the initial consonant to define her entry with the twang of a tobacco-chewing swamp-dweller.

The tempo was a little slow for Mrs Ford-Hughes's breath control. Not one who usually forged ahead, she found herself unequal to the phrases stretching over two bars, and decided that saving breath was synonymous with slipping flat off the bottom of the note as the scale fell, ending up sounding like a pair of leaky bellows which had just been jolted off a moving cart going over a pothole. Gwynneth and Charlie did their best, but there was a general feeling of relief when the double bar line approached, heralding the transition into the next movement. Joshua was careful to widen his movements to attract the attention of even the distracted outriders of the choir, and somehow safely gathered them up and set them running into the '*Omnes generationes*' fugue-like explosion that crashes into the end of the introspective and introverted solo movement. It was almost as if Bach had kept his orchestration for this very moment in order to expunge, in an instant, any memory of a dire soprano solo. Eliot led the basses in chanting '*omnes omnes*' with a gusto worthy of the football terrace, setting up such a powerful energy treadmill that the other singers found it easy to step onto the moving escalator at the right speed and go for it themselves. Joshua smiled at them, and managed to turn and nod his appreciation at a retreating Mrs Ford-Hughes without losing the choir's attention. Mrs Ford-Hughes graciously slid away towards her husband at the back of the hall, and aside from a tickle of perfume in Joshua's nose he managed to put her out of his head for the remainder of the movement.

Chapter 28

The pub was emptier than usual after that rehearsal. Joshua, with a new and, at least to him, surprisingly uncomfortable awkwardness around Erin, decided that since Fenella wasn't there it was probably time he paid some attention to his wife. When he got home, his wife had already gone up to bed. Unable ever to admit his secret gratitude every time this happened, he took a beer from the fridge and wandered over to the breakfast bar to scan the paper for late-night bachelor TV viewing possibilities. A piece of paper was propped against the pepper mill. His wife's handwriting looped around the information that he was to call a Ms Horowitz as soon as possible, giving a United States telephone number. The facts were sketchy, apart from it being something to do with an audition. Joshua turned the paper over, hoping for more details on the reverse but, since it merely revealed a torn-off shopping list that included sausages, avocado and panty liners, it was not strictly relevant. He turned it back and stared. Who the hell was Ms Horowitz? He swallowed a gulp of cold beery fizziness and felt it slide down.

He checked his watch. Just gone eleven o'clock. Not knowing the US state codes by heart, he wasn't sure where in the country he'd be calling, but since they were at least five hours behind it had to be worth a try. He picked up the phone and dialled.

After only one ring, and before he was really ready to speak, the line clicked open and a voice brimful of American youth and enthusiasm chirruped at him.

'Hall & Pritchard, how may I help you?'

'Um, yes. Hello. I'm – I've been given this number to speak to a Ms Horowitz.'

'That's correct, sir, would you like me to connect you?'

'Er, yes. Yes please. Thank you.'

'You're welcome.'

He swallowed another mouthful of beer while trying to whip his brain up to daylight American speed rather than dark London evening wind down time. What the hell was Hall & Pritchard? It sounded like a solicitor's office. He began the uncomfortable prickly soul-search that is usually generated by seeing a blue light of a police car in your rear-view mirror.

Another click, and then he was treated to a brief concert of an indeterminate Vivaldi season played on panpipes, before it was cut off mid-toot and another female voice muscled itself stridently into its place.

'Summer Horowitz.'

It was a statement, devoid of the professional welcome to which the receptionist had treated him.

'Ms Horowitz? Hello, this is Joshua Blake. I had a message to call you?' And what kind of name was Summer? It must belong to a long-limbed, tanned blonde, perhaps with siblings called Leaf and River. He figured he'd called California rather than the east coast. Perhaps he should have at least checked that before. Any clue would have been beneficial at this point: he was feeling distinctly at the low end of the food chain so far. She did not give his imagination long to develop.

'Oh, Joshua – great to hear you.' Her voice floated up instantly through several stratifications of social warmth, confusing him. 'How are you doing?'

'Er, great. Thank you.' He tailed off, hoping she would tell him why he just called her. And he wasn't great. He was bounced into saying that because he was talking to an over-enthusiastic American. He was just ordinarily, Britishly fine.

'That's great. Now, Joshua, I got your number from some of our people in London, England, and we have a great opportunity for you.'

There were many great things in America, it appeared.

'We've gotten involved in a showcasing opportunity for young conductors, which is gonna give a huge kick to careers here and over with you in Europe, including London, England.'

She stopped, appearing to want approbation for her keen grasp of global geography. Joshua cleared his throat in what he thought might be an enquiring manner, while he waited for her to come to the point.

'Here's the thing: we have ten places for conducting plat-forms in our gala evening next week. There's been a lot of stomach flu going around the Bay Area, and unfortunately we've had three of our conductors pull out. We wondered if you would be interested in taking up this opportunity?'

Bay Area? So she was talking San Francisco. Joshua was torn between cynicism about any legitimacy of a conducting competition he'd never heard of with a frisson that always affected him about events in the States.

'Um… what exactly would this opportunity involve?'

She seemed surprised that he hadn't bitten off her hand in his haste to secure his place. 'Well,' – that single syllable dropping him subtly down her friendship scale – 'each competitor conducts a movement from a symphony of their choice and, at the end of the evening, our panel of exclusively invited professionals from the classical music industry vote for their favourite. All travel expenses are paid for by our sponsor. The winner is invited to participate in a shared guest season with the San Francisco Concert Orchestra, with all the attendant opportunities that would offer.'

Joshua listened to her list of benefits with growing interest. A free trip to the States. Conducting exposure. Publicity.

'This certainly ticks a lot of boxes. And when did you say this was?'

'This week: Saturday. Can I put you down for a place?'

He thought quickly. Saturday. Doable. Just. He could be back for the last Monday rehearsal in Stockwell.

'Well, Summer, this all sounds most interesting. Yes, please.'

'Oh that is awesome!' He was right up there on her favourite list again, he could tell. 'If we can just take some contact details for you we can be in touch about what you want to play, and the other logistics of the whole thing.'

Email addresses exchanged, she thanked him again in her profuse, tanned way, and disconnected, leaving Joshua standing in his kitchen holding the phone and wearing an absent smile.

He swallowed some more beer, feeling as if he had achieved something instead of merely agreeing to whatever an enthusiastic West Coaster had suggested. He dug out some pretzels from a low cupboard and walked through to the sitting room, letting himself fall backwards onto the sofa and putting his feet up on the coffee table all in one smooth movement. He fired the remote at the TV with all the pinpoint accuracy of one of Clint's great shootouts, and settled down to watch some other Americans chase bad guys all over a city that had more sunshine and bullets than London ever seemed to.

Throwing a pretzel up high in the air, he caught it in his mouth. Living the dream.

Chapter 29

'To the States? When?'

'This Saturday. Flying out on Friday. There'll be plenty of time for me to get back for the rehearsal on Monday.' Joshua's voice crackled out of David's telephone.

'Well, it's hardly the time… oh, I suppose you're right.'

David was finding this an unwelcome call from Joshua, but his office colleagues' eavesdropping meant that he felt he had to remain calm and in control.

'There really is plenty of time. It's only the Saturday afternoon and evening thing there. I can be on a plane on Sunday and be back easily.'

'Well, we don't want you wrung out with jet lag – too tired to conduct properly.' David was not convinced. This was no ordinary concert.

Joshua laughed like an excited schoolboy. 'David, stop worrying. They're flying me out business class! Can you believe it? I'll sleep on the flight, won't be there long enough to change time zones, and snooze all the way back too. Stop worrying.'

'Well, if you're sure…' said David. 'I'll let Rafael know.'

'Thanks. Aren't you going to wish me luck?'

'Oh, of course. Yes. Best of British. Now, I really ought to go. Bit busy here.'

'Ciao!

***

By the weekend, the news of Joshua's trip had spread, with just a couple of tweets and a few phone calls. Fenella, unlike David, was not treated to a personal telephone conversation, and had to make do with finding out from other members of the orchestra on Twitter. She typed out a couple of passive-aggressive texts to him, hovered her finger over the 'send' button, and carefully deleted each one slowly, letter by letter. Irritating though Fenella was, even she was aware of a credibility gap widening in her relationship with Joshua and she couldn't escape the fatalistic feeling of an end just ahead. The passive-aggressive text is reserved for those who are secure in their assessment of loyalty in their lover: it uses up a lot of slack goodwill. Already taut relationships tend to snap. She wasn't ready to snap this just yet.

Joshua flew out to California on Friday, giving his wife a dry cheek peck before he walked to the tube station. November was beginning to dovetail into December, and he walked along the pavement pulling his wheeled flight bag behind him, ticking its small wheels across every join in the paving slabs like a small, demented flamenco dancer trying to keep up with his long strides. His roll of batons was wrapped in his tailcoat: Summer had been careful to check that he had tails and would bring them to wear for their gala concert. Not for the first time, Joshua had stared at that email from her, wondering what kind of set-up he was flying blindly towards. How far into their careers were his fellow conducting competitors if they had to be nannied into remembering the international uniform for their chosen profession? But as soon as he arrived at the business lounge at Heathrow and sipped his first glass of wine, he decided to surrender all reservations he might have about the trip and embrace the positives. God, he was starting to sound like Summer. He drank himself unsteadily onto the flight, and found the hospitality in business class far too alluring for him to sleep much. There was a particularly attractive member of the cabin crew whom he was keen to engage in conversation, quite forgetting, as he found himself somewhere between the fifth and sixth glass of wine, that she was being paid to be nice to him. The fact that her professional attitude hid that fact from him was to her credit, and his feeble and doomed flirtation lost momentum as they crossed into US airspace for their long push to the Pacific coast.

Chapter 30

Ann poured tea into Erin's mug and handed it to her across the kitchen table.

'Come on, then. How's it going?'

Erin pulled a face as she sipped, her eyes sliding away from Ann to look over the cluttered windowsill into the garden. Cobwebs looped over dilapidated shrubs and tried to knit together the strands of Ann's rotary washing line.

'I'm not ready.'

Ann gave her a steady look.

'You're never ready for your first concert. At least, you never feel as if you are.' She took a gulp of tea and levered a digestive biscuit out of the packet. Munching the first bite, she waved the biscuit around as she continued, with her mouth full. 'It's only when you get as old as me that things tend to fall into perspective a bit more easily.' She swallowed, and took another gulp of tea. 'I wouldn't say you *feel* ready for a performance, exactly. It's more a case of *knowing* you've done all the work you need to do. And knowing you're not going to freeze onstage when the bastard bits come up.'

Erin smiled. 'Is that a technical term?'

'Abso-bastard-lutely. And another thing – you're not doing it from memory. That was always my worst fear: going blank the bar before I was supposed to come in.'

'As long as I don't pull it off the stand when I turn a page…'

'Yes. Do you want to practise your page turns this morning?'

Erin flicked a look at Ann to check that this was indeed a joke, and then laughed. Tension bubbled up out of her in a sudden deflation of the shell she had felt growing more brittle around her as the days went on. She helped herself to a digestive.

'I don't know why I let you talk me into doing this.'

'So you'd have someone to blame when you started getting cold feet.'

'It's cold hands this morning.' Erin pressed her fingers around her mug. 'Bloody freezing on the way here.'

'Have another biscuit. Blood sugar and ability to do semi-quavers are inextricably linked.'

'And the ability to fit into one's concert dress?'

Ann snorted into her tea. 'I have a wardrobe full of old concert dresses I can lend you if you reach that stage. All embracing the idea of comfort. Anyway,' she looked over the table pointedly, 'by the time you finish that Elgar they won't be remembering you for your dress, believe me.'

Erin took another biscuit. 'It's so unfair on female per-formers: we have to glitz up and the blokes just put on their old jacket and trousers and get on with it.'

'And sweat like billy-o in the summer, and then can't be bothered to have them dry cleaned between every concert, so you end up sitting next to someone who smells like the tramps Tory cabinet ministers complain about when they're coming back from the opera. If only they sat a bit closer to the orchestra they might rethink the subject of their rants.' Ann leaned into the worn wooden back of her kitchen chair and dragged another closer to put her feet on. 'And don't you believe it about the waistline thing being only for us girls. Maybe it's because I spent so much time in a cello section and it affords – how shall I put it? – more camouflage than other instruments, but I've had to sit next to many a pot-bellied male who found on the day of a concert that his paunch exceeded the last extension button on his trousers and sat through the entire thing with the button and half his flies undone.'

Erin laughed. 'Was anyone ever half mast when you all took a bow?'

'There was one time dear old Ralph had to try and catch them as they went south and he went north, as it were. For a moment it was a toss up between holding on to his trousers or his cello.' Ann put the last bit of biscuit into her mouth and chewed philosophically. 'Doubt anyone noticed.'

They were sitting at Ann's kitchen table drinking tea on Saturday morning, just as Joshua was getting to know the intimate details of his hotel room ceiling while he waited for America to wake up. Erin finished her second biscuit and changed the subject.

'What is this thing Joshua's gone to the States for? Do you know?'

'Some competition I think – I just heard the fag end of the story from David. God knows. Chasing his dream of being discovered.'

'Not great timing.'

'Well, he's due back tomorrow, so it shouldn't affect us.'

'He's always hustling.' Erin looked out of the window again. It was such a busy word, 'hustle'. Sounded like what it meant. Quite the opposite of the way 'calm' sounded, like the millpond it conjured up. The cobwebs on the washing line were quite still. Mesmerising, with all the water droplets beading along them.

She heard Ann's mug going back onto the table and her feet being replaced on the floor. Time to work.

'Ready?' Ann asked.

'Yes,' said Erin. 'Well, no. But yes.'

They went into the music room where Erin got the Strad out of its case. Ann sat on one of the two upright chairs facing each other on the rug, tightened her bow and extended the spike as she lay her cello on her lap. Erin settled herself on the other chair and did the same. Both did these things without conscious thought, the muscle memory in their fingers knowing exactly when to stop stretching the horsehair on their bow as it reached the optimum tension for bounce and strength on the string. With spikes it was slightly different, as each chair could be a different height, but a cellist develops an almost supernatural ability to glance at a chair and know exactly how far out their spike must go to let the cello sit at their accustomed angle. It's a skill not famed for its transferable qualities, but very useful in a supermarket if you're trying to work out whether you can reach the top shelf in those heels.

Erin loved the way Ann taught. When they first ran through the Elgar together, Ann had played a piano reduction of the full orchestral score, to give an idea of what the whole performance would sound like. Now Erin had absorbed it so intensely that she no longer needed to hear what the accompaniment would be doing: it looped itself automatically in her head when she played. So now, Ann sat with her own cello as they worked on it at a micro-level, as a poet will analyse a single word in a line or a single comma, and decide whether it fits in the whole or jars the structure.

They slowly worked through the second movement, the one that has the cello skittering above the orchestra in an endless *spiccato* version of the tune: lots of tiny, light notes played with a bow bouncing over the strings.

Ann watched Erin's first few bars before stopping her just after Erin's left hand had climbed to one of the ridiculously high harmonics Elgar put in to make the cello sound like a yodelling violin.

'Try to relax your wrist a bit – the bowing arm, I mean,' she said, straightening up and readying herself to play her own cello. She set up a quiet thrumming *spiccato* rhythm on one of her open strings, and spoke to Erin over the top. 'Look. I'm hardly moving my arm at all. You just want to drop these notes onto the string before you're hovering in the air again: it's not an effort. Like dancing on cling film.'

Erin watched Ann's arm hang almost motionless, with just her hand and wrist quivering a tiny amount to make the bow tremble up and down, like a hummingbird's wings fluttering while its head is held completely still.

'Try it,' Ann said. 'Just get a feeling of lightness. That way you can skittle through this movement without breaking a sweat and save your muscle strength for the real stuff a bit later. This is just a bit of fun.'

Erin started her own bow going, trying to copy what Ann was doing.

'Yeah – that's much better. Keep going.' Ann dropped out, letting Erin's stream of notes fall out of the Strad like a line of dots being released into flight. 'Can you hear the difference? That's sounding like an engine ticking over now. You can run for ever like that. Keep it going, and then just run into that passage we were on just now. Keep that feeling of weightlessness.'

Erin slipped smoothly into the *arpeggio* passage, and found the cello supporting her on the way up in a way that had never happened on her own instrument. It was like being bounced on a trampoline, almost effortless. She grinned at Ann.

'OK. Got it, I think. Feels much better.'

'Sounds better too. Great. Let's start this section again and keep going.'

They worked with deep concentration all morning, with Erin peeling off layers as she warmed up. She was surprised when she discovered it was well into the afternoon and they had been playing for three hours. While Ann put the kettle on and dug into her fridge for something to put in a sandwich, Erin checked her phone.

'Ha! Charlie's been busy,' she called, walking into the kitchen.

'What's he done now?' said Ann, piling assorted salad items on top of cheese slices and giving them a dubious look. 'Thank God I played cello. I'd have never made it in the catering industry.'

'Oh, don't worry, I'm grateful for any food. Suddenly famished. No – he's been googling that conducting competition Joshua's gone to. Just got a text... let's see.'

They sat at the kitchen table, where Ann offered Erin a jar of mayonnaise. 'It might act as cement and keep structural integrity. You never know your luck.'

Erin was peering at her phone, zooming on to a website with her finger and thumb to read the tiny print.

'Oh God. It's apparently run by some media company in California. Hall & Pritchard. They do reality TV stuff…'

'Reality TV? Oh Lord.'

'Their names are hilarious. All this copy on the "About us" page is written by someone called Summer Horowitz. "We unlock the potential encased in each and every one of us to succeed and become a beacon of talent for our generation." Who knew?'

'They did. I'd rather listen to The Who singing about their generation than that kind of twaddle.' Ann took a large bite out of her sandwich that was more vertical than horizontal, managing to catch the escaping mayonnaise on her plate, and carried on talking through it. 'Joshua's a thrill-seeker. It'll be just up his street.'

'Brilliant,' Erin sighed, closing the site and turning to her own impressively sized sandwich. 'Charlie wonders if Joshua will be seduced by the tans and blinding American teeth and fail to return altogether.'

Ann snorted, nodding. 'Well, now you've nicked his girlfriend's nice cello, what is there for him to come back for?'

'Ha!' Erin felt happier than she had for weeks, and almost forgot the terror of the concert being only days away. 'You're so bloody right.'

'Bloody am!' said Ann. 'Up the women. And the cellos. Eat up. We've got the last movement to go over before I'll let you out. Technically, this is kidnap.'

'But I like it here.'

'Yeah yeah. Finish your food, I need a fag. And I'm damned if I'm going outside for one just because of you – it's too pissing cold.'

'The more I get to know you,' said Erin, 'the more I admire your forthright views. I think I'll make it my aim in life to become you. Basically.'

Ann's chuckle turned into a cough as some cucumber skin caught in the back of her throat. She flapped her hand at Erin, although whether it was an 'I'm OK don't worry' kind of flap or a 'Do you know the Heimlich manoeuvre?' flap was unclear. Recovering, she took a gulp of tea.

'Don't be tempted, my young friend,' she said. 'I can't even feed myself properly.'

Chapter 31

As Sunday's dawn raced west around the planet, London was waking to more autumnal drizzle as Joshua found himself at a late after-concert party. He was eight hours behind London, and this knowledge seemed to act as a reality buffer. He had eight free hours to use as he liked before having to enter the real world again. His brain, soaked as it was in a fine, estate-bottled Napa Valley Malbec, did not factor in that those same eight hours must be subtracted over the Atlantic before landing back in Blighty. But he was talking animatedly to one of Summer Horowitz's underlings about tempo changes in Bruckner symphonies and didn't notice either the mathematics of global travel or the pained look of tension crystallising behind her professional smile. He had just been voted runner-up and was milking the celebrity status it afforded. Summer was busy conferring temporary-but-slightly-higher-celebrity status on the conductor who had won, amid flashing photography bulbs and the sound of money being made.

Joshua's flight was at 3:35 p.m. on Sunday, which was due to arrive in London at 9:55 a.m. on Monday, having sucked up all those eight hours borrowed on tick on the way out. He had ages. He could sleep in all morning and get to L.A.

airport by lunchtime. Those were the last coherent thoughts going through his head at the end of that late, late party, with the flowing Malbec and the smiling minions, and the music, and the swimming pool, and the fucking glamour of it all. He had surely been born to be a rock star. Who had started him on this classical shit? By the time he started kissing one of the production crew, he didn't know how to begin to answer that question.

* * *

In London, the orchestra was scattered out over a wide area, mostly south of the river. If Schrödinger had looked down at that moment, he may have opined that the orchestra did not exist as an entity in itself. Quantum mechanics might view each player as a string which can join and split. Individual decisions bleed consequences into the whole.

* * *

David was stuck in rush hour traffic on the Clapham Road, taking his ten-year-old to football. His overall mood was not improved by losing the Battle For Control Of The Radio, so he was being assaulted by some frenzied music with sub-beats he didn't understand coming out of the car speakers. His ten-year-old picked his nose and didn't hear his father ask him to stop. David's phone was in his back pocket, making his right buttock aware of every bump in the road with a lurch of alarm in case it was alerting him to something that could possibly go wrong with the concert. He was already exhausted with mental scenarios he had conjured and solved hourly. He liked to think that if a real situation arose he would have already thought of the answer. Meanwhile, his right buttock remained on high alert, making him sit slightly askew to the left, although he was unaware of it. His back would remind him later.

* * *

Pearl was walking to the shops, humming to herself and pulling a leatherette shopping basket on wheels alongside her. She had reached the age when getting up late was simply not an option, even if she no longer had to get to work every day, and the weekends were indistinguishable from weekdays. A retired person's day stretched ahead of her: punctuated by a trip to the library and cups of tea. She had six hardbacks in her trolley ready for quick-drop return (four Catherine Cooksons, a Danielle Steel and a Norma Roberts), after which she planned to spend some of the orchestra's petty cash on some luxury biscuits worthy of the last rehearsal before such an important concert. Pearl was inclining towards white chocolate chip cookies, and wondered if she dared slip a couple of packets of Duchy Original dark chocolate-dipped gingers in there as well. She could eke it out with rich teas after Christmas to make up for it.

* * *

Rafael was already in his study at home, but the spreadsheet he had open on his laptop was the orchestra's, not one for his firm. He was using the quiet of an early Sunday morning to go over different outcomes of Saturday's concert. Every one that didn't involve a full house of ticket sales and a substantial proportion of money from the Ford-Hugheses back on track soon decayed into red on his graphs. Rafael sighed, and gnawed already-red fingers where his nails used to be. He went to get another coffee before opening up another tab to try a new combination.

* * *

Marco, curser of dead conductors, was still asleep in the bedroom he'd grown up in. Student finances being what they were, he'd chosen a course at a college close enough to his parents' house to let him stay at home while he studied. The smell of cooking bacon crept under his door and started to draw him out of a particularly intense REM sleep stage, and his dream (a recurring one he had experienced ever since Oscar's demise) started to turn a falling Oscar into an enormous cartoon ham which shot him a look of pained betrayal. Marco woke distressed and sweating, as he had done every night since it happened. His mother, concerned about her son's increasing exhaustion, had no idea her idea to cook him a fortifying breakfast had just added another layer of bizarre surrealism onto his anxiety dream. She put a second egg in the pan and wiped her hands on her apron.

* * *

Maureen was on the Northern Line reading *Fifty Shades of Grey* on her Kindle and heading for her kickboxing class.

* * *

Fenella stared over the grey river, making coffee. She hadn't slept well. Her arm made sleeping in any position other than flat on her back impossible, and any attempt to turn in her sleep woke her with sharp pains. She popped a couple more painkillers out of a blister pack while the kettle was boiling, and swallowed them with juice. She was trying to decide whether or not to go to the concert. Her biting jealousy of Erin bagging the Elgar was battling her sense of entitlement of some of the adulation: after all, it was her Stradivari even if she couldn't play it. Joshua had said the place would be crawling with press, and some could even be from the national papers. Surely they would want to see the owner as well as the player? Fenella imagined it might be akin to being in the parade ground of a racecourse after winning a race, with the horse, jockey and owner all given their chance in the limelight. Her head gave an involuntary toss, lifting her hair over one shoulder, as if to plump up her sagging confidence. Or she could have been channelling the equine theme. Since she was unaware she did it, we'll never know.

* * *

Ann had lit her first cigarette as she lay in bed. The Nicorette patches were there on the bedside table, next to the fag packet. It wasn't as if she didn't want to give up, it just never seemed the right time. That week she reminded herself of the air traffic controller in *Airplane!* who decided it was never the right time to give up smoking, drinking, amphetamines and finally glue-sniffing. At least she stuck to the smoking. Mostly. But frankly, with Erin to nurture, she couldn't afford any other distractions. Next week, she would quit. Probably.

* * *

Noel Osmar had been at his desk for so long he had already gone to make his third coffee. Weekends for him bled seamlessly into weekdays, just as they did for Pearl, but for Noel they always meant work. As he sat down again with the mug, he clicked a minimised icon on his laptop, and the map unfolded across his screen with that familiar winking cursor showing where the Strad was. When it hadn't moved for a few days after leaving Fenella's flat, Noel had gone on a discreet reconnaisance and, after a few more computer enquiries on the police database, had discovered quite a lot about Erin. He had already bought his ticket for Saturday's concert, and was looking forward to hearing her play. He hadn't mentioned it to Frank, only partly for fear that he might be nicknamed 'Morse' at the station if his foray into classical music were to be discovered. There were some things he could do without.

* * *

Charlie was running late for lunch with his sister. He'd been having difficulty sleeping since he'd realised that he'd regressed to his teenage years in his need to obsess over his latest crush. He'd found himself thinking about Erin when he should have been sleeping and then, when he did eventually fall asleep far too late, she intruded into his dreams as well. He'd hit the snooze button twice and then dropped off again, so now he was trying to make up lost time by running for a bus and doing up his cuffs at the same time, his Oyster card between his teeth. His contact lenses were in a pocket, and the drizzle was collecting on his glasses as he ran, making it as difficult to see the number of the approaching bus as he would have found it without them. The bus happily managed to distract him from that by soaking his trousers from the knee down as it overtook him via a puddle and braked at the bus stop with a squeal.

Charlie snatched his Oyster out of his mouth to have a proper swear without having to clench his teeth through it.

'You bloody, sodding, fucknuckle bastard!' he said, slowing to a walk as he realised the queue would hold the bus at the stop for quite long enough for him to approach. His wool trousers clung unpleasantly to his calves and he could feel his socks wicking moisture inside his shoes. 'It's bloody Sunday. I'm prepared for this on Mondays, but Sundays? You're spoiling me.'

He stopped talking out loud after people started staring at him, and just shuffled forward in the queue looking morose. He was momentarily cheered though, as his monologue had at least reminded him that it was Sunday, which meant that he would see Erin the next day. By the time he pressed his Oyster card on the reader, he had even forgotten to give the driver a dirty look for his soaking, and so was completely taken by surprise by a sudden:

'Sorry mate. Think I got you back there. No room on this road to move out. That's the cycle lane shenanigans for you. Nightmare.'

Charlie grinned at him and went to sit down, squelching slightly, but not minding half so much.

* * *

Mr and Mrs Ford-Hughes were sipping their morning tea, brought to them by their maid, Paola, who had returned downstairs to the kitchen to prepare their breakfasts. Mr Ford-Hughes turned to his wife.

'How are you feeling this morning, my dear? Did you sleep any better?'

'Do you know, honey, I think I did.' She leaned over, picked two sugar lumps from the bowl on the bed tray and stirred them into her tea. 'I feel quite refreshed.'

'That's marvellous. I was beginning to worry that you could have been overdoing it.'

She shook her head, and put her spoon on the saucer before lifting the cup to her lips.

'No, I'm fine. Really. So looking forward to singing. LOOKING FORWARD TO THE SINGING.'

She was adept at noticing when he hadn't heard, and had adopted the peculiarly English method of being understood by merely raising her voice and enunciating more clearly.

'You'll be the toast of the concert. I'm so proud of you.'

He squeezed her hand and they drank in companionable silence, looking at their view over Battersea Park. It was one of the reasons they had bought this house, with its floor-length windows.

Presently, Mrs Ford-Hughes stirred and readied herself to rise for breakfast: never an operation to be undertaken without careful planning. Her night attire was reminiscent of Hattie Jaques' in the *Carry On* films, with ruffles and bows aplenty. She wafted towards her dressing gown hanging on the back of the door.

'I can't laze around today, honey. It's the last rehearsal tomorrow, and we have to whip that orchestra into shape! Can't let Mr Strauss down, now, can we?'

Mr Ford-Hughes smiled adoringly as he watched his wife leave the room. She still had the power to overcome him, and he drank the last of his tea feeling his temporary erection subside under the duvet. He reached to his bedside table and fitted his hearing aids before joining her downstairs for eggs Benedict.

* * *

Erin balled her fingers inside cold mittens as she walked round the park. No point even trying to get back to sleep once she'd woken, even though it was only just struggling to get light. A quick stride out to the baker's on the other side of the park, then back for a piping hot coffee and croissants before her morning's practice. She exchanged nods with dog walkers and kicked through the trough of leaves blown to the south side of the path, humming bits of the slow movement when she was out of earshot of anyone else. The music rode into the cold air on the plume of her breath and feathered away behind her. She had been worried that playing a melody about such loss and longing would prove difficult with Joshua conducting, but had found her heart healing remarkably quickly in the weeks since he'd dumped her. Realising that a former lover is a complete dickhead is always beneficial to this process.

* * *

Five thousand miles away, Joshua's phone alarm tried to wake him. Buried, as it was, in his jacket pocket on the production assistant's couch, it had no chance of being heard on the other side of her apartment, where she and Joshua slept, naked limbs as carelessly entwined as one could ask for in a one-night-stand cliché.

Chapter 32

'What do you mean, "problem"?'

David's right buttock had been proved correct about incoming trouble at around eleven o'clock that evening, when his television viewing had been interrupted just as he was about to switch it off anyway and head to bed.

'I'm in a cab now and we're heading for the airport, but—'

'Joshua – what time is it? Shouldn't you be on a plane?' David felt for his TV remote control, turned it off and twisted his wrist to look at his watch. 'What's going on?'

The crackle and external noise from the connection to Joshua made him hold his own phone away from his ear.

'Nearly at the airport now. I guess we'll be there in – What? What did you say? – right, the cabbie reckons in about twenty minutes. There's still a chance I'll get on.'

'What happened?'

'Long story, David. Long story. But listen, I was runner-up! Got a bit on the local news channel and Summer's promised that there'll be a lot of interest—'

'Joshua. Are you telling me you might miss your flight?' David raised his voice to cut through the noise of an American freeway, but not loud enough to wake his wife who had gone upstairs before *Newsnight*.

'Er – no. Not exactly. Well, maybe. Gotta see how things pan out at LAX.'

David's body drooped until his head was entirely propped by his hand.

'Right. Well. I can't say I'm overjoyed at this news, Joshua.'

'Yeah. Sorry. I'll let you know when I'm checked in.'

'You do that.'

David disconnected, swearing to the blank television screen. It was Sunday night. There's still time, he told himself. Even if Joshua missed his flight, there would be others to get him home during Monday, in time to take Monday evening's rehearsal and in time for the concert. He tried to stop his adrenaline pushing over the dominoes in his head to arrive at a disastrous conclusion before it was required.

He walked to the kitchen and opened the fridge, looking for something easy to eat. He couldn't go to bed now. Quite apart from the fact that Joshua would be calling back soon, he was far too jittery to sleep anyway. Cheese. That was the thing. He cut an irregularly shaped triangle off a crumbly Wensleydale and munched thoughtfully, bringing up a new text screen on his phone and typing Rafael's name. Then he paused. It was late. He didn't even know if Joshua was going to miss his flight yet. There seemed little point in worrying Rafael over something that might not even happen. What was the maxim? Absorb and deflect. Or was that Iron Man talking to Pepper Potts? He shook his head.

He put a couple of oatcakes on a plate with some butter, snapped off a branch of grapes, sliced some more cheese and wandered back to the sofa with his phone back in its accustomed right buttock position.

Fifteen minutes later it buzzed.

'Yep. What news?' David was not in the mood for small talk.

'Ah, David. Well, not great news, to be honest.' Joshua's voice was unusually hesitant. 'Check-in staff won't let me through. I've tried to reason with them but – I mean the flight doesn't take off for… what… twenty minutes at least.'

'They won't let you through, Joshua.'

'Well, I—'

'Forget it. They won't. You'll have to get another flight.'

'Shit. You're probably right. Shit.'

'Go back to the airline desk and sort it out from there. You'll be able to change your ticket I should think.'

'Yeah. Yeah. Summer will probably have all the details. I'll maybe talk to her.'

'You do that, Joshua. And for God's sake get back here fast. Text me. I'm going to bed.'

David cut the phone before he said any of the things he was thinking. Absorb and deflect. Just try not to deflect it all into an ulcer. He went upstairs to lie awake next to his sleeping wife, trying not to move every time he felt restless. He wondered, not for the first time that autumn, why exactly he had offered to do this job. Eventually he fell into a fitful sleep without answering that question.

He woke early and reached for his phone before his eyes had even properly opened. Four texts from Joshua lined up on his screen with all the inescapability of a tax bill. He tapped on them in order, hoping he might placate whatever gods might be looking down into making the fourth one a happy ending.

Summer's looking into it. She'll get back asap.

Some problem with ticket. Let you know.

Threatened this pisspoor company with legal action if they don't get me back.

Bunch of arses. Stranded on non-flexi ticket. Cards maxed. SOS.

David put his phone down on his stomach and closed his eyes, feeling his tic jump-start. He pressed his palm over the twitching eye and swore silently. His wife had not stirred. He eased himself out of bed and went down to the kitchen, where he could start whatever Plan B he could think of over a mug of tea. He began to compose a text to Rafael.

Chapter 33

Erin's phone rang on Monday morning while she was practising. She stopped bowing and peered down at her phone on the floor, quite prepared to carry on again if it wasn't urgent. When she saw David's name there she switched her bow into her left hand and leaned down to answer it, resting her cheek on the side of the cello.

'Hi, David? Everything OK?'

'Ah, hello, Erin. Not exactly – um, we've heard from Joshua.' David's voice was hesitant.

'Oh? When's he due back? Is he delayed or something?'

'Well, yes. It appears that he missed his flight yesterday and is having some considerable difficulty booking another one.'

Erin sat upright, holding the neck of the cello and her bow with a straight left arm.

'What? He's still there?'

'Er – yes. I've been speaking to Rafael, and we're trying to contact Eliot Yarrow – the choir chap, you know? – to see if he can do tonight's rehearsal if Joshua can't make it which, frankly, at this stage, it's looking unlikely he can. There's been some sort of mix-up with his ticket.'

'Oh for God's sake. Bloody Joshua. What's he playing at?'

'Quite. Anyway, I'm waiting to hear back from Eliot, and if he can step in for tonight we can keep things ticking over until the afternoon rehearsal on Saturday. I'm sure Joshua will have found a way to return by then.'

'What are we doing tonight apart from running the Elgar?'

'Joshua was planning to top and tail the Strauss...'

Erin groaned, but could hear David manfully trying not to succumb to despair about Mrs Ford-Hughes.

'Sorry,' she said. 'Go on. Elgar and Strauss.'

'Yes, and that would leave the bulk of the Bach to run through on Saturday with the choir before the concert. Eliot will have been preparing them so they shouldn't need more detailed time with the orchestra. I'm sure he'll know the Elgar, even if he's not actually conducted it before.'

'Yes, you're right,' said Erin, staring through her window at the leaves she still hadn't swept. 'Well, it's not ideal but I guess – well, I just hope Eliot can do it. But what if he can't?'

'Let's cross that bridge when we come to it,' said David, with brisk optimism that it wouldn't come to that. He sounded confident. 'I'll let you know as soon as I hear.'

'OK, thanks. Bye.'

Erin sighed, and let her phone drop on the carpet. First she was bounced into playing a concerto on someone else's cello at short notice. Now she could be playing it with an unknown conductor on half a rehearsal. She was nervous before and this really wasn't helping. She reached down for her phone again and rang Ann.

'Hi, Erin. How's it going?'

'Hi. Um, not well, suddenly. You haven't heard about Joshua, I take it?'

'No.' Ann's voice was wary. 'What's he done?'

'He's only gone and missed his flight back. God knows how. David's just called me. And so he won't be back for tonight's rehearsal, and—'

'Whoa. Stop a minute. Slow down. Start again and tell me what David actually said.'

Erin took a breath, and let it out slowly before she started speaking again.

'He said that Joshua had missed his flight and there was some problem with his ticket. That he can't book another one, or something. Anyway, he – Joshua – won't be back in time for tonight's rehearsal and he – David, I mean – has asked Eliot Yarrow to do it.'

There was a short silence as Ann processed this information. 'Bugger.'

'Quite.'

'Joshua should stop chasing his tinsel dreams and sort out where his professional priorities lie.'

'I agree.'

'Eliot – does he have any orchestral experience? If he's just done choral… well, no matter how good you are with a choir it's a different ball game in front of an orchestra.'

'I don't know. Oh God…'

'Look, don't worry about it now. I shouldn't have brought that up, just thinking out loud. You know the music. The orchestra knows it. It's just tonight's rehearsal. We'll be fine.'

'If you say so.' Erin sounded miserable.

'I do bloody say so. Joshua needs a kick up the arse. How on earth did he miss his flight? Did David say?'

'No. I don't know. Maybe he won the competition and was too drunk to find the airport.' Erin's voice carried the sound of a small smile which had appeared on her face to Ann.

'Unlikely. Well, the winning. Not the drinking. Let's focus on what is actually in our control. Look – how is the Elgar going?'

'Oh… OK, I suppose. Doing a bit of the fourth movement now.'

'Good. You'll be a star. Shall I see you tonight a bit early? I can get there a quarter of an hour before, to sort any last minute hitches?'

'Yes, that would be great,' said Erin. 'Thanks.'

'Sock it to 'em. See you later.'

Erin dropped her phone onto the carpet for the second time, feeling much brighter than after the first.

* * *

By half past six that evening the rehearsal hall was already brightly lit and getting busy. Erin pushed through the doors, leaning the Strad away to stop it being hit as they closed behind her, and turned to see who had already arrived.

Pearl and Rafael were carrying chairs from the stacks at the side of the hall and arranging them in the familiar orchestra shape in the middle of the floor. There were a few players opening their instrument cases and a couple more helping with the chairs and music stands. David was talking to Eliot by the stage, and when he saw Erin he waved at her, clearly pointing her out to Eliot, who turned round and smiled. She walked over to where they were standing, still carrying the cello. She wasn't about to let it leave her side, even if it was just across a school hall.

'Hello, Erin,' said David. 'Have you met Eliot properly? I know you were here when the choir came to run through the Bach, but perhaps you haven't…?'

Erin smiled and held her hand out to Eliot. 'No, not properly. Hello.'

Eliot shook her hand and grinned back. 'Hi, Erin. Very nice to meet you. Properly.'

'Well,' David flustered, trying to sound as if he was very much on top of the situation that had very nearly got away from everyone, 'I was just telling Eliot about the proposed running order for tonight's rehearsal. We're planning to do some Elgar before the coffee break, and Mrs Ford-Hughes is due to join us later on to run a bit of her Strauss.'

'Yes,' agreed Eliot. 'I was about to say that I've actually done both of those. I clocked up quite a bit of orchestral experience at university and was lucky enough to conduct both pieces in my final year there.'

Erin's face must have betrayed her relief.

'Don't worry,' Eliot went on, talking directly to Erin. 'We'll be fine.'

'As long as I don't cock up,' she said, smiling as one layer of tension dissolved. 'And then you have the delights of Mrs Ford-Hughes after the break. Has David…?'

'Ah, yes, I was just coming to that,' said David.

'I believe I had the honour of hearing her at our last Bach rehearsal with you,' Eliot said, raising his eyebrows. 'I am… forewarned, I think is the correct term here.'

'Well, you know why we're putting on this concert, don't you?' David said.

'I gathered. Fundraising kind of thing?'

'It's just that – er – Mrs Ford-Hughes used to, well… gift us an annual bursary. And she has been forced to reconsider since her injury at our last concert.'

Erin put her case down on the floor and put her arm round it. She felt she ought to help David explain this, not least because she still felt a sense of responsibility of letting Mrs Ford-Hughes talk them into the Strauss in the first place.

'We need her money back,' she said to Eliot. 'We thought we could get away with giving her a bit in the Bach, but she wanted the Strauss.' She shrugged at David, who was looking faintly aghast at her candour. 'What? I think Eliot needs to know.'

'I was about to allude to it now. As delicately as I could.'

Eliot laughed. 'I get it. You need her dosh so I have to be nice? Is that it?'

David and Erin both laughed too.

'Er, yes. In a nutshell.' David was relieved Eliot seemed to be taking all this very much in his stride.

'We're very grateful,' whispered Erin. 'Please don't leave!'

'OK,' Eliot whispered back. 'But you might owe me a pint afterwards.'

'Ha! Let's see if I can get through my bit first. You might change your mind.'

Erin walked over to the rest of the cellos and put the Strad case next to Ann, who was tightening her bow.

'Joshua still in the States then?' she said, tipping her head over to where Eliot had been released by David into the wild and was chatting to some free-range violinists.

'Yeah. And the doghouse. Apparently there's been no news of him since that SOS message for money. Wanker.'

'He is. However, he is thousands of miles away. You, on the other hand, are here. With what looks like a capable conductor, and most of an orchestra. How're you feeling?'

'Surprisingly OK, actually. It may not last.'

'You'll be fine.'

Erin took the Strad out of its case and leaned it towards her as she reached back in for the bow. She had gone past the stage of sweating every time she had to move it, fearing it could splinter into a pile of overpriced matches if she slipped.

'Alright – can we make a start, please?' called Eliot, having made the mistake of trying to engage Maureen in social chit-chat. He looked bruised, but determined to recover.

Erin carried her cello and music to where David had put a chair and stand near Eliot's place in front of the orchestra, while the strings tuned to the oboe's A. Eliot took a step towards her.

'How do you want to do this? I was thinking we could run most of it and go over some of the joins if we need to. Does that sound OK?'

Erin nodded. 'Yep. Sounds good. I've not performed it before, but I ran most of it the night when – er – when Fenella was mugged. Not on this cello, of course.'

'Well, we'll crack on then and see where we end up.' Eliot gave her a smile of such absolute confidence Erin felt herself able to rely on him. Suddenly the prospect of playing without having to filter everything through the Joshua complication seemed a relief.

The rehearsal went as planned, with Eliot breaking the flow only where necessary, to clarify a tempo with Erin or tidy up a ragged entry from the orchestra. They built a solid Elgar wall of sound that had no terrifying unplayed stretches

– always the danger when a piece is topped and tailed for the tricky bits and the perceived simple passages are simply not rehearsed and, therefore, can lay surprising traps during a concert. Erin found herself catching Charlie's eye sometimes, from her place opposite him on the violin side of the orchestra. He was leading the cello section with a skill Fenella never had, and the result of having him at the front and the ever-reliable Ann at the back was that the section was playing out of its skin. Erin was absurdly proud of them.

Eliot piloted the first half of the rehearsal skilfully into the coffee break right on time, making it look effortless. He rose in all the players' estimation from then on. Pearl had already scuttled out, but before everyone else followed her there was a spontaneous round of applause for Erin. From the warm whistles of appreciation and foot-stamping it was clear Erin had the support of the heart of the orchestra. Eliot added his sincere claps to the noise, nodding enthusiastically and laughing as Erin flushed with pleasure. He slapped her on the back as she returned to the cello side of the hall.

'Well done indeed! You've got nothing to worry about on Saturday.'

'Thanks. Feeling better about it now.'

'No, really. You were fabulous. I'll be here – if I survive the Bach sandwiched between my tenors and basses – and cheering you on.'

Erin was surrounded by a congratulatory cello section as she put the Strad back in its case. Ann nodded to her with a smile, and mouthed 'Very nice'.

'Oh God,' groaned Charlie, looking over her head. 'And it was all going so well.'

Erin turned to look. Making her way through the door held open by her attentive husband was Mrs Ford-Hughes. She wore a floor-length velvet coat that added to the regal effect to which she was undoubtedly aspiring.

'Impressive though,' said Ann. 'It's not everyone who can stop the tide of this orchestra flowing to coffee. She'd have taught Cnut a thing or two.'

Indeed, as soon as the Ford-Hugheses had cleared the doorway, the scramble to exit was as if a cork had been popped from a bottle. The velvet-clad mistress of the waves surveyed the crowds eddying around her with detachment, took her husband's proffered arm and drifted towards the centre of the hall.

'Does Joshua have someplace else he'd rather be?' she asked of nobody in particular, lowering her eyelids as she searched the room, ending up back at her husband's face. He looked at David, who was bustling towards them, two fingers pressed to his twitching eye.

'Well?' Mr Ford-Hughes almost growled.

'Joshua has been unavoidably delayed, I'm afraid... he was attending another professional engagement and there were a number of unforeseen travel hitches.' David massaged the side of his head and threw out his arm towards Eliot as a distraction. 'We've been most fortunate to secure the services of Eliot Yarrow, who has stepped up to the plate, as it were, with aplomb. Eliot, allow me to introduce Mrs Ford-Hughes, our Strauss soloist.'

Eliot, who had decided to throw himself fully into the sycophantic side of his new role, strode to David's side and clasped Mrs Ford-Hughes's hand in both of his. She allowed him to hold it for a moment, as if processing the baseball idiom coming out of David's mouth took all her active thought.

'Delighted to meet you,' Eliot was saying. 'The *Four Last Songs* are a favourite of mine; I'm so looking forward to tonight's rehearsal.'

'You've done them before, then?' Mrs Ford-Hughes was not yet won over.

'Oh, absolutely. In fact, I'm glad we have a chance to speak for a moment before we dive straight into the music. Let me find you a coffee…'

Erin, Charlie and Ann watched as Mrs Ford-Hughes allowed herself to be guided gently towards the swirl of caffeine-hunters, who parted like the Red Sea once more to let them through. It was as if Mrs Ford-Hughes possessed the human equivalent of a hydrophobic sheen.

'Eliot's earning whatever we're paying him for this rehearsal. I'm impressed,' said Charlie. 'Mrs Ford-Hughes looked almost docile.'

'He's wisely getting all his brownie points in early so he can start ahead of the game,' said Ann.

'Divide and conquer,' added Erin, nodding at David and Mr Ford-Hughes, who had been left together by the success of Eliot's charm. David's facial spasms were easing off a little, now the initial news-breaking appeared to have gone so well. They began to follow Eliot and Mrs Ford-Hughes towards refreshment.

Charlie finished strapping his cello in its case, and glanced at Erin's arm draped over hers.

'Shall I bring yours back here? You're not leaving that cello, are you?'

'Er, no. Yes, that'd be great. Milk and sugar, thanks.'

'Ann, can I get yours too? I can try and snaffle some biscuits, unless they're all now ring-fenced for the Ford-Hugheses' delectation.'

'Shh!' Erin widened her eyes towards Mr Ford-Hughes's back. 'Go on, before you blow all of Eliot's hard work.'

'Just milk for me, thanks,' said Ann. 'Shoo.'

Erin sat sideways on one of the cello chairs near her case and Ann joined her on the desk behind.

'Five days. Then all this will be over,' Erin said, looking round the hall and circling her left wrist with the fingers of her right hand, stretching the tension out and clenching her fist, then wriggling her whole left hand.

'First one down. I hope many to go.'

'Hold your horses. I haven't done this one quite yet.'

'But you will. And you'll do it well – better than you give yourself credit for. Would be a shame to stop there.'

'What do you mean?'

'I mean, you idiot,' said Ann, with a smile in her voice, 'that I don't waste my time on people who aren't worth it. Christ knows I don't need to these days. You need to believe in yourself a bit more. What was that shitty job you had? Remember, the one you were always complaining about?'

Erin rubbed both eyes and yawned. 'Yeah. Databases. Boring as fuck. You're right.'

'Well then.'

'Well, what?'

'Don't make that mistake again. You can play. Better than a lot of people I see at music college. Don't waste it.'

Erin looked at Ann and, for once, didn't feel the need to slide into self-deprecation or evasive humour. 'Is this one of those evenings we'll talk about later: one of those "I

281

remember the evening when Ann sat me down and changed my life" kind of things? That's what it sounds like.'

'I've been trying to have this conversation with you for weeks. As I think you've noticed and tried to ignore. I'm only doing better tonight because you can't leave the Strad. It's like an invisible tether.'

Charlie returned with coffees balanced in his hands, wearing the internationally recognised facial expression to convey panic about there being no suitable place to put something down that was currently lava temperature. They hurried to relieve him of his burdens and he dug around in his trouser pockets for some biscuits.

'Sorry, nowhere else to put 'em,' he said, shaking each one to make sure it was free of pocket fluff before proffering. 'I've got garibaldi crumbs down my leg now. There must be a hole.'

'I was going to say thank you, but now I'm not sure,' said Erin, peering at her biscuit before taking a bite.

'Hey – tell you something: Eliot's buttering up Mrs Ford-Hughes brilliantly. He's got her on to stories of her youth in Arkansas.'

'If she stays in a good mood maybe we'll all survive the second half then,' said Ann. 'If she doesn't try and tell Eliot what to do, like she did with Joshua.'

'I think Eliot's on top of things,' said Charlie, trying to drink his coffee without skinning his tongue. He turned to Erin. 'And at least I get to sit next to you instead of Fenella this time. Much more fun. Though of course you should be leading us all, now you're the soloist 'n' all.'

'No way. Getting quite enough of the limelight as it is, thank you.'

They sipped their way down their coffees as the rest of the orchestra began to straggle back into the hall and resume their places for the Strauss. Mr Ford-Hughes took his, now accustomed, seat by the door, while his positively simpering wife arrived with Eliot and made her way across the floor within her velvet folds.

The rehearsal achieved none of the musical development of the first half, but confirmed to the orchestra that they could indeed survive the worst Mrs Ford-Hughes could throw at them without breaking down which was, in itself, no small triumph. She seemed to have taken so well to Eliot she even allowed him to bring her off some of her longer pauses without demur. There was a general air of renewed orchestral vigour which, given the potential for mishap only hours earlier, bolstered everyone's confidence. Even David's tic had subsided by the end of the evening.

Chapter 34

The rest of that week had the sort of elastic time that expands or contracts depending on what waits for you. For Erin, the Saturday concert seemed to rush at her, with days evaporating before she felt she had practised enough.

For Joshua, still in California, each morning the sun rose with the smugness of an overconfident yoga salutation. Each morning he made more calls to try to arrange a flight home. Summer's willingness to help never really made it back up to the level it was before the gala concert. Joshua had the dual discomfort of being aware there were some hours of that night his memory was hazy over, and of not knowing how much Summer had witnessed.

David watched the Joshua disaster unravel across the screen on his phone as he received texts updating him on a situation that seemed to remain static. No money, no flight then sudden, giddy hope about getting a flight followed by news that he had not managed it. David did not feel inclined to step in. A short conversation with Rafael had made it plain there could be no bail out from the non-existent orchestral funds. He had had a quick chat with Eliot after the rehearsal about a possible Plan B should Joshua fail to return. Since Eliot already knew the Bach, Strauss and Elgar, it was just the Mendelssohn that could prove a problem. Eliot said he would get a score and have a look, just in case. David had left the hall on Monday night as boosted by Eliot's unflappable confidence as Erin had been during the Elgar. Clearly on some cosmic karma scale, the payment of a singing Mrs Ford-Hughes in any situation allowed for a hefty plus on the other side.

By the time Joshua texted on Friday with concrete news, David had given up checking. Joshua's wife had arranged a loan from her parents and bought a ticket for her husband. What she hadn't bothered to tell Joshua was that she had gone to stay with them indefinitely. There would be no warm homecoming for him.

Eight hours ahead of Joshua, David had simply gone to bed and switched his phone to silent. He spent the night unaware that Joshua was booked on a United non-stop flight out of Los Angeles late afternoon and would arrive in London at eleven thirty on Saturday morning.

* * *

Erin arrived at the hall early for the two o'clock rehearsal. As she pushed the door open, she could hear Joshua arguing with David.

'What do you mean? I texted you. I said my flight would be in at eleven thirty. Delayed in the end – I've come straight here from the sodding airport – and now you say you don't need me after all?'

'If you could just calm down, Joshua—'

'I will not fucking calm down!' Joshua's voice cracked with exhaustion and dehydration. 'You would not believe the week I've had.'

Erin carried the Strad over to the side of the hall, set it down and leaned on it. She felt she might as well enjoy the show.

Charlie, who had arrived behind her, came over. 'Bloody hell. When did he turn up?'

'No idea – just arrived. He was like this when I got here.'

'Awkward.'

David was scratching the side of his head as if trying to think of the right thing to say. He caught sight of Erin and Charlie over Joshua's shoulder, and threw them an exasperated look before turning back to Joshua.

'Look, we simply didn't know if you were going to make it back. You can understand us needing to plan for this eventuality.'

'No. Not "this" eventuality, David. "That" eventuality. The one that didn't happen. Because, if you notice, I'm fucking here. Ta-fucking-da.'

'Shall we try and avoid the gratuitous language? People are arriving.'

They were indeed, and were as transfixed as Erin and Charlie. Joshua swung round to see.

'Oh hello, everyone! You're just in time to see David try to muscle me out of my own shitting concert.'

David tried once more to take charge. 'Good afternoon. Come in, come in. As you see, Joshua has arrived unexpectedly... er...'

He tailed off as Eliot appeared at the door and walked towards them. His footsteps sounded unnaturally loud in the almost silent hall.

'OK,' said Charlie in Erin's ear. 'A fiver says Joshua clocks him one. Tenner says David steps in and gets flattened by mistake. Has Joshua been drinking?'

'He looks awful,' said Erin. 'Not in a fit state to conduct anything.'

Eliot kept walking until he was a few feet from Joshua, then stopped, unbuttoned his coat and unlooped his scarf a few times from round his neck. He was smiling.

'Hello, David. Joshua – welcome back. When did you get in?'

'Apparently, too late to stop you muscling in on my orchestra. Well, I can take it from here.'

Eliot wandered to the side of the hall to put his coat and scarf over the back of a chair. 'The thing is, Joshua,' he said, 'we weren't sure if you'd make it back on time. I suggest you go home, have a shower and a nap. You must be jet-lagged.'

Joshua lunged after Eliot and was caught off-balance by David.

'You can't take my sodding concert!'

David pulled him back. 'Joshua, Eliot's right. You're exhausted. It must have been quite a week. Now I'm not one to censure musicians' alcohol intake,' (he ignored the chuckles rippling round the listening orchestra), 'but I can certainly smell whisky. There are things at stake today that are bigger than you.'

'You wouldn't even have lured that fat diva back if I hadn't gone to see her,' Joshua shouted.

'Here we go,' whispered Charlie to Erin. 'He doesn't look as if he could land a punch straight, though.'

'Shh,' said Erin. 'I've never seen him like this.'

'Firstly,' said David, 'I believe that was Erin's idea. Secondly, I feel any conductor who uses that kind of description about one of our soloists is perhaps better off not attending the concert.'

Joshua stared at him. There was a belligerent sway to his legs. 'Fuck off.'

David glanced over to Erin and Charlie, who were just moving towards him when Carl stepped away from his trombone case and strode over. Carl was one of those brass players who resemble an oak tree in winter: stout of trunk without any foliage on top. He wouldn't have looked out of place on guard at a nightclub door. He nodded to David.

'I'll take it from here. C'mon, mate. Let's get you a taxi.'

Quite how he propelled Joshua out of the hall was unclear to onlookers. At one point they were not even sure if Joshua's feet were touching the floor. David watched them go, putting his hand up to his eye as if to reassure its tic that it was not necessary to spring into action.

Eliot walked back to the centre of the hall. 'I owe Carl a pint later.'

David laughed out his excess tension. 'Never thought I'd say this, but I've never been so glad to see him.'

'Right then,' said Eliot. 'While we wait for Carl to return, maybe we could all sit down and tune?'

The players settled into their seats, taking a moment as Carl walked in through the doors to give him a few whistles of appreciation and brief applause. Carl nodded, and updated David as he went past. 'All sorted. One pissed conductor in a cab. I had a quick word, and I don't think we need to worry about him for this evening. All yours, Eliot.'

'Thanks,' said Eliot. 'I'll get my round in later.'

Erin, Charlie and Ann exchanged relieved expressions, and the orchestra went about its final rehearsal with the air of a ship crewed by mutineers.

* * *

By seven o'clock that evening, most of them were back at the hall. The room behind the stage was full of open instrument cases and the sound of warming up: the decoy duck call of an oboe reed, watery parps of the horns testing all their natural frequencies and the chirruping of a second violin trying some semiquavers. There were a few sightings of boxer shorts, as some people changed into concert black having cycled there. A drift of nervous sweat hung about the place, masking the whiff of slightly moist cyclist.

Erin stood on one side, not noticing the underwear and hairy legs to her left. She wiped her palms down her skirt and wished she didn't feel quite so sick.

On the other side of the building, Noel Osmar was walking through the doors and trying to find a seat that would let him have a good view of the cello soloist. He stopped, uncertain, as he scanned the chairs on the stage. Because the programme was due to start with *Fingal's Cave*, there was no seat set out for Erin. Noel, not having previously been to a classical concert – apart from that time that he had been called to sort out a sudden death – had no idea where she would sit. He made his way as far forward as he could, and hoped it would do. He had watched the wink of the tracking curser move to the hall earlier and had felt a prickle of excitement about hearing the Strad played at last.

David and Rafael were in the foyer, trying to arrange an impromptu press conference between several local papers and Fenella, who was flicking her hair like a red-carpet A-lister and lapping up the attention while she could. Her cast was draped in a cashmere pashmina which artfully, and only partially, obscured it. The metal external pins glinted for the cameras.

'Where's Joshua?' she asked David, through a wide smile at the flashbulbs. 'Shouldn't he be here too?'

'Ah, yes,' said David. 'I'm afraid he won't be coming – don't worry!' He forestalled Fenella's look of horror. 'All is well. Eliot Yarrow will be conducting. Anyway, I'll leave you to it, and get myself round the back. We'll be on in a few minutes.'

Ann and Charlie each gave Erin a quick hug as they arrived, but didn't try to start any conversation. Eliot walked over as they were all getting their cellos out and tightening their bows.

'OK, Erin?' he said.

'Not really.'

'Ah – you'll be fine. Play half as well as you did at the rehearsal and you'll storm through it. I was wondering – did you want to sit out of the rest of the concert? Since we're doing the Elgar last, I don't want you to be tired before you start.'

'I'd rather play, I think. I'd go mad back here on my own with nothing to do.'

'No problem. Just thought I'd ask.' Eliot squeezed her shoulder and wandered over to the door towards the stage.

Ann smiled at Erin. 'Go easy then. Don't knacker your hand before the important stuff.'

'Yes, boss,' said Erin. 'God, I wish my voice worked properly. My mouth is so dry. But my hands are so wet! Can't my body sort itself out?'

'It'll settle down,' said Ann.

David appeared in the doorway and held up his hands. 'Alright, everybody. Nearly time. It's a full house, thank goodness! Well done on all your ticket sales. I think Mrs Ford-Hughes has invited half her county set as well.'

'Where *is* our delightful soloist?' called Carl.

'She's in the administrator's office,' said David. 'It has proved extremely useful as a dressing room.'

Indeed, as he spoke, the warblings of a nervous soprano warming up drifted along the corridor.

'Right then, let's go,' said David, standing aside to let the orchestra troop past him onto the stage. He heard the applause swell from the hall and caught Rafael's eye as he walked past. They shared a look of something close to relief. Latent worry about surviving the next two hours was a feeling they both ignored. Sometimes, you have to embrace triumph when you can. David turned and followed his fellow players onto the stage.

Eliot bounded on after everyone else and raised his arm to acknowledge the audience, bowing low and turning towards the orchestra in one smooth movement. He looked round at everyone, smiling and making eye contact, willing them to trust him and ride on his confidence. There is alchemy to conducting. It is more than technique and musicality alone. Eliot could feel the crackle of energy in the air as he gathered the players ready with both arms outstretched. He grinned quickly, and set off in Mendelssohn's boat towards *Fingal's Cave*.

As the last chord echoed around the hall (Brian some-how managing to keep his pitch up on his last flute note as if skewered to the wall by Eliot's baton), the audience erupted into a roar of appreciation that took the orchestra by surprise.

'Let's hope we haven't peaked too soon,' muttered Charlie to Erin as they stood to take their bows.

'At least the first half dozen rows seem to be the Ford-Hughes supporters' club,' she said. 'They'll be reliable clappers no matter what happens next.'

As they settled again in their seats, Eliot turned to the audience.

'As you know, this concert is a fund-raiser for the Stockwell Park Orchestra. We are immensely proud to introduce a debut soloist for our next piece: the *Four Last Songs* by Richard Strauss. Please give a very warm welcome to this evening's soprano: Maryanne Ford-Hughes!'

The orchestra were left mouthing their surprise to each other over Mrs Ford-Hughes being in possession of a first name, let alone it not being Dolly, as she made a regal entry from the wings. The bias-cut hem of her silk dress set up a waveform round her feet like the legs of a millipede, mak-ing her appear to levitate towards Eliot. He took a couple of steps towards her and kissed her on both cheeks. The front rows of the audience went wild. Noel Osmar, trapped at the edge of the third row, shrank a little into his collar as the waves of noise and perfume broke together over his head.

Mrs Ford-Hughes opened her score. Eliot fixed the orchestra with a determined look, mouthed 'Good luck' to them all, and pushed them into Strauss's thick-textured world of reflection and death.

It wasn't exactly that Mrs Ford-Hughes had improved as a singer, or a musician. Rather, Eliot seemed able to force her to look at him and could exert some peripheral control over her excesses. Her pronunciation was still worthy of Dolly Parton. Her tuning was wayward. Her timing was approximate. Somehow, though, Eliot steered her through the four songs with the force of his will and they all arrived at the other side more or less intact. It helped that the end of the fourth song, *Im Abendrot*, had a full twenty-one bars of the orchestra alone, at a speed of *sehr langsam* (very slow). By the time the *pianissimo* chords dissolved under the last few woodwind trills, Mrs Ford-Hughes had stood for so long with her eyes shut it was as if she was erased from the performance. There was an extended moment of absolute stillness after the music stopped, as Eliot held his position. When he finally let his arms drop and grinned his triumph at the orchestra, the applause rolled towards them in a deafening wedge. Eliot nodded his thanks to the players before turning to Mrs Ford-Hughes and inviting her to take all the applause herself. She beamed at her friends, and clutched at her throat as if the whole experience threatened to overwhelm her. On her second curtain call, the small florist shop that had been ordered by her husband was delivered to her onstage, and effectively cut short any further milking of the applause on account of the fact that nobody could see her anymore.

Pearl had already darted around to the tables at the back of the hall and was pouring wine. Eliot watched helplessly as his choir trooped up in formation and necked at least a glass each before most of the paying guests could decently get there. Short of hailing them across the moneyed VIP heads, there was nothing he could do.

Charlie came up behind him and followed his gaze. 'The Bach might have rugby boots on, then, do you think?' he said. 'Don't worry. We'll get through it. Bloody well done with the Strauss, mate. Tell you something, Joshua couldn't have pulled that one off.'

'Ha! Thanks. You guys were outstanding.'

'We were, weren't we? Let's hope we can keep it up.'

'How's Erin doing?'

'She's staying round the back. Said she didn't want any wine.' Charlie smiled. 'Can't imagine why.'

They moved towards the bar together as the crowd eddied. Noel Osmar stood at the side of the hall, sipping a glass of red that had not been left to breathe for long enough to begin to disguise its price bracket. Fenella saw him and walked over.

'Mr Osmar! I wasn't expecting to see you here tonight.'

Noel straightened and nearly clicked his heels together. 'Miss Stroud. How lovely. How are you feeling?'

Fenella grimaced. 'Oh – it has its good days and bad days. But on the whole, I suppose it's mending as fast as it can. Clearly not fast enough for this concert…'

'Yes,' Noel wondered how delicately he could put it. 'I saw in the programme you weren't playing your Stradivari. Is it…?'

'Yes, it's here. But you're right, I'm not playing. But,' she sighed, 'I was persuaded that the orchestra needed my Strad, so I've lent it for the Elgar. I've just been telling all those reporters about it.' She pointed to where the gaggle of press was paying homage to Mrs Ford-Hughes through the gate-keeper of Mr Ford-Hughes. 'Erin is taking my place. I hope she's up to it.'

'I am looking forward to hearing your cello played, very much indeed,' said Noel.

'Well, the Elgar is marvellous. If Erin can get to the top of those scales in the first movement we might have a decent performance, I suppose. Oh, please excuse me. I must just talk to—' She made a line for one straggling journalist who had been separated from the scrum around Mrs Ford-Hughes. Fenella was not going to let an interview opportunity pass her by.

Twenty minutes later, Eliot began to herd his choir toward the stage. The noise level in the hall had risen to pub decibels as the general blood alcohol levels rose. Eliot reasoned that at least if the choir were pissed, half the audience were too, so perhaps it wouldn't matter quite so much.

Rafael caught Eliot's eye from his vantage point as a Mrs Ford-Hughes outrider, and prepared to extricate her from the paparazzi.

By the time the orchestra were seated again, with the choir behind them, the hall had taken on a rather dissolute party air. Pearl hadn't had time to clear the long table of drinks, and some members of the audience took the opportunity to refill their glasses as they resumed their seats. There was a rumble of oiled conversation.

Eliot looked at the singers from his place at the side of the stage. The men in particular seemed rosier of cheek than they had been earlier, and he sighed. He wasn't even going to be able to sit between the tenors and basses to keep them on track. Mrs Ford-Hughes bustled up behind him and giggled coquettishly, kissing him on his cheek. He caught the scent of alcohol on her breath too. Better and better.

'Shall we go on together?' he asked, leading the way to the podium. Mrs Ford-Hughes walked onto the stage for the second time that evening, in a slightly more parabolic arc than the first.

When the applause had died down, Eliot turned to the singers and stretched his index and middle fingers towards his own eyes, in the hope some of them might get the hint that he wanted them to watch him. Unfortunately, some of the more mature altos interpreted this gesture as him giving them the V-sign, and there was a rustle of slightly tipsy affront among them.

The best that can be said of the Bach was that the musicians (and singers, if one categorises them as separate from musicians, as some do) arrived more or less safely on the other side. If Eliot had to sing the tenor lead occasionally to get them back on message, the audience was at least shielded from that knowledge by the basses roaring out their part as if they were on the terraces at an FA Cup final. Nuanced and articulate baroque singing it was not. Still, their overall enthusiasm seemed to suffice, as in the boisterous recordings from the 1960s before anyone had heard of period instruments and baroque pitch. Even the swoops and involuntary harmonies provided by Mrs Ford-Hughes on his left seemed not to dent the chorus's enthusiasm to race towards the final double bar line, and thenceforth to the pub.

It was received with rapture.

Eliot bowed, and ushered Mrs Ford-Hughes offstage as quickly as he decently could. In the third row, Noel sat up straighter in his chair. The rows in front of him thinned as the varying ranks of Mrs Ford-Hughes's acquaintance hurried to the administrator's office to start their backstage congratulatory party. Noel saw David walk out carrying a chair and music stand. He set them up in front of the violins, on the left side of the stage. Noel would be within ten feet of the Stradivari, with a view uninterrupted by anyone. He felt a rush of anticipation.

Eliot returned and, as the entire cello section stood and began their chair-swapping, he spoke.

'Ladies and gentlemen, we now come to the final piece in tonight's concert. As you see, our cellos are migrating…' He turned as a ripple of laughter ran through audience and orchestra. The chorus had long evaporated from their seats. 'The reason for this is because we have within their ranks a gifted young player, who has stepped in at a relatively late stage to play the Elgar for us.' Erin smiled at him as she crossed the stage to the lone chair, and started settling her music on the stand.

Eliot continued. 'It's a bit convoluted, but the cello you see her holding is not hers. It belongs to Fenella Stroud, who has generously lent it to Erin for this evening's concert.' He gestured to where Fenella sat in the audience, and there was a short round of applause for her generosity. When quiet had resumed, Eliot said, 'This is no ordinary cello. It was made in the early seventeen hundreds by Antonio Stradivari and is one of perhaps sixty left in the world.' He turned to Erin. 'So don't drop it, for God's sake.'

The hall laughed, and Erin eased out of her tension a little. Eliot could feel the audience coming with him, as he could feel when an orchestra did. He needed them on Erin's side. He glanced at the rest of the cellos. 'All set?' They nodded. He faced the hall once more. 'The Elgar Cello Concerto.'

He waited until Erin was ready, then nodded at the orchestra. They looked back at him, alert for his signal. He had never been prouder of a load of amateur musicians. This wasn't their job. They were there for all sorts of reasons but right then, in that hall, they were doing it for Erin and so they could carry on playing together, drinking together and eating Pearl's biscuits. For once, they were all on the same side.

Erin's first chords rang out over the heads of the audience with the authority of a seasoned professional. The cello had played those notes many times in the last hundred years of its existence and, although Stradivari had not conceived of thick-textured music like Elgar's, he had embedded enough indescribable magic to let his cello soar.

Noel was transfixed. Erin tipped the instrument as she crossed the strings, and the varnish caught the light and seemed, to Noel, to change colour note by note. He remembered the first time he had seen it, in that lock-up in Petersham. Somehow he had known it would sound like this. There had been a quality about it, a presence of spirit almost and of purpose. Of something made to be heard.

By the end of the concerto, every person in that hall had become locked in to the music. Wine was left undrunk under chairs. People who usually fidgeted during concerts were motionless. Then, even before the echoes of the last chord had died, their applause was ripped out of its box by spontaneous shouts of appreciation. Noel roused himself from his trance-like state, and discovered he could still move his arms. He clapped in amazement, for a performance he had not understood but needed no translation. A performance that went straight to his gut. He was on his feet before he knew quite what he was doing, and the whole room followed him.

Erin gasped in disbelief as she saw her standing ovation. She looked over at Ann, who was joining the applause and nodding her congratulations.

She bowed, holding the neck of the Strad steady as she did so. It trembled slightly in her hand as it picked up the thunderous noise in the hall. Sound is energy.

Chapter 35

The concert would end as all concerts do: in the pub, the nineteenth hole for musicians. Erin found herself squeezed from all angles as people hugged her before they left the hall, promising to buy her a drink when she reached the pub.

Fenella came backstage, and the knot of people round Erin melted aside as she approached.

'Well done, Erin,' she said. 'You played beautifully.'

Erin grinned. 'Thanks. It was amazing to play. Thank you so much for lending it to me. It's been – quite the experience.'

Ann called over from where she was putting her own cello away. 'Well, now you've got that one under your belt, it's time we got you doing another.'

'Damn right,' said Charlie.

'What is this, a press gang,' said Erin. 'Give us a chance. I barely survived this one.'

'I think you should,' said Fenella. They all turned to look at her, and she gave her hair a small flick, as if to steady herself. 'You play better than I do. Even I can hear that.' She coughed and blinked, and looked straight at Erin. 'This cello deserves to be played. I'd like you to keep it, at least for a while – I'm not going to be playing for months. If ever.'

Erin stared at her. 'Really?'

Ann was quick. 'That's amazingly generous of you, Fenella. I think it's a great idea. You can use it to audition for music college and take it from there.'

'Hang on,' said Erin. 'Let's not get ahead of ourselves.'

'Ah, come on,' said Charlie. 'It makes perfect sense. You should play it, and Fenella can become the famous and generous benefactor who gets all the credit... all the column inches...' He grinned.

'It's quite common, you know,' said Ann. 'Most of the Strads played around the world don't belong to the players themselves. They're on loan from museums or – well, people like Fenella.'

They packed up, retrieved coats and scarves and walked through to the hall, which was almost empty. Pearl was clearing the last of the wine table, and Rafael and David were by the doors to the foyer with Eliot. Rafael saw Erin and smiled.

'Fabulous, Erin. Well done indeed.'

'How are the finances?' called Charlie, as they walked across the hall.

'They are a bit fabulous too,' said David. 'Tell them, Rafael.'

'Well,' said Rafael, 'we had a record take for tonight, plus the retiring collection basket we put out. A complete sell-out.'

'Now we just need the Ford-Hughes's fortune and we'll be home and dry,' said Ann. 'Any news on that?'

Eliot cleared his throat in an unnecessarily tubercular fashion, and the entire party gleaned they could be receiving imminent news on that front. Her perfume arrived first.

Mrs Ford-Hughes led a small group of her friends out of a side door that came from the administrator's office and pressed herself against Eliot's jacket. He caught Erin's eye over Mrs Ford-Hughes's fascinator, and tried not to sneeze as its feathers brushed his nose.

'Eliot, honey, I wanna thank you from the bottom of my heart for one of the best days of my life.'

'Er – I'm very glad,' he said. There was a short silence as Mrs Ford-Hughes leaned into him, until her husband touched her gently on the shoulder.

'Darling, hadn't we better be going? It's late.'

She peeled herself off Eliot immediately. 'Oh, sure. Sure. I wanna say to y'all that I had the most peachy time tonight! And I wanna thank you for that.'

It was David's turn to clear his throat. 'I'm so pleased. You sang magnificently.'

'Why, thank you! But before I go, I also wanna tell you we're reinstating our bursary. Maybe we can make this thing an annual event!'

She rescued anyone from having to respond to that by sweeping out of the hall on her husband's arm, followed by her friends. The room seemed very quiet after the door had closed.

'Did she say "annual event"?' said Charlie.

'I prefer to concentrate on the bit where she said we could have her money,' said Rafael.

'We did it!' said David, slightly dazed. 'We bloody did it!'

'Erin did it,' said Ann, and gave Erin an enormous bear hug, which turned into one of those group hugs British people are supposed to abhor as the rest of them joined in. They finally broke apart, laughing.

'Well,' said Charlie. 'There's only one thing for it.'

'Pub,' said Erin. 'You're buying.'

Acknowledgements

I have so many people to thank:

Abbie Headon is a wonderful commissioning editor but, before that, she was a friend I made on Twitter. She hounded me until I confessed to having written a comic novel, and then didn't hate it. Caroline Goldsmith and Abbie Rutherford copyedited and proofread with skill and patience, and saved you from having to read any number of awful things in here. Clare Stacy at Head Design produced the beautiful cover, which I adore.

Thank you to all the orchestras and choirs in which I've ever played or sung, and probably won't be allowed back into now. And, honestly, I didn't use anybody real for a character. Not a whole one, anyway. One trait per person, tops. I can see a lawyer waving at me now – ooh look, squirrels!

Now, listen. This is important. Twitter pals: writers and editors and agents and jokers and teachers and poets and fictional nobility and musicians and ranters and bookshops and engineers and painters and weird cartoon people and historians and old friends discovered round the world and new friends made and yes I said yes I will Yes. You drank tea with me during edits and talked me through nights of insomnia. You make me laugh every day. I can't fit you all in here but if I tried and one of you got missed off we'd have tears and Such Umbrage Taken. There would be a great unfollowing flounce and frankly I'm not up to that. You know who you are. Every single one. I couldn't have done it without you. Idiots.

Both Joanna Cannon and Lee Randall (via Twitter, naturally) steered me toward the correct pronunciation of 'vibrio parahaemolyticus', which saved me from anxiety dreams in case I ever have to read page 8 out loud.

Finally, thank you to Zig, who is a Good Boy and doesn't care about grammar as long as we've been for a walk, where he prefers sniffs to chasing a ball, leaving me time to work out the next bit of story.

About the Author

Isabel Rogers writes poetry and fiction, but never on the same day. She won the 2014 Cardiff International Poetry Competition, was Hampshire Poet Laureate 2016, and her debut collection, *Don't Ask*, came out in 2017 (Eyewear). *Life, Death and Cellos* is her first novel to be published.

She had a proper City job before a decade in the Scottish Highlands, writing and working in the NHS. She now lives in Hampshire, laughs a lot and neglects her cello. She is on Twitter @Isabelwriter.

Note from the Publisher

To receive updates on new releases in the Stockwell Park Orchestra series – plus special offers and news of other humorous fiction series to make you smile – sign up now to the Farrago mailing list at farragobooks.com/sign-up.